The Ghost of Emmett Till

Based on Real Life Events

By

W. James Richardson

authorHOUSE

1663 Liberty Drive, Suite 200
Bloomington, Indiana 47403
(800) 839-8640
www.authorhouse.com

First published by AuthorHouse 01/22/05

ISBN: 1-4184-6478-3 (e)
ISBN: 1-4184-6477-5 (sc)

Library of Congress Control Number:2004094103

This book is printed on acid-free paper.

Printed in the United States of America
Bloomington, Indiana

Chapter One

Sunday, August 28, 1955

Moses Wright's worst nightmare unfolded: Armed white men came to his home and carried away his fourteen-year-old great nephew into the night. He felt helpless, understanding that white people in Mississippi practically did whatever they wanted when it came to Negroes and got away with whatever they did. The last words he heard as the men left were "We're gonna teach the niggah a lesson…."

Moses whiffed the countrified air that was imbued with the familiar scent of farm animals. He stood on the rickety front porch of his home and peered heartrendingly into the uninterrupted darkness across the landscape that consisted of his vegetable garden and acres of plantation cotton that was the estate of Mr. Frederick, the white boss he worked for. Cedar, persimmon, pecan, and cottonwood trees sat silhouetted at the edge of the cotton fields like motionless sentries under the dim moonlight.

Moses wondered where they'd taken Emmett. He found the night air to be as still as death and strangely absent of the usual sound of trilling killdeer that huddled at the not far away lake. Tears trickled down his furrowed, ebony cheeks.

1

He mopped sweat from his brow with the back of his hand and hurried back inside his home. His dark, scarred, callous, trembling hand picked up the telephone receiver.

"Operator, I'd like to place a call to Chicago and speak with Mrs. Mamie Till." Tears swelled in his tired, red eyes.

* * *

Mamie Till's head jerked on top of the pillow. "My God!"

The noise jolted her and seemed to emanate from a megaphone. It was the phone ringing. She felt disoriented and struggled to raise her eyelids, thinking she'd over slept. She turned on the lamp on the nightstand next to the bed and read the oval-face clock. It was three-ten, not late for work, and not late for anything. She wondered what day it was. She tossed the bedcover off of her, sprang out of bed, and rushed a few steps from her bedroom to reach the incessantly ringing phone in the cramp living room of her modest home. She wasn't certain as to whom the caller might be, but thirty-one years of living had edified her that good news seldom traveled in the middle of the night.

"Hello," Mamie answered while feeling a bit winded as the palm of her free hand shot to her chest and as if to slow her heartbeat.

"Mamie, da took Emmett!"

"Uncle Moses, is this you?" She heard him sniffling.

"Yeah Mamie! Da jes' came to the house and took Emmett away! I'm so sorry. But there wuz nothin I could do. It wuz three of 'em and da had a gun."

"My God! Please calm down Uncle Moses. What are you talking about? Who took Emmett?"

"Two white men! A man named Roy Bryant and another man. Some other men wuz involved. Three came to the house and I saw two other men in the back of the truck when they took Emmett with 'em."

2

"Oh my God! Why did they take Emmett? What did they want with my child?"

"Mr. Bryant claimed Emmett insulted his wife by whistlin at her."

"Oh no, Uncle Moses! No! Oh Jesus! Not my child! Oh God, not Emmett!"

"I'm so sorry, Mamie. I wish I coulda did somethin. Mr. Bryant said dat he wuzn't gonna stand for Emmett bein fresh with his wife. The other man had a gun. We wuz all sleepin when da came. Da made Emmett get dress. I begged Mr. Bryant not to take Emmett, but it wuz jes' like beggin the devil. I begged him to jes' give Emmett a whippin 'cause he wuzn't from down here. I told him dat Emmett wuz from Chicago and dat he didn't know no better 'bout what he did. Da didn't listen to me and hauled Emmett away in a truck. Mamie, da gonna do somethin bad to Emmett. I jes' know it."

"Oh my God! Oh Jesus please help me! Where did they take Emmett?"

"I don't know. Da didn't say. Da jes' took him away and had a gun pointed at his head. I think da gonna hurt Emmett."

"Oh God! Please don't say that Uncle Moses. Please don't! Did you call the sheriff's office?"

"I called, but dese *crackers* down here ain't gonna do much. The sheriff asked me if I wuz certain dat Emmett didn't leave on his own and dat I should wait 'til mornin to see if he return and if he don't, for me to come to report it then."

"My Lord, Uncle Moses! They took my child?" Mamie's legs gave out. She slumped on a nearby chair.

"Yeah Mamie. Da did! Da sho' took him. I'm so sorry. It really hurts me, but what could I do? Nothin a colored person can do to white people down here. Da can do whatever da want with coloreds and get away with it. Mamie, yah know dat from havin lived down here. Mr.Bryant had more evil in his eyes than I ever seen a man possess. Yah gotta get down here and see 'bout Emmett."

"Did Emmett ever mention anything to you about whistling at a white woman?"

"No. First I heard told of it when the men came lookin for Emmett."

"I don't believe Emmett messed with that white man's wife because at the train station, and just before he left, I told Emmett that Mississippi was different than Chicago. I told him that when he got to Mississippi to say yes ma'am and no ma'am and yes sir and no sir. And I sure told him that if he saw a white woman coming down the street that he should step off the sidewalk and drop his head to respect her. I told him don't even look directly at a white woman or say anything to her. I told Emmett all of that before he left and I know he understood. After I told him all of that I don't believe he would whistle at a white woman. Maybe the woman thought Emmett whistled at her because he has a stuttering problem. I taught him to perch his lips and sort of whistle to help pronounce his words. Maybe Emmett did that and the white woman thought Emmett was getting fresh with her. When did Emmett supposed to have whistled at the woman?"

"It wuz day before yet'erday. No, the day before dat. Three days ago when Emmett was in town and went to the store to buy candy and bubble gum at the Bryants' grocery store. You know Emmett love him some bubble gum; always chewin it and blowin bubbles."

"Lord, I sent my child down there on a vacation and never thought something like this would happen. Oh, my Lord! Lord Jesus I pray they don't hurt my child. Did Emmett have his wallet on him when the men took him away?"

"I, I don't know. Why?"

4

"Because he had a picture of a white woman in his wallet."

"A white woman? Why?"

"It was one of those pictures that came with the wallet. Emmett purchased a new wallet just before leaving to come down there. Oh, my God! I pray he didn't have his wallet with him and that picture in it."

"Me too, Mamie. Me too. Emmett was in trouble enough. If dose men see dat picture in his wallet, no tellin what da might do."

Mamie hanged up the phone with tears streaming down her tan face. She attempted to bring some order to the chaos and confusion roaring in her head like a storm. Although it was unseasonably warm for Chicago at nearly four in the morning in late August, Mamie felt a chill. She folded her arms for warmth as she sat, still trying to make sense of everything. She deliberated that it all would be only a nightmare if she was dreaming. But she was hauntingly and painfully awake.

Mamie pondered that her present ordeal was all too similar to when she'd received a letter ten years past from her husband Louis, an Army private at the time, stating that he was accused of rape and was being court marshaled. She recalled her husband having declared his innocence and her bemoaning that Louis never stood a chance and was not allowed to testify on his own behalf and was subsequently hanged to death for raping an Italian woman.

Tears streamed down Mamie's face as she hoped and prayed for Emmett's safe return home. She thought about needing to call her boss to let him know that she wouldn't be in for work today in regard to her civil service job and the reason why. It dawned upon her that today was Sunday – no job to go to, but a day of worship.

* * *

Roy Bryant, in his early twenties, and his half-brother J.W. Milam, five years older, came looking vigilante-style for their human prey and found him in the person they'd declared to be *a young, sassy nigga boy* from Chicago whose name they'd learned to be Emmett Louis Till. They'd also discovered that Emmett was visiting relatives in Money and had been reported and identified as the boy who four days ago whistled at and insulted Roy's wife at the grocery store they owned. And Roy was hell-bent on teaching the boy a lesson as to how niggers were supposed to comport around white people and particularly with white women. So Roy enlisted the help of his stepbrother to come and drag Emmett away from his great- uncle's home without a court-ordered summons. The men understood that they didn't need legal papers or authority in the Mississippi Delta to spirit away Negroes for any purpose a white man desired. And it was Roy's desire to teach the boy from up North a "solid lesson" regarding *nigger decorum* around white folks in the South.

After terrorizing, torturing, beating, maiming, and shooting Emmett in the head, Roy and J.W. weighed the boy's body with a near one hundred-pound rusty iron cotton gin fan attached to his raw fleshy neck before tossing his deformed body deep in the Tallahatchie River from an old fishing boat. Emmett's body splashed loudly in the quiet of the night, followed by the rhythmic clanging sound of the chain against the boat, and concluding with a clamorous splash emanating from the cotton gin fan.

"That niggah's fish bait now, " Roy rejoiced as Emmett's body sank underneath the quiet surface of the river glistening under the light of a half moon. Roy dipped his bloodstained hands in the river and washed off the blood, and as did J.W.

On their journey home from the bank of the Tallahatchie, Roy boasted, bragged, and reveled in regard to the murder of fourteen-year-old Emmett Louis Till. J.W. joined in on the jubilee by sharing a jar of moonshine liquor and smoking a fat cigar.

J.W. said, "White people in the North might allow niggers to get away with messin with white women, but niggers got a rude awakenin when they bring their black asses down here." He took another swig of the liquor and said, "Damn that nigger made me angry. He was a little cocky sonnabitch." J.W. wiped sweat from the top of his balding head with his bare hand. He removed the cigar from his mouth and said, "When other niggers 'round here discover that Chicago boy missin they'll be reminded about the consequences of messin with white women."

Roy said, " And it didn't matter how old he was because niggah boys grow up to be niggah men. The boy had to be taught a lesson. Don't care where he was from. That niggah made me crazy with anger when he claimed to be just as good as a white person. That's the kinda crazy thinking niggahs in the North possess. Well, that Chicago boy's mother won't be able to recognize him if his body ever shows up, which I doubt."

J.W. accepted the jar of moonshine back from Roy and said, "That nigger's attitude would've upset any white man. And he never apologized. We were right to do what we did to him. Any white man down here would've felt like we did. It's still hard to believe that the nigger had a picture of a white girl in his wallet. That was just too much." J.W. swallowed from the liquor jar and passed it to Roy who said, "I know I ain't gonna no more think about killin that niggah than if we'd slaughtered a hog."

The men finished off the jar of moonshine and felt satisfied that Southern justice had prevailed and had been rightfully served on the Negro boy from Chicago who they'd assessed as not knowing his place. Roy's conscience was sedated because he was of the opinion that the flirtatious and disrespectful boy had committed a felonious act against a white woman – his wife. So he felt justified in regard to the homicide he committed. He drove his truck down dusty dirt roads and past cotton fields to drop off J.W. and thanked him for his assistance.

When Roy arrived home he primed a water pump in the back yard of the old, two-story, two-bedroom house where he and his wife Caroline and their two young boys lived. He ran water in a banged up tin tub, splashed the cold water on his face, and scrubbed his hands with a bar of Lava soap that he kept next to the pump. He removed his muddy boots, disrobed, and deposited his bloodstained clothing in the tub of water. He entered the house and the bedroom where his wife lay in wait and eager to know the nature of the business he and J.W. had taken care of with the Chicago boy.

"What happened?" Caroline asked.

"We taught that boy a lesson like I said we would. He didn't apologize 'bout nothin and had a picture of a white gal in his wallet. Can yah believe it?"

"My God! What did you do?"

"Never you mind. Don't be concerned about it. But yah won't be bothered by that niggah again or no other niggah 'round these parts."

"Well, whatever you did that boy brought it on himself. Goodnight Roy. We need to get some sleep so we can open up the store in the morning"

"Goodnight Caroline. There's a couple of things I need to attend to before I come to the store in the morning, so I'll be a little late."

Roy got underneath the covers, kissed his wife, and extinguished the kerosene lamp next to the bed. As he lay there his mind revisited his and J.W.'s scenario with the boy from Chicago. Roy mulled that everything that happened was the boy's fault and that he would've been less than a man if he hadn't dealt with the boy like he did. Roy rationalized that if he'd allowed the boy to get off without punishment, that other Negroes would be in his store flirting with his wife. No sooner than sleep crept upon Roy he was suddenly awaken by an eerie clamor outside his house. The noise sounded like something weighty splashing in water and chains rattling. At first he thought he was dreaming, but he was awake and the sound was prominent. He wondered how could it be while understanding that he lived several miles from the river or any body of water that would produce the repeated sound he was hearing. He got out of bed, raised the shade, parted the shear curtains, and looked out the bedroom window from the second floor. He saw no one or anything he thought could be making such a racket. He looked over at Caroline who was fast asleep. The noise got weirdly louder: *splash, clang, clang, clang, clang ... splash.*

Roy figured he was hallucinating. He went to the bathroom and ran cold water in the sink. He dipped both hands in the water and applied it to his face. He peeped through his fingers and became startled by the mysterious crimson rash on the palm of his hands. He ruled out poison ivory, but had no notion what could have infested his hands. His hands didn't itch but the rash had an appearance of bloodstains. Feeling perplexed he ran his hand from the top of his head through his thick dark hair down to the nape of his neck. He felt something foreign in the back of his head. He picked at the substance in his hair and produced a piece of gummy bubble gum pinched between his fingers.

"What the hell!" Roy wondered how the gum got in his hair. He went to his bedroom and saw a wad of bubble gum stuck to the pillow he'd rested on. It didn't make sense to him, knowing that he nor his wife chewed bubble gum. He wondered if his kids were the culprits.

Splash, clang, clang, clang, clang ... splash. The sound grew louder.

* * *

An hour after J.W. was dropped him off at home, he was in a more sober state and found it difficult to sleep. He left his house and went to the backyard in a fresh change of clothes. He became ill upon seeing the blood and particles of human flesh on the clothes he'd worn earlier, and now he was depositing them in a pit he dug. He vomited in the pit, wiped his mouth with a handkerchief, and soaked the clothing with gasoline. He struck a match, lit a cigar, puffed on it, then flicked the match into the pit, producing a roar of a brilliant flame that erased the peripheral darkness of the early morning. He stared into the flame and recounted how he and Roy dragged the Chicago boy away from Moses Wright's home with the intention of scaring him, but which they were unsuccessful in doing because of the boy's conviction that he was just as good as white people. Roy mused that murder wasn't the initial intent, but no less the outcome. He reflected that the boy was spared death from his initial lynching and that the noose was taken from around his neck so that he could be beaten some more, which produced broken bones and crushed cartilage. He recalled the boy's head being repeatedly stumped until it was reduced to mush and much like a crushed ripe watermelon after he was shot in the head.

J.W. visualized the grotesque disfigurement of the boy's face and body as he stared into the fiery pit. The dying flame grew brighter and a white plumb of smoke rose more than five feet above the ashes and meandered back and forth. The phenomenon at first astonished J.W., but now he was startled by the misty life form of a person the smoke took on. He turned and ran inside his house, closed and locked the door. He braced his back against the door with his eyes closed. He took deep breaths in an effort to convince himself that he was imagining things, then saw bubble gum wrappers strewed across the floor that weren't present when he earlier entered the house.

* * *

The morning sun shone through the living room window. Mamie hardy slept after speaking with Uncle Moses. She hadn't had the strength to get up from the large padded chair. She felt weighed down by her heart and mind. She'd occupied the chair as sedentary as a rock since her phone conversation. She'd dozed off a few times but only to awaken to the angst that was stacking up in her head like pallets.

Mamie considered what all she needed to attend to before leaving Chicago to go to Mississippi to see about Emmett. She considered that she wouldn't get paid for another five days, so she would need to ask her mother to borrow some money to catch the train. But first she would need to call her supervisor to apprise him of her situation. Then next she needed to press her hair, but to do that she needed to go to the corner store when it opened at eight, in about three hours, to purchase some Dixie Peach hair dressing because she'd almost run out.

As long as Mamie thought about all she had to do before departing for Mississippi, she felt less encumbered in regard to thinking the worst. She opened up the bible on her lap, read another scripture, and prayed to God that He would answer her prayer regarding Emmett's safe return home. She suddenly was reminded of something else she needed to do before leaving for Mississippi, which was to call her pastor, Reverend Harem Williams, to ask him to have members of the congregation to pray for Emmett and her, hoping that the mass prayers would bring Emmett safely back home.

* * *

Roy Bryant was tired from not sleeping well last night, and hardly at all because of the bizarre noise he heard throughout the night and which didn't end until daybreak.

His wife Caroline prepared breakfast and left to open up the grocery store. He told her that he would arrive before noon after taking care of some business. Roy appreciated the fact that his wife was a good old Southern girl who didn't ask a lot of questions. He considered her to be as loyal as a puppy.

* * *

Vera Franklin checked herself out in the mirror and felt pleased. She thought her jet- black hair that flowed to her shoulders looked perfect. She realized that she had unusual, as some claimed, unnatural looking hair for a dark-skinned colored girl. But she understood that she'd come by her grade of hair naturally, as well, her hazel brown eyes, long eye lashes, thick eyebrows, and pointed nose. Her mother was a full-fledged Cherokee Indian who died giving birth to her. Her father was a tall Negro with dark complexion who'd gone off as a soldier in war in Korea and died, leaving her to feign for herself. She discovered that her good looks attracted both black and white men but found that it was white men who could do the most for her financially, such as Roy Bryant. Living rent-free in one of his rural rental cabins suited her just fine.

Vera enjoyed the largess Roy bestowed upon her in the form of nice gifts and such as the white pearl necklace and matching earrings, as well as the pretty sundress she was wearing at his request for their rendezvous this morning. And she wasn't repelled to pleasing him in a womanly way because of his benevolence toward her, which she'd done for three years since she was nineteen. She mused that none of it had anything to do with love but just the survival of a pretty black woman in the Mississippi Delta. She fancied herself to be as dark as a Hershey's candy bar and no less sweet when it was to her advantage. She pleasured in the knowledge that her black, female nectar intoxicated Bryant and made him drunk with desire.

Chapter Two

August 29, 1955

Shortly before noon, Mamie boarded the Illinois Central train, *The Spirit of New Orleans*, at the bustling Englewood Station at Sixty-third and Woodlawn in downtown Chicago to make her heavyhearted journey to Money, Mississippi.

Her hair was freshly pressed and neatly styled. She wore a white blouse and a Navy blue full-length skirt, wanting to look respectable, but feeling downcast. She boarded with one large suitcase and carried hope and faith along with her. She also brought along some fried chicken and a hefty piece of pound cake wrapped in wax paper and placed in a brown paper sack. But her appetite was no larger than a sparrow's.

Mamie leaned her head back against the seat on the passenger train and closed her eyes. She recalled the words Pastor Williams had spoken to her over the phone, encouraging her to travel to Mississippi with faith and to anchor herself in God, no matter what she discovered. She reminisced growing up in Mississippi and recalled the inferior facilities reserved for Negroes, including schools, which white people deemed separate but equal under southern *Jim Crow* laws, but which was simply rhetoric and a farce as far as most Negroes were concerned. She considered the accommodations in the South to be about as equal for Negroes as T-bone steak was to potted-meat. She thought that not much had changed in Mississippi since she lived and grew up there.

The train whistle squealed and ended Mamie's musing. She was once again reminded of Emmett and the purpose for her trip. She kept her eyes closed, clutched her hands tightly, and mumbled, "Please, Lord, let Emmett be all right. He's a good son."

She recalled the happy times she'd spent with Emmett and particularly last Christmas. She removed photos she'd taken at Christmas and looked at them as tears trickled down her cheeks. She hoped and prayed that Emmett was safe. She held onto Pastor Williams' words of comfort and latched onto her faith that God would make everything right.

The train stopped in Caro, the last stop in Illinois, and where Negro passengers had to abandon their seats and move to the segregated front car behind the train's engine if they weren't already sitting there before travelling into the southern states.

In Memphis, Tennessee, the train dropped off a few passengers and picked up new ones. Mamie focused her sight on an elderly Negro woman with silver-gray hair who boarded, wearing a yellow sundress with daisy patterns. Mamie guessed that the woman was in her late seventies or early eighties. She noticed that the woman was clutching the handles of a crocheted brown bag with stitched designs. The woman's shoulders were hunched and she walked with the aid of cane.

"Miss, is this seat vacant?"

Mamie looked into the pleasant black face of the elderly woman and said, "No one's sitting here."

"Good, I'll just park my tired body next to yah, if yah don't mind."

"No, not at all."

Mamie watched the woman moved slowly, grasped the seat in front for support, turned and dropped her full weight onto the seat. She placed her bag between her feet and held onto her cane. "Where yah headed young lady," the woman asked.

"Mississippi," Mamie answered.

"Me, too. What part?"

"Money."

"I'm headed to Greenwood, not far from Money. Yah got people dar?"

"Yes. I used to live there but moved to Chicago when I was twelve. I'm going to see about my son."

"What's wrong? Is he sick or somethin?"

"No, he's not sick but he's in trouble." Tears gushed from Mamie's eyes as her shoulders heaved.

The elderly woman took an embroidered handkerchief from her bag, wrapped an arm around Mamie's shoulders, and turned toward her. She handed Mamie the handkerchief and asked, "Lord, child, what's the matter? What kinda trouble yer son in?" She waited for Mamie to gain her composure.

Mamie dried her tears, lifted her face from the handkerchief, and said, "I received a call last night from my Uncle Moses in Money where my son was staying on summer vacation. He told me that two white men came and dragged my son outta his house and took him somewhere and no one has seen him since."

The vintage Negro woman looked sorrowfully deep into Mamie's swollen, red eyes and said, "Oh, baby, I'm so sorry. Why did the men take yer son?"

"They accused him of getting fresh with the wife of one of the men and claimed he whistled at her."

17

The woman emitted a sympathetic grunt. She patted Mamie gently on her hand that rested in her lap. She reached down and retrieved her brown bag from off the floor and pulled out a Mason jar that was three-quarters filled with dark soil.

Mamie stared at the jar, perplexed about its contents.

"Open up yer hand, baby."

Mamie did as the woman requested without question. She watched as the woman removed a pinch of the dark soil from the jar and placed it in the palm of her hand.

"Close yer hand," the woman directed.

Mamie complied.

The woman said, "I had ancestors who wuz slaves and led outta slavery to Canada through the Underground Railroad by Harriet Tubman. When they reached Canada, Harriet told the runaway slaves to dig up a handful of soil and save it in order to always remind 'em of their freedom and for it to be a keepsake for generations to come. The soil came to be known as *Freedom Soil* and over the years used in rituals for good luck, health and prosperity. Some claim that if yah squeeze the soil in the palm of yer hand and close yer eyes that good visions will come during times of trouble. Lean back, close yer eyes, and jes' relax yer mind. I'm gonna do the same. Baby, give me yer free hand to hold on to."

Mamie and the aged woman leaned back against their seats with their eyes closed, both clutching the *Freedom Soil.* The elderly woman counted silently to eighty-seven, which was the age of the oldest living person in her family, and hence a part of the ritual. She opened her eyes and instructed Mamie to do likewise.

"How do yah feel, baby?" the woman asked.

"More at peace, but I didn't experience a vision."

"Not everyone sees a vision, but I did."

"What did you see?"

"I saw lots of people in a circle rallyin 'round a young boy about thirteen-years-old or maybe fourteen or fifteen. A soft-spoken Negro woman with light-colored skin and wearing glasses stepped inside the circle next to the young boy. She wuz upset about an injustice dat she experienced. People boycotted 'cause of the injustice against her. Then I had a vision of a young Negro man, a minister, with a powerful voice. People listened to his messages and followed him from city to city while he preached, marched in protest of injustices, and spread messages of love. They referred to him as some kinda prince. The young boy in the middle of the circle wuz the focal point of everything and wuz at peace."

"I wonder if the boy in the circle was supposed to be my son Emmett?" Mamie asked. She found herself being jostled. She looked up into the face of a Negro sleeping car porter wearing a gray uniform and a matching cap with a black bill.

"Are you okay, Miss?" the porter asked. "You've been asleep for a long time and were apparently dreamin. We've reached your stop."

Mamie cleared her eyes and asked, "Where did the woman go that was sitting next to me? She had gray hair and walked with a cane."

"There's wasn't a woman sittin next to you. A young man boarded the train in Evansville and was sittin next to you all the time."

"Are you sure?"

"Yes, I'm sure. Part of my job is to keep track of the riders. Those gum wrappers must be his."

Mamie looked down at the seat next to her and saw three empty bubble gum wrappers; the same brand Emmett was so fond of. "Where did the boy go?" Mamie queried.

"He got off jes' a minute ago."

Mamie grabbed her belongings and rushed from the train. She searched frantically but neither saw a young boy or the elderly Negro woman. She walked to a water fountain situated below a sign that read *Colored Only*, which was next to a water fountain that had a *Whites Only* sign above it. Mamie drank from the colored fountain and went to the outdoor pay phone to call Uncle Moses to pick her up.

She waited on the porch along with other Negroes outside the small train depot. She swatted pesky mosquitoes and thought of Mississippi as being a place where Negroes stayed emotionally thirsty and never able to clinch their thirst for equality and justice. She felt life in Mississippi for Negroes to be as searing as the noonday sun. She began questioning her maternal judgment for sending her son to a place where she and her family had literary escaped from when she was a young girl. She watched white people go inside the station to attend to whatever business they well pleased and where fans hummed and cooled them off from the humidity and stifling heat. The Negroes fanned themselves outside on the porch and endured.

Mamie viewed in the distance the bright orange aura of the descending evening sun and looked around at the red Mississippi clay. She cuffed a hand into a tight fist and thought about the dark *Freedom Soil* as well as the venerable Negro woman and the vision she'd shared. Mamie's thought focused on the young boy in the middle of the circle who the woman said was happy and at peace. Then it dawned on her that she was holding an embroidered handkerchief that wasn't hers.

* * *

For a third consecutive night, Roy Bryant found a good night sleep as difficult to achieve as reading a Chinese novel. It was 3:00 A.M. and the noise in his head had him tossing and turning like a man possessed. He surmised that the sound was not external but rather harbored in his mind because his wife Caroline had denied hearing anything of that nature; and, unlike him, she had no trouble sleeping throughout the night.

Roy rose from his bed for the umpteenth time and thus the same ritual since… He shut down his contemplation like always in desperation, not wanting to attribute the sound in his head and his insomnia to any guilt for having murdered the boy from Chicago. He trudged from the bedroom to the kitchen, filled a glass with water from the faucet, and sat at the kitchen table in deep thought as he stared at the red rash on the palms of his hands. He was reminded that the stains first appeared after…

"Hell no! No damn way!"

Roy was determined not to accept that the rash on his hands was a manifestation, and that the incessant sound in his head was some form of retribution for killing the boy. But he couldn't make sense of it and considered that he might be going crazy, which he could accept over any feeling of contrition.

After an hour Roy went back to bed.

Splash, clang, clang, clang, clang… splash.

The sound returned and woke Roy again. He pressed a pillow over his face and covered his ears.

Splash, clang, clang, clang, clang… splash.

The sound was still audible. He was desperate for sleep but couldn't rid himself of the discordant and stentorian rhythm in his head, which after the second night had made him conscious that the metallic, clanging sound was a replica of when he and J.W. threw the boy's body overboard into the river with a chain around his neck and a cotton gin fan serving as an anchor.

Splash, clang, clang, clang, clang… splash.

Roy was obstinate about conceding guilt, concluding in his mind that he'd rather die first. With his head buried underneath the pillow, he contemplated smothering himself in order to lose consciousness.

Splash, clang, clang, clang, clang... splash.

* * *

J.W. Milam was sleeping intermittently at night and he knew why without surmising in the least. Since beating, lynching, and murdering the boy from Chicago, he felt haunted. He was often seeing, if not imagining, mystical images that took on human forms via smoke from fires, blowing dust, misty images, and shadows on the walls of his bedroom – like now. He could make out the silhouette of a body hanging from a tree branch.

J.W. jumped out of bed and grabbed a heavy blanket to cover the bedroom window, wanting to cast the room in total darkness and to eliminate the shadows on the walls. He couldn't understand why he was being haunted and tormented and not Roy while understanding that it'd been Roy's idea to teach the boy a lesson; no matter that he himself shot the boy in the head. J.W. conjectured that he'd gone along with Roy that night for the amusement and joy of seeing the boy squirm and plead. He hadn't expected or anticipated murder; not at first until the boy starting saying things about being just as good as white people.

J.W. couldn't understand why he was being tormented while Roy didn't seem to be bothered, since he never heard him express any feelings to the contrary and seemed to go about his business like nothing ever happened.

J.W. dozed off, but within seconds a heavy wind arose that shook the house, rattled the windows, and blew the blanket off the bedroom window across the room. The racket woke him up. His sight riveted on a shadow on the wall that had the appearance of a human-like form that seemed to struggle for life with a noose around the neck and hanging from a barren tree. He heard the wind making eerie and guttural sounds like someone dying in agony. His eyes bulged and grew as large as half-dollars. His breathing was fast and shallow. Beads of cold sweat surfaced on his face and hands. A pain pierced his heart as though skewered by a dull knife. The scream in his head lodged in his throat like a cork.

Chapter Three

The Mississippi Delta

Herbert Cunningham gathered with his fraternal brothers in an isolated, wooded area during the late evening in front of a towering bonfire with leaping flames where their Klavern was located. All the brothers were mutually clad in full-length white robes and matching peaked hoods. They were equally agitated and incensed after being enlightened by the Exalted Cyclopes that the local NAACP was encouraging Negroes to register to vote in an attempt to upset the social order of things white people cherished and held sacred in Mississippi.

Brother Cunningham listened intensely as he contemplated the reprisals suggested by the Exalted Cyclopes against any colored person foolish enough to register to vote and go to the polls in LeFlore County. He heard the Exalted Cyclopes say, "Brothers, we'll deal with our niggah situation later. Our primary purpose for gatherin here tonight is to induct twelve worthy members into our fold. And what makes these men worthy is that they are white Protestants who hate the blacks, Jews, and Catholics who have debased America and its heritage. Escort the men to the sacred alter to be anointed with oil and administered the oath."

Brother Cunningham glowed as the men were guided to the altar. He watched the inductees kneel before the Exalted Cyclopes who applied a drop of oil from a vessel to the forehead of each recruit and then commanded them to stand.

The Exalted Cyclopes thrust both his arms forward and cited, "With this transparent, life-giving, powerful God-given fluid, more precious and far more significant than all the sacred oils of the ancients, I set you apart from the men of your daily association to the great and honorable task you voluntarily allotted yourselves as citizens of the Invisible Empire."

* * *

Emmett's disappearance had Mamie Till on edge. She couldn't sleep and no matter how tired she felt. She held a photo of Emmett in her hand as she longed to hold him in her arms and hear his voice again. She thought about his favorite song *Why Do Fools Fall in Love* by Frankie Lymon & The Teenagers and how he'd sing it off-tune and make her laugh. All she wanted to do was to get him safely back home. She vowed to herself that she would never again fuss at him, about his messy bedroom, or about the bubble gum wrappers he would leave all over the house. She longed to cook his favorite meal: pancakes with lots of Aunt Jemima syrup and pork link sausages. Tears fell from her eyes. She'd been crying all through the night and waiting for the morning sun to show itself and not set one more day in Mississippi without her seeing her son.

As the sun rose in the eastern horizon, so did Mamie's hope of seeing Emmett alive. Uncle Moses was up early. He came into the living room where family portraits and religious symbols lined the off-white walls. He sat next to

Mamie on the sofa where she'd remained through the night, holding onto the photo of Emmett. Uncle Moses handed her a cup of coffee, which she accepted. She took a sip and asked, "What time do you think we can go and see the sheriff?"

"I wuz told 'round nine o'clock when I called."

"What's the sheriff's name?"

"Herbert Cunningham. He's been the sheriff for 'bout ten years."

"What kind of person is he? Do you think he will help us?"

Uncle Moses got up from the sofa and walked to a window. He peered out at the rows of potatoes, tomatoes, green beans, turnips, mustard, and collard greens he'd planted in his garden and at a tractor that was as old as Emmett that stood near an old gray shed. His tongue was still but his mind was racing.

"Uncle Moses, I asked if you thought Sheriff Cunningham would help us."

"I heard yah, Mamie." He turned around to face her and said, "Mamie, jes' don't count on Sheriff Cunningham doin a lot. White people are the same as da wuz when y'all packed and left from down here. I'm jes' sayin don't get your hopes too high 'cause white people is gonna support each other no matter what when it come to us coloreds. And no matter what Mr.Bryant and those men did with Emmett, yah can expect white people down here to stick together. Dat's jes' the way thangs is down here. Nothin changed. Nothing changed at all. Thangs is jes' the same as it always wuz."

* * *

It appeared to Uncle Moses that the sky was posturing for rain as he drove Mamie to the LeFlore County Sheriff Department. He felt distraught about Emmett's abduction, which hounded him to no end. He recalled how brazen the men were when they came to his home early in the morning and entered, as though they'd owned it and everybody in it. Although he was born and raised in Mississippi, he'd always begrudged the manner in which white people, and white men in particular, disrespected and treated colored people. He contemplated that white men reveled in belittling colored men, making them submissive, and treating them like big children. He pondered being sixty-four years of age and never treated as a man by white people. Moisture came to his eyes as he loathed not being able to stand up to the men who invaded his home and spirited away his great nephew at gunpoint. And he didn't feel at all optimistic about what they did to Emmett.

Uncle Moses rolled the driver-side window fully down to take advantage of an easterly breeze. He took a handkerchief from the back pocket of his freshly starched coveralls, dabbed the tears in the corner of his tired, reddish eyes, wiped sweat from his brow, and rubbed his callous hands through his, short, thin, gray hair.

Mamie festered on the inside with her own thoughts and was relying on prayer. She struggled to be optimistic with the passing of time. The magnolia trees and cotton fields along the side of the road starkly reminded her that she was in the Deep South and where her son had disappeared.

* * *

A young white sheriff deputy tapped on Sheriff Herbert Cunningham's office door, heard "Come in", and entered. He said, "That colored woman from Chicago who called to say her son is missin is here to see you, sheriff. She's here with an old colored boy."

"I'll see 'em after I finish my breakfast. Tell 'em to wait."

28

The deputy left the sheriff's office, approached Mamie and Uncle Moses and said, "The sheriff's busy. He'll see you shortly. Take a seat over there." He pointed to an area where other Negroes sat and away from white people.

Sheriff Cunningham took his time finishing his breakfast, in no hurry to assist Mamie Till or any of the coloreds; nor anyone else who he didn't consider a constituent and supporter of him at the polls come election time. And he knew very well that the coloreds were no factor during an election because they couldn't vote or were afraid to vote. He thought about what the Exalted Cyclopes enlightened the brothers about in regard to the NAACP encouraging the coloreds to register to vote. The contemplation angered him as he scooped heavily buttered grits from his plate with a fork and ate them. A broad smile appeared on Sheriff Cunningham's reddish face as he recalled the Exalted Cyclopes' describing the NAACP as the "Nigger Association of Apes and Colored People" at last night's meeting.

The sheriff completed his breakfast, took a sip from his coffee cup, wiped his mouth with a paper napkin and buffed his badge with it before discarding it in the wastepaper basket next to his desk. He lit a cigarette then buzzed the inter-office. He directed a deputy to bring Mamie Till to his office.

Mamie stood along with Uncle Moses and primped her neat, glossy black hair with her fingers. She tugged at her blue sundress as they followed the sheriff deputy. Upon entering the sheriff's office, Mamie's and Uncle Moses' visions glued to a large Confederate flag on the wall behind the sheriff's desk, along with photos of white men in gray Confederate uniforms. The words *The South Shall Rise Again!* were written in black cursive letters underneath the flag.

The sheriff remained seated at his desk, leaned back in his chair, and crossed his ankles on the corner of his desk, making the soles of his boots visible. He blew smoke from his mouth and didn't bother to offer Mamie and Uncle Moses a seat. And had no intention to do so. "Now, what's this about your son missin? And who's this ol' boy?" Sheriff Cunningham asked.

"This is Moses Wright, my son's great-uncle. He was home when the men came to his home and took my son away at gunpoint. He called your office after it happened and was told that we needed to wait forty-eight hours to make a missing person report. Sheriff, out of due respect, I don't understand why this is being treated as a missing person case. My son was kidnapped at gun point."

"Girl, are you from down here? And do you work in law enforcement?"

"I'm originally from here and no sir I don't work in law enforcement."

"Then girl don't come in here tellin me what kinda case this is. I'll decide that. Is that clear?"

"Yes sir." Mamie said, humbly.

"Okay. Now we're understandin each other." The sheriff combed his fingers though his brown mane that was highlighted by strands of gray at his temples. "So, boy, you say that you saw two men come to your house and take away this girl's son?"

"Yessuh."

"What time of day was it? And what did the men look like?"

"It wuz between two and two-thirty in the mornin. The men wuz white. I knew one of 'em. His name is Roy Bryant who owns a grocery store in Money. I didn't know who the other man wuz, but his head wuz bald at the top and he wuz the same height as Mr. Bryant, but older. Maybe thirty-somethin."

"So, you claim that Roy Bryant and another man came to your house with guns and took this girl's son with 'em?"

"Dar wuz only one gun, suh. The other man with Mr. Bryant had a gun."

"Are you certain there was a gun involved and couldn't this girl's son have gone with the men willingly?"

"Sheriff, I'm sho' dar wuz a gun; a pistol. And my nephew didn't go willingly. He wuz cryin and beggin when the men took him."

"So, did you say anything to the men?"

"I begged 'em not to take my nephew and do him harm."

"Why did they say they came for this girl's son?"

"Mr. Bryant claimed that Emmett insulted his wife at his store. Said somethin 'bout Emmett asked his wife for a date and then whistled at her when he left the store."

The sheriff lifted his upper torso like a King Cobra. His blue eyes enlarged and froze into a glare at the witness.

Uncle Moses dropped his head and looked off, understanding that it wasn't acceptable for coloreds to look white people in their eyes. He cleared his throat and said, "Emmett claimed he didn't do any of what Mr. Bryant claimed he did. Mr. Bryant grabbed Emmett by the neck and the other man pointed a gun at his head and asked if Emmett wuz callin his wife a liar. I told Mr. Bryant that Emmett wuzn't from down here and if he did what he claimed, it wuz 'cause Emmett didn't know better. I promised Mr. Bryant dat on my dead mother's grave dat it'd never happen again, but he didn't listen to me and took Emmett away anyhow. He said he wuz gonna teach Emmett a lesson."

Mamie sniffled. She detected a scowl on the sheriff's face.

Sheriff Cunningham summarily ended the meeting after hearing Uncle Moses' account of what happened and the reason the men came looking for Mamie's son. He simply said he had enough information and sent them on their way.

Mamie's optimism that the sheriff might assist them evaporated like ice under the scorching Mississippi sun. The sheriff let it be known that Roy Bryant had a right to be upset by Emmett disrespecting his wife. The sheriff was also emphatic in stating that any white man worth his salt would be offended, including himself.

As Mamie left the LeFlore County Sheriff Department she noticed a hunched-over elderly colored man sweeping the floor. She felt as though she and Uncle Moses had been treated no better than the trash the man was taking a broom to.

The sheriff caused Mamie to feel trivial and defeated. She was desperate to learn of Emmett's whereabouts but was at a lost as to what to do next. She didn't know where else to turn and didn't want to lose hope as she struggled with the tears building inside of her, but she didn't want the white people to see her cry.

Mamie felt herself living a nightmare. Never could she have contemplated that putting Emmett on a train from Chicago to Mississippi would turn out to be a train-ride to hell. Tears gushed from her eyes as she reached the truck. It seemed to her that the sky began to cry in concert with her as a heavy rain fell.

* * *

After Mamie and Uncle Moses left, Sheriff Cunningham felt full of himself and righteously haughty about not being accommodating. He was in a gleeful mood and felt like sharing his elation with the clerks and deputies in his office. Smirking, he asked, "What do you call a nigger in a sauna?"

His staff laughed but no one articulated an answer.

"What?" someone asked.

"Tar!" the sheriff bellowed.

Everyone laughed.

"What do you call a pool of water with a dead nigger's body in it?" the sheriff quizzed.

"What?" a deputy asked.

"An inkwell!" the sheriff shouted with mirth.

"Okay, okay, I've got another one. What do you call a nigger who whistles at a white woman?"

"What?"

"A tree ornament!" the sheriff whooped. "Got another one. What do you call…"

Chapter Four

Tallahatchie County, Mississippi
August 31, 1955

It was the twilight of the evening. Two middle-aged Negro men were fishing into the murky water of the Tallahatchie River from the thicket of the riverbank. Mosquitoes were annoying and plentiful, but the fishermen endured because the fish were biting just as well. Suddenly they witnessed a strange occurrence. A stream of water rose and levitated more than five feet above the surface of the river, momentarily subsided, then rose again as though it had life and then disappeared. One of the fishermen saw the bobble tied to the line of his cane pole disappear under the surface of the water and then felt a tug on his fishing line.

"Feels like a Mississippi cat," said the fisherman as he struggled to haul in his catch. He grew disappointed upon discovering what looked like a piece of clothing hooked on his line. He pulled his snare to the riverbank where the two men examined it and discerned that it was a T-shirt with the inscription *Chicago White Sox*. They gazed at each other with thoughts of suspicion. They both were from Sumner and had heard talk about the missing boy from Chicago. Knowing that bit of information, the men's Mississippi upbringing and Southern acclimation cause the shirt to become suspect. They agreed that they needed to keep their discovery unrevealed to the local authorities and, instead, acknowledge it to someone who would not disregard their finding or suppress it. They agreed that Reverend Patrick Taylor, pastor of the Bedrock African Methodist Episcopal Church in Sumner, would be the ideal person to contact. The fishermen placed the shirt in a bucket underneath fish they'd caught, hurriedly packed their gear, and scampered up the embankment to their truck.

* * *

Reverend Patrick Taylor's heartbeat quickened during his telephone conversation. He contemplated that if the men's discovery was what they all speculated, then he would need to consult with and defer the matter to someone else in the Negro community who commanded more resources and influence. He immediately thought of Reverend Johnny McAfee, president of the Tallahatchie County Branch of the NAACP.

Reverend Taylor was engaged in deep thoughts when he heard a firm knock at the back door. He knew who it was because he'd instructed the men to come to the back of the house. The time on his watch was ten thirty-three. His wife and children were asleep, which he thought to be a good thing, so as not to have to explain the situation regarding his late evening guests. He hurried to open the door and discovered that it was the men he was expecting: one was the caller and a member of his small congregation and the other he knew as a general laborer. The men visages didn't go unnoticed by the reverend; both appeared fidgety. But so was he.

Reverend Taylor grabbed a lantern off the kitchen table, closed the door behind him, and led the men to a field behind his house next to a wooden shed. One of the men carried a plastic lard bucket attached to a metal handle. He sat the bucket next to the shed. The light from the lantern exposed the fish in the bucket. The man who carried the bucket stuck his large, dark, crusty hand deep into the bucket and withdrew a shirt. Under the glow of the lantern, Reverend Taylor observed the suspected incriminating piece of clothing to be just as it was described over the phone: torn and stained. The reverend blew out the flame to extinguish the lantern. He instructed the men to wait as he hurried back to the house to make a phone call and to fetch his car keys.

* * *

Reverend Taylor felt tense as he sat behind the wheel of his 1950 Oldsmobile heading south to Greenville. All the windows of his car were down that allowed him and his passengers to take advantage of the late evening breeze that flowed through the car as it steadily moved along. They passed a county patrol car sitting off on the side of the road near the woods in the dark.

The reverend observed the speedometer and felt comfortable that he was inside the posted speed limit. He saw the patrol car pull away from its perch and huddled behind his car. The men grew nervous and concerned about the package they were transporting in the trunk of the car. Their fear elevated when the officer activated his flashing lights.

The reverend pulled over on the shoulder of the two-lane road.

The men sat motionless and speechless, hoping for the best. They knew they hadn't violated any traffic laws, but they also understood that Negroes were subject to being stopped for any reason.

The otherwise quiet of the night was encroached by the sound of crickets chirping and owls communicating in the woods.

The men heard the officer's car door open and shut, then the sound of his boots pounding the asphalt as he moved toward them while shining a flashlight inside their car.

"Yah boys got some I.D.? What y'all doin out here this time of the night?" the white sheriff deputy inquired. "Yah not runnin moonshine liquor, are yah?"

"No sir. I'm Reverend Patrick Taylor. We're headed to Greenville, officer." He reached for his wallet to produce his driver's license.

The deputy examined the IDs the men produced and handed them back, with the exception of Reverend Taylor's.

"Headed to Greenville did yah say, reverend?"

"Yes sir."

"Y'all boys are from Sumner, so why the need to go to Greenville this time of the night?"

Reverend Taylor said, "Sam here (referring to his front seat passenger) got a very sick relative in Greenville and wanted me to come and pray with the family."

"Is that so? Why you? They got preachers in Greenville. Y'all coloreds don't lack for preachers. Y'all have more preachers than legitimate children." The deputy chuckled, amused by his own remark, then said, "Hear talk that the preacher who's head of the NAACP is getting the coloreds riled up about voting. Y'all know anything about that, preacher boy?"

"I heard some talk, but don't know too much about it," Reverend Taylor answered.

The deputy handed Reverend Taylor's license back and said, "Preacher boy, I hope y'all don't get yourselves involved with that voting nonsense because if yah do there's certain to be a heap of trouble between the whites and coloreds. Now, y'all don't want trouble between the whites and coloreds, do yah?"

"No, sir."

The deputy shined his light in the face of the front seat passenger and asked, "What about yah, boy? Yah want that kinda trouble?"

"No, sir."

The deputy rotated the light to the face of the passenger in the backseat. "And, boy, what about yah?"

"No, sir, officer, I don't want no trouble."

"Good. That's good, boys; real good. And be sure y'all tell the other coloreds that it'll be lots of trouble if they register to vote. White people 'round these parts like things the way they are. So there's no need to try to change things. Things are good between the whites and coloreds the way it is. Now what's in there?" The deputy illuminated the glove box with his flashlight.

"Just papers," Reverend Taylor answered.

"Let see 'em. Take 'em out."

"Yes, sir."

The deputy examined the papers, didn't detect anything bothersome or suspicious, then asked, "What's in the trunk?" Just then something in the woods caught the deputy's attention and suddenly the crickets stopped chirping and the owls stopped hooting. The deputy rubbed and squinted his eyes, attempting to clear his vision – but to no avail. He saw a hazy figure moving through the trees and hovering above the ground. The deputy's stomach began to rumble as he experienced an urging in his bowels.

"Y'all boys take off," the deputy instructed.

Reverend Taylor and his passengers did just as the deputy instructed – took off.

The deputy ran to the edge of the woods on the opposite side of the road. He hastened to unfasten his gun belt, then dropped his trousers behind a tree and squatted to relieve himself of the sudden bout of diarrhea. He shone his flashlight to search for leaves to wipe his posterior and was surprised to discover scattered bubble gum wrappers among the leaves. He wondered why would any kids be in the woods along this remote portion of the road. He finished cleaning himself and heard crickets suddenly chirping again, as well as owls hooting once more. The hazel figure he thought he saw in the woods had disappeared.

Down the road, Reverend Taylor and his passengers wiped sweat from their faces and counted their blessings. "That was close!" His passengers agreed. They all wondered what would've happened if the deputy had discovered the package in the trunk.

"Men, I feel a prayer inside of me," said the reverend. He pulled over on the side of the road.

* * *

Reverend Johnny McAfee, president of the Tallahatchie County Branch of the NAACP, was on the phone early the following morning. He'd hardly slept last night after the visit from Pastor Taylor and his companions. He was speaking with a FBI agent, edifying him about the situation regarding the boy from Chicago who was kidnapped in Money at gunpoint and never to be seen again. He told the agent that local law enforcement had refused to investigate. He also informed the agent about the nature of the shirt in his possession that was fished out of the Tallahatchie River and delivered to him for safekeeping.

"Negroes in Mississippi need justice," Reverend McAfee beseeched before ending the telephone conversation with the agent.

On the evening of the following day, a FBI Recovery Team searched an eerily calm Tallahatchie River under a gray sky for a body. Tallahatchie County Sheriff Clarence Studder, several of his deputies, and a crew of FBI agents stood on the bank in the midst of moss-laden cypress trees watching the operation. The sheriff thumped a cigarette from his Lucky Strike pack into the palm of his hand and lit it. He watched the operation with a disposition as bitter as vinegar, feeling most irritated about the FBI's involvement and what he'd said to be "interference in local affairs."

Curious bystanders, black and white, witnessed the operation from the bank of the river. Mamie Till, family members, and well-wishers huddled together on a grassy knoll as they watched.

Uncle Moses questioned his manhood for not being able to defend Emmett from the men who grabbed him from his home. Mamie stood on the bank in a numb trance. Her skin felt icy cold. Her innards turned like a rotisserie. Her mind was torn: wishful to see her son alive but also doubtful that she would. She fought against allowing her doubtful contemplation to overpower her hopeful musing. She felt drained.

Three hours into the search the recovery team hauled a body from the river. Two veteran recovery team members became sick and gagged upon seeing the gruesome condition of the body.

* * *

Before noon the next day, Roy Bryant and J.W. Milam were arrested and brought to the Tallahatchie County Jail without handcuffs by sheriff deputies. The men were arrested for the murder of Emmett Louis Till.

Sheriff Cunningham got immediately on the phone and called the Exalted Cyclopes, informing him of the arrest of Roy Bryant and J.W. Milam who both had been considered for induction into the Invisible Empire. The Exalted Cyclopes thanked the sheriff, hung up, retrieved a telephone number from his personal directory and made a call to brother Curtis Sterlings.

* * *

Roy Bryant and J.W. Milam got arraigned on the morning after their arrest and were present in court still without handcuffs and with their lawyers.

The court's bailiff announced, "All rise. Court is now in session, presided over by Circuit Judge Curtis Sterlings."

Judge Sterling, a tall, slender white man with curly brown hair and in his early forties, entered the courtroom from his chambers. The bailiff said, "All may now be seated. Court is now in session."

A young white female clerk with long blond hair said, "The first case this morning, judge, involves Roy Bryant and J.W. Milam, accused of murdering Emmett Louis Till in LeFlore County, Mississippi." The clerk handed the judge the file case and said, "The defendants are present and represented by their attorneys."

Judge Sterling said, "The defendants and their counsels may approach the bench. How do the defendants plea?"

"Not guilty," the two men said in unison.

"Bail is set at one hundred dollars each."

No one from the prosecutor's office objected. Roy Bryant and J.W. Milam smiled and left with their attorneys to post bail. Judge Sterling asked for the next case.

Later that evening Moses Wright's phone rang close to midnight. "Hello."

"Is this Moses Wright?"

"Yeah, it is. Who's callin?"

"Niggah, don't worry about who's callin. Jes' be careful about what you say in court when the time comes or else be concerned about your own body being dragged outta the river." Click.

* * *

An elderly white man who worked the night shift as janitor at the Tallahatchie County Court House used his key to enter the courtroom of Judge Curtis Sterlings. The janitor slid across the floor on his frail legs and lost the cigarette from his mouth. He caught his balance on a bench. He turned on the lights and discovered patches of water. He'd seen spills before but nothing like the uniform pattern he was viewing. He followed the trail of water that led him to one of the benches in the courtroom. He took off his hat and scratched his gray head upon seeing bubble gum wrappers scattered on the bench. He was puzzled as he left to fetch a mop and bucket.

* * *

Sheriff Cunningham of LeFlore County arrived at his office earlier than usual, upset about the FBI's presence and involvement in the death of what he'd labeled the smart-mouth, disrespectful nigger boy from Chicago who insulted a white woman. The sheriff mused that the boy's disappearance was a cogent and fitting message for all the coloreds in regard to the consequence for not properly comporting around white people. He detested the Yankees, liberal media, communist sympathizers, and race-traitors coming to Mississippi to cover the homicide. He thought all the hoopla and focus had caused his office to appear inept for not earlier arresting Roy Bryant and J.W. Milan for kidnapping. He fumed at the thought. Blood rushed to his face turning it red.

Sheriff Cunningham rested his wide-brim Stetson hat on a coat rack and went to his desk to make some telephone calls.

"What the hell!"

The sheriff popped up from his chair with both his hands pressed against the seat of his trousers. He looked down at the chair and discovered a puddle of water. He looked up at the ceiling, thinking that perhaps it had leaked but saw no tell-tell evidence. He secured a cloth towel to soak up the water, dried the chair, fanned his butt, and sat back down. He opened his desk drawer and became stunned to see bubble gum wrappers inside.

* * *

Roy Bryant's black mistress, Vera Franklin, had her mind made up about what she planned to do after over hearing Roy discuss killing the young boy from Chicago and bragging about getting away with murder while talking to his stepbrother J.W. Milam over the phone. She knew Roy thought she was asleep in her bedroom at the time, but she pretended to be asleep, just like she faked having orgasms with him. She cogitated about Roy being real tired and explained that his sexual dysfunction was a result of not sleeping well at night, which she mused little mattered to her.

Vera knew she would place her life in danger if she revealed that she'd over heard Roy confess to the murder. She understood that there was no way she was going to volunteer to be a witness at the murder trial. She also felt that she couldn't live with herself by doing nothing. She flung her long flowing jet-black hair out of her face like a white woman and paid the store clerk for the rat poison. She left the store and pleasured in the thought that her purchase would take care of two-legged rodents as well.

Chapter Five

News of Emmett Till's death traveled to Chicago and around the nation and other parts of the world before Mamie arrived back home. She felt overwhelmed as she witnessed throngs of people in front of her house, and most notably the people with cameras, as she embarked from the cab she'd taken from the train station. She felt relieved to see Reverend Harem Williams emerge from the crowd and approached her. He assisted her with her bags and hurriedly escorted her to the front door of her house.

Reverend Williams turned to the crowd and said, "Please my good people, Mrs. Till is no doubt experiencing a lot of strain. She's obviously in mourning, so please give her the opportunity to rest and get herself together. I'm sure she will have a statement to make later regarding the murder of her son in Mississippi."

* * *

Mamie used Reverend Williams' broad shoulders for comfort and to cry on. Her tears flowed unabated and prolonged as the reverend sat next to her on a sofa, held her, and administered empathetic pats to her back. Mamie raised her head and said, "They killed my child, Pastor!"

"I know, Sister Till. I know."

"Why, Pastor? Why did they have to do that to Emmett?"

"We don't always know why people do the evil they do, but God will be their judge."

"Why couldn't God protect Emmett? Where was God when they came and got my child, tortured him, and murdered him? Why did God let 'em do this to him? He was just a child; a child I carried inside of me for nine months and raised for fourteen years and these men came along and ended my child's life in moments." Mamie hung her head and cried into the handkerchief she held in her hand.

"It wasn't God's doing. It was the ungodliness in those men that caused Emmett's death, Sister Till. God's role isn't to control the hearts and minds of man. Scripture says that he who believes in God shall not perish and will find their reward in his kingdom. And those who don't believe and not confess their sins will perish in hell. It's times like this, Sister Till, that you need to be strong in your faith, trust in God's wisdom, and bask in the glory of Jesus Christ, our Lord and Savior."

"I want to be strong, Pastor. I'm trying, but my soul is weary. Identifying Emmett's body was the hardest thing I've done in my life. It was horrible, Pastor. One of his eyes was hanging from his face and the other one was missing. Parts of both his ears were missing. One side of his face was crushed to the bone and the back of his head was nearly separated from his skull. His mouth was wide open and his tongue was hanging out. He had only three teeth left. In order to identify my son, I started at his feet because it was hard looking at his face. I recognized his feet and knees and the teeth that were still in his mouth. I also recognized the color in the hanging eye. He had on his father's ring with his father's initials. I saw a hole in his head and assumed it was a bullet hole. I could look through the hole and see daylight on the other side. And I wondered why did they have to shoot him, too."

Reverend Williams grimaced at Mamie's detailed and graphic description. He gently held Mamie's trembling hands.

"That's what they did to Emmett, Pastor. That's what those bastards did!" Mamie blubbered. "Excuse me, Pastor."

"That's okay, Sister Till. I understand your hurt and pain. Just let it out."

Mamie stared at the photo of Emmett that she held in her hand. Her tears fell and soaked into her blouse and skirt. She said, "They beat Emmett so bad that he looked like a monster. I sent my child to Mississippi whole and now he's coming back home with parts of him missing. Emmett was a good-looking boy." Mamie looked again at the photo then said, "My child looked more horrible than Frankenstein after what they did to him. It hurts, Pastor. It hurts! Dear God help me. Please!" Tears gushed from her eyes.

Reverend Williams reached for Mamie's hands, held on to them, and said, "I know it hurts, Sister Till. I know. And God is with you."

"I wanted God to be with Emmett! Why couldn't God have been with Emmett so this wouldn't happen? They hurt my child; hurt him real bad. I can't imagine how scared he must've been. What they did to Emmett no one shouldn't have done to a dog. A dog, Pastor! A dog!" Tears exploded from Mamie's tear ducts and ran down her face.

"Sister Till, God is with Emmett. God never abandoned Emmett and He won't abandon you. Your faith is being tested. Read scripture tonight, pray, and commune with God. He will answer you and help you through your pain and sorrow."

"You think God has that much time to spend on me?"

"God's time is eternal. You are a child of His and He will spend as much time as it takes."

"What about the men who killed Emmett? Are they children of God?"

"Yes they are, but sometimes in families children go astray. Make no mistake about it, our Father in Heaven will appropriately take care of his wayward children. Their evil will not go unpunished."

Mamie thanked Reverend Williams for coming, for his words of comfort, for his prayers, and for the assurance that the church and community would take care of Emmett's funeral and proper burial. She got dressed for bed, opened her bible, knelt on the floor by her bed and prayed. She finished and went to Emmett's room one more time this evening, and each time wishing that he were home safe and sound in his bed. This time she saw something on the floor next to his bed that she hadn't notice before: bubble gum wrappers. She picked up the wrappers but didn't discard them like she would when Emmett was alive. Instead, she folded the wrappers, took them to her bedroom, and stuck them inside her bible.

* * *

The next morning, Mamie was up early after sleeping intermittently and dreaming off and on. Her decision had come in a dream. She called Reverend Williams and apologized to his wife for calling so early and was told that an apology wasn't necessary. The reverend's wife offered her condolences then called her husband to the phone.

"Good morning Sister Till. How are you feeling this morning?"

"Still hurting, but better. I realize I need to be strong for Emmett so that his death won't be in vain."

"Good to hear you're better. Prayer certainly make things better. What can I do for you this morning, Sister? Nothing is too great or too small. The members of the congregation and I are here for you. And like I said yesterday evening, don't hesitate to call if you need anything. Anything at all."

"Thank you, Pastor, I really appreciate it."

"You're welcome Sister Till. To God be the glory. So what is it that you need?"

"Pastor, it's nothing I need, but, rather, something I want to do."

"And what's that, Sister Till?"

"I want an open-casket funeral for Emmett. I want people to see what they did to my child in Mississippi because words alone can't describe it."

There was a period of silence before Reverend Williams asked, "Are you sure, Sister Till, that you really want to do this, understanding the condition you said Emmett's body is in? The undertakers can't perform miracles. I'm sure you know that."

"I'm not looking for a miracle, Pastor. I'm looking for justice for Emmett. I don't trust those white people in Mississippi to provide justice to what happened to Emmett. And since the media is so interested in what happened, I want an open-casket funeral so the world can see what those animals did to my child…"

* * *

After hanging up the phone, Reverend Williams wasn't certain that he agreed with Mamie about having an open casket funeral because he thought it might be too gruesome, although he empathized with her rationale. He also understood that she was insistent.

Clad in pajamas, Reverend Williams pondered the matter as he stroked his neatly trimmed black beard with his long, thick fingers. He lifted his six-two, hefty frame from a chair in the living room and went to his study to sit and ponder. He recalled Sister Till telling him that Emmett had been lynched and aside from all else that was done to him. It seemed to Reverend Williams that he needed to do more, realizing that he was hailed as a leader in the Negro community. He pondered as to what he could do since the crime against Emmett happened in another state. He leaned fully back in a large padded chair and closed his eyes. He visualized young Emmett being hanged. Suddenly the words "strange fruit" came to mind. He opened his eyes, went to his record collection and found an LP by Billie Holiday. There it was—her record recording of *Strange Fruit*. He removed the record from its sleeve, placed it on the turntable, lifted the arm of the turntable and guided the needle on the record. He sat back down and listened to the lyrics:

> *Southern trees bear a strange fruit,*
> *Blood on the leaves and blood on the root,*
> *Black body swinging in the Southern breeze,*
> *Strange fruit hanging from the popular tree.*
>
> *Pastoral scenes of the gallant South,*
> *The bulging eyes and the twisted mouth,*
> *Scent of magnolias sweet and fresh,*
> *And the sudden smells of burning flesh.*
>
> *Here is a fruit for the crows to pluck,*
> *For the rain to gather, for the wind to suck,*
> *For the sun to rot, for the tree to drop,*
> *Here is a strange and bitter crop.*

Tears clouded Reverend Williams' eyes. "Strange fruit," he murmured as he visualized young Emmett Till hanging from a tree in Mississippi. He'd seen a number of photos that depicted jubilant, smug-faced white men with bold postures hanging Negroes and posing along with the corpses with a sense of impunity and as though they'd bagged wild game as trophies. And their brazen acts of openly taking photos of their horrific deeds more than suggested to him that the scofflaws didn't fear prosecution in regard to the lynchings that produced the *strange fruit*. His mind was made up. He knew now what he needed to do. He recalled that the NAACP had been working for years to get a federal anti-lynching bill passed by Congress. He decided to join their efforts so that state laws – particularly in the South – wouldn't any longer protect white men from stringing up Negroes at their discretion, murdering them and going unpunished. And the more he thought about it an open-casket funeral for Emmett now sounded like a good idea.

* * *

Reverend Williams accompanied Mamie Till and family members to the A.A. Rayner Funeral Home in Chicago where Emmett's body had arrived in a rubber bag inside a wooden freight crate from Mississippi.

"Open it up!" Mamie shouted in agony and with her face soaked with tears. "Open it up and let people see what they did to my child." She leaned over Emmett's body and cried, "Darling, you have not died in vain. Your life has been sacrificed for something, and I will see to that. I promise, darling. I promise."

* * *

Upon Mamie's insistence, Emmett's body was put on display in an open-casket. Pastor Williams suggested that his body be allowed to lie in state at the funeral home so that people could pay their respect and witness the brutal slaying first-hand. Four days were agreed upon. More than two hundred thousand mourners and curious minded individuals lined up for blocks outside the funeral home to view Emmet's disfigured body.

Mamie Till was most pleased in regard to how the public responded. She was satisfied that she'd made the right decision to have an open-casket funeral, though many fainted upon viewing her son's mutilated body and required assistance. Visitors deposited flowers, cards, and various items inside and outside the casket. *Jet Magazine,* black-owned and headquartered in Chicago, took exclusive photographs of Emmett's deformed corpse and published them. Additional newspapers and magazines published the revealing photos across the country and worldwide, which horrified and enraged people.

* * *

Throngs of people came and left. It was time for Mamie to bid farewell to her only child. Before the casket was closed, Mamie looked down at Emmett with red, swollen eyes and reiterated her promise," Baby, I'm going to see that your life stood for something as long as I have breadth in my body and a tongue to speak."

The casket was closed and Mr. A.A. Rayner, owner of the funeral home, approached Mamie and asked, "What do you want done with all the flowers, cards, and things left by people?" He held a Mason jar in his hand with black dirt inside and said, "This was one of the items left inside the casket. I don't know what its significance is. Do you want us to throw it out?"

"No!" Mamie insisted. "Give it to me. It's *Freedom Soil.*"

"It's what?"

"*Freedom Soil.*"

"And how do you know?"

"I just know. Trust me."

* * *

Mamie felt exhausted when she finally got to bed late. Relatives and friends were still up; she could hear their chatter on the other side of the closed bedroom door. She rolled over and picked up the Mason jar that contained the black dirt that she knew to be *Freedom Soil.* She held the jar close to her heart, shut her eyes, and recalled the elderly Negro woman who'd enlightened her about the soil and who'd had visions of seeing lots of people in a circle rallying around a young boy. She recollected the woman saying that a soft-spoken Negro woman emerged from the circle who was defiant on an injustice she experienced and that people boycotted in her support. Mamie also recalled the woman mentioning that a young, Negro minister rose with a powerful voice and communicated messages that people listened to and that people followed him from city to city while he preached and marched in protest and spread messages of love and peace. What Mamie most remembered was the woman telling her that the young boy in the middle of the circle was the catalysis of it all and that he was happy and at peace.

Chapter Six

Detroit, Michigan

Jamal Peterson observed the commotion from a barstool at Bakers Keyboard Lounge on Livernois Avenue as patrons circulated a September 1955 copy of *Jet magazine*. The hubbub was in reference to an article about the boy from Chicago by the name of Emmett Till who had been brutally murdered in Mississippi for "allegedly whistling at a white woman". Jamal had read the article at home and had seen the horrible photo of Emmett, so he passed when Kim, the cute, high-yellow, late thirty-something barmaid, offered the magazine to him. She handed it to an interested petite female patron with small legs but decent size teats that Jamal was observing at the bar.

Jamal always disagreed with claims that he was a womanizer and would be the first to tell anyone that because he observed women, flirted with some of them, and admired many of them; it didn't mean he was shopping. He fancied himself to be a connoisseur of women. He credited himself with studying women, understanding their likes and dislikes, knowing what turned them on or off, and having mastered an eclectic approach to women for the purpose of getting his way with a number of them. He mused that his ex-wife, Francine, never accepted his explanations whenever she discovered women's phone numbers in his pants and shirt pockets, the rouge on his suit-coats, and lipstick on his shirt collars when he would finally arrive home late and sometimes early in the morning smelling like a distillery, in his ex's words. He recalled Francine telling him that his explanations were as flimsy as piecrust.

Jamal stirred the scotch and coke in his glass and recalled the "Bullshit!" response he often got from Francine whenever he would claim that nothing was going on with the women he kept company with at the bar, which sometimes got reported back to her. He suspected the informants were likely women who wanted him badly or else low-down bitches who'd been with him but got dismissed because he had a bout of guilt for cheating on his wife, whom he affectionately referred to as *Babycakes*. Or maybe things ended because someone more appealing came along. One or the other, he mused.

Jamal pondered that the statement, "We're just friends" was normally his guilty mantra whenever Francine questioned him about the female company he kept. And he recalled using the word *platonic* as if it were a vitamin pill – that is, until the day Francine strolled into the bar and caught him with a scotch and coke in one hand and his other platonic hand between Jasmine McKnight's big, pretty legs. He remembered that his well-used penis was as hard as a brick when she arrived unexpectedly, and just before Jasmine and he were about to leave for the motel to borrow some love from one another. He recalled quickly removing his hand from between Jasmine's thighs when Francine approached their table and asked, "What are you doing, searching for your friend's pussy? Can't you smell it? I'm getting a divorce, you lying, cheating bastard!" He remembered Francine making the statement so loudly that it drowned out the jukebox and commanded everyone's attention in the lounge. He reminisced feeling more embarrassed than if he'd shitted in the middle of the floor.

Jamal pondered that Francine rarely swore, but didn't hold back that night, then doused his neatly pressed suit (a birthday present from her) with his drink before leaving. He called to mind how fine and sexy his own wife looked as she strutted out the lounge, and how foolish he felt as he noticed other men admiring Babycakes and checking out her cute, tight ass in the slacks she wore. Suddenly he was reminded that his wife was s*teak,* filet mignon, and that he was out in the streets flipping and sampling hamburgers. He recalled that it was the same night when he found his car on four flat tires in the parking lot outside the bar and his clothes were on the front porch when a male friend dropped him off at home. And he would grant that he was certifiable drunk when he arrived, figuring he needed to self medicate in regard to the inevitable pain he anticipated when he arrived home.

Jamal got Kim's attention and requested another drink. He told her that while she was at it to serve a round to the two foxy ladies who had just come in and were sitting at the table by the wall next to the framed, autographed photo of Louis Armstrong. Jamal's radar was on, and he really couldn't remember a time when it was off whenever a fine woman – or one just a little cute – was in his sight. He'd experienced on a number of occasions that the more he drank, the more the whiskey altered the not-so-attracted women's appearances by giving them physical makeovers that made them suddenly desirable to flirt with and hopefully to get lucky with after the *last-call* for alcohol before the bar closed. But then after going home with some of them and waking up sober, he, too many times, discovered that the women's features deteriorated, and they didn't look as comely as the night before.

Jamal recognized that he'd come by his way with women naturally because he was just like his *old man,* God rest his soul, who was dead. His mother divorced him for his own brand of cheating that produced children with two other women. At least Jamal knew he didn't have any kids outside his marriage because he always practiced safe sex. So the only child he had was with Francine, a son, Thurgood, named after Thurgood Marshall, the NAACP lawyer who last year successfully argued the case before the Supreme Court that established segregation in public schools was unconstitutional (*Brown vs. Board of Education of Topeka).* It was a case that Jamal relished covering as a freelance journalist. He enjoyed the flexibility in regard to being self-employed after fifteen years working for others with a degree in journalism from the University of Detroit. He'd banked that his sterling credentials would land him some plum contracts and assignments as a freelancer, which he wasn't wrong.

Jamal mulled that most of his assignments kept him on the road but not out of bars or out of bed with other women, which he realized were the reasons Francine divorced him with a four-year-old child whom he loves and misses. He would admit that he still had feelings for Babycakes and knew that he was the one who fucked up the marriage. "Got feelings, hell!" Jamal murmured, "I sill love Babycakes." He pondered that he hadn't wanted a divorce and desired to work things out, but recalled Francine telling him, "You work out finances, household bills, schedules, and a lot of other things in a marriage, but you don't work out infidelity." And he knew Babycakes was right on that account. Nonetheless, he tried to convince her to reconsider. He still could feel the verbal dagger Francine thrust in him when she told him that he was nothing but a "low-down, mangy dog". And added that her mother always told her that if she lay down with canines, she would catch fleas, which was exactly what she'd done with him. He recollected that it was a rather quick divorce after his father-in-law, an attorney, found out about the cheating and used his influence to accelerate the divorce.

"The ladies said thanks for their drinks and said you're welcome to join 'em if you would like", said Kim. She took the twenty-dollar bill Jamal handed to her and went to the cash register to make change. Jamal turned around on the barstool and raised his glass to the two young women whom he'd purchased drinks for and whom appeared to be in their late twenties, early thirties top.

Kim returned with his change. He tipped her and left his barstool to join the women at their table with the knowledge that his clean-cut, handsome features and suits and ties often got him invitations with the ladies, such as the one he was now accepting. He stroked his thick black mustache with his index finger and headed to the table.

"Hello, lovely ladies. I'm Jamal Peterson and would very much like to make your acquaintance." He extended his drink-free hand, his right.

"Hello, Jamal, I'm Tessie Robinson and this is my friend, Vivian DuPree. Have a seat."

"My pleasure. I've never seen you ladies here before. Are you from Detroit?"

"We both live in the Brewster Projects."

"Black Bottom, huh? I know a few people who live there. In fact, several cousins of mine live there. Do you know any Sanfords?" Both women appeared puzzled and shook their heads.

Tessie said, "You look like a professional man. What kinda work do you do?"

"I'm a freelance journalist and a columnist for the Michigan Gazette."

"No kidding? How interesting and very impressive."

Jamal reciprocated Tessie's smile, although hers was brighter. He felt buoyed and encouraged whenever he'd impressed a pretty woman. And he was impressed that terms like *freelance journalist* and *columnist* didn't go over Tessie's head, so he surmised that she was sufficiently educated – thus his type of woman, along with other attributes. He was actually beginning to like her for more than her anatomy.

It didn't go unnoticed by Jamal that Tessie was doing all the talking and was obviously interested in him. He appreciated women who knew what they wanted, especially if it were he. He found Tessie very attractive, but would give Vivian a slight edge in the face department. But Tessie's full lips were more inviting. Vivian's nose was pudgy and cute, but Tessie's eyes were hazel and alluring. Vivian's hair was short and stylish. Tessie's was long and striking. He noticed that both women's fingernails were polished and not chipped. Vivian had a gap in her teeth on the top-front. Tessie's dental was pearly white and even. Both were smartly dressed. Vivian had nice breasts, but was a little heavier than he preferred. Tessie was taller with a thinner waistline. He imagined Vivian had a nicer ass, but Tessie's legs were shapelier. Vivian had light complexion. Tessie's was the color of coffee with a dash of cream like Babycakes. No *ash* showed anywhere on their epidermis; refreshing, he thought. Vivian wore a wedding band. Tessie didn't. It was settled. It was Tessie's panties he wanted to take off tonight.

"Who all have you written for, Jamal?" Tessie inquired.

"Man, it's too numerous to remember them all from off the top of my head. Some are The National Press Association that I'm under contract with, Global News, Post, Time, Newsweek, Look, Life, The Washington D.C. Gazette, The Chicago Daily, The Los Angeles Sentinel. I can go on and on. I recently did a story on Josephine Baker for the *Sentinel*."

"No kidding? You met Josephine Baker?"

"Sure did. I interviewed her at the hotel she was staying at in L.A. She's a very sophisticated woman, aside from being a very talented vocalist and good looking. I'm heading to Chicago tomorrow to interview Emmett Till's mother."

"You're talking about the boy from Chicago who got killed in Mississippi for whistling at a white woman?"

It was the first time Vivian had said something. Jamal looked at her and said, "Yes. The journalist in me tells me that her son's murder is going to significantly change how Negroes are treated in this country. I've got a gut feeling about it."

"I hope you're right," said Tessie. "It was terrible as to what they did to that boy. I don't care if he did whistle or flirted with a white woman." She changed her frown to a smile as she asked, "Jamal, have you ever flirted with a white woman?"

"No I haven't. Never saw a white woman I cared to approach in such a manner because my eyes are always glued to chocolate, molasses, almond, and peach-colored women like y'all."

"You know what to say to us colored girls, don't you, Mr. Jamal?"

"More important, I know how to treat colored women. You are queens like Queen Nefertari of Egypt, a black woman – an African queen. I'm merely your humble servant..."

* * *

The alarm clock went off at six o'clock the next morning. When Jamal awoke, Tessie had breakfast prepared for him at her apartment. Jamal's bags were packed in his car. He was to catch a train to Chicago in three hours. Tessie brought Jamal's breakfast to the bedroom. "Want me to feed it to you? I will. You're no longer my servant. You're my king and, baby, last night you gave me the royal treatment…"

Jamal drove into the Corktown section of Detroit off Michigan Avenue to board a train out of the Michigan Central Depot. The towering train depot with marbled floors and gold-plated chandeliers always impressed him. He found the depot humming with pedestrian traffic. He rested his luggage next to a pay phone inside the depot and although his time was tight, he called Tessie like he promised. He hung up after assuring her once more that last night wasn't just a one-night stand. He promised he would call her when he arrived in Chicago and returned home to Detroit. And although he enjoyed Tessie's company last night, and especially sharing her bed, he was more excited about his interview with Mamie Till regarding the brutal murder of her son.

Chapter Seven

Montgomery, Alabama (1955)

Rosa Parks, a cultured, Negro woman and well respected in Montgomery in regard to her civic involvement and religious activities, had seen many injustices toward Negroes as a resident of Alabama and the South during her thirty-eight years of living. She mused that nothing had tugged at her heart, mind, and soul like the article in *Jet magazine* regarding young Emmett Till's death.

Rosa sat in a comfortable chair in her living room while in quiet contemplation after returning home this evening from her job as a seamstress at a downtown department store. The image in regard to the photo of Emmett Till's mangled body still lingered in the recesses of her mind. She wondered when Negroes would ever achieve justice in America. She thought about all the indignities suffered in Montgomery in regard to riding the Montgomery City Bus Line. She meditated about the police arresting Negro children like fifteen-year-old Claudette Colvin, one year older than Emmett Till, and eighteen-year-old Mary Louise Smith. And in each case they were arrested for not relenting their seats on the buses to white people although they had been sitting in the *colored* section, which was the law.

Rosa felt things needed to change for the benefit and welfare of Negroes. And with young Emmett's death, she thought the injustices were far more than enough and that things couldn't be allowed to go on like they have.

* * *

Martin Luther King Jr., a young, well-educated man of small statue with a thunderous voice that electrified people when he spoke, especially each Sunday when he preached a sermon as pastor of Dexter Avenue Church, was a popular figure in Montgomery. Some referred to him as "reverend", "pastor", or "doctor", depending on their preference and which made him no mind because he was quick to tell people that he wasn't concerned about degrees and titles but, rather, with serving the Lord, preaching the gospel, and serving humanity.

This evening, in the solitude of his study inside his church that overlooked Dexter Avenue, Reverend-Doctor King's heart was heavy as he read for the second time the story about Emmett Till's murder in the Mississippi Delta. He pondered the inhumanity some men perpetrated against others. His theological teaching led him to believe that such men were destined for hell. He felt it was his mission to be dutiful to God and of service to humanity in a way God would direct and approve. He reminded himself that it wasn't his role to judge the men who brutalized young Emmett, although in this instance he felt it difficult to repulse.

As he sat in deep contemplation, Revered-Doctor King deliberated about there having been discussions in Montgomery for years in regard to the fifty thousand Negroes who lived there boycotting the Montgomery City Bus Line. He realized that nothing of the sort had happened beyond the meetings and conversations. He thought that in a day-and-time when white men could boldly violate Negroes by coming to their homes and taking away their children and murdering them – like what had happened to Emmett Till – that it was time out for inaction and apathy. He jotted on a piece of paper the words: *An individual has not started living until he can rise above the narrow confines of his individualistic concerns to the broader concerns of all humanity.*

He laid the ink pen down on his desk next to a writing tablet. He opened up a desk drawer and removed scissors to cut out Emmett Till's picture from the magazine. He rested the picture on the desk and observed it once more. Reverend-Doctor King thought about how Emmett's mother must be suffering. He considered that the time would come when he and his wife, Corretta, would have children. He fancied the kind of world he would like to see them live in. He knew it wasn't a world where people could do what they did to Emmett Till and not all people being repulsed by it. He surmised that if ever there was a time for action; the time was now.

Chapter Eight

South Side Chicago (Black Metropolis)

Jamal Peterson observed a state of chaos when he arrived at the door of Mamie Till's south side residence. Her home was packed with people, and everyone seemed to be in a twitter. A young girl with a tan complexion, big eyes and long, twin pigtails, wearing bobby socks and black and white saddle shoes opened the door for him and walked away without saying anything, leaving him standing near the front door like furniture, so he thought and felt. There were photos on the wall and an assortment of plants and flowers throughout the house that would have given him the impression that he was at a funeral home or florist shop if he didn't know better. He scanned the living room to see if he could recognize Mrs. Till from her photo in *Jet magazine,* but to no avail. There were lots of women in the room but he couldn't discern any of them to be her. He saw a tall, distinguished-looking man with a beard and of medium brown complexion look his way and made eye contact. He watched as the man glided around and through sitting and standing bodies as nimbly as a panther. The man approached wearing a smile, extended his hand and said, "I'm Pastor Harem Williams. And you?"

"I'm Jamal Peterson on assignment with *The National Press Association* to conduct an interview with Mrs. Till. Pleased to make your acquaintance."

"Pleased to meet you also, Mr. Peterson."

"Please call me Jamal. It makes me feel old when people older than ten refer to me as mister."

Pastor Williams chuckled and said, "Well, I'm well over ten, so Jamal it is. Mrs. Till is here but I'm afraid she's not going to have time to conduct an interview. Things have been coming to her fast and furious as you might imagine. She was just recently informed that the trial for the two men accused of killing her son starts in five days. She wants and needs to be present for the trial so there are a lot of arrangements to be made and the reason so many people are present. Mrs. Till apologizes and still wants to honor the interview, but perhaps it has to be by phone or she can do it in Mississippi if you plan to attend the trial."

* * *

After calling a cab, Jamal returned to his room at the Palmer House Hotel. He made a phone call to his contact person at *The National Press Association's* New York office to get clearance to travel to Mississippi in order to cover the trial and conduct a personal interview with Mamie Till. With that done, everything approved, and a train reservation made, he had time to kill before catching the Illinois Central train south the next day. Some food and drinks sounded good. And maybe some female company, which reminded him that he needed to call Tessie Robinson to apprise her of his situation and the change in his itinerary.

After speaking with Tessie, Jamal hung up the telephone. He left his room and went out to purchase a bottle of Johnny Walker Black whiskey, a bottle of Coca-Cola to serve as a chaser, some barbecue ribs, and a copy of the *Chicago Defender* newspaper, which he brought back to his room. He combed through the newspaper and came across a picture of Dorothy Donegan, a jazz pianist who he'd heard raves about but had never seen her perform live. The article read:

> *Dorothy Donegan is a most talented jazz pianist who brashly mixes swing, boogie-woogie, vaudeville, pop, ragtime and Bach -- sometimes within a span of ten minutes – and who is known for an outrageous sense of humor. She is appearing Thursday-Sunday at Chicago's London House, 22569 S. Michigan Avenue & Wacker, showtime at 9 p.m.*

Jamal took a cab to the London House that evening and was on his fifth drink into the second half of Dorothy Donegan's performance. The music had his head bobbing, his feet patting, his shoulders swaying, and his hands clapping as he sat at a table full of strangers, except for the new female friend he met this evening at the club. Her name was Stephanie Parker. She was in town from Cleveland, Ohio visiting friends. She was thirty-two-years-old, a teller at a bank (largest in Cleveland), had one child and was married once and currently divorced for two years.

As Jamal chatted with Stephanie he kept the drinks flowing and the good time escalating. He told his new female friend that her body was telling time. She responded with a seductive smile and inquired as to how it was that her body was telling time. Jamal sipped the whiskey from his glass and told her that she had an hourglass figure. He also told her that she must have descended from heaven because she had the face of an angel. He stated that her lovely brown eyes were hypnotic and that she had him in a trance. He assessed her thighs to be soft and smooth for that's where the *Johnny Walker Black* had his hand applied above her garter and underneath the table covered with white linen. Stephanie appeared to be unfazed by his roaming hand. She matched him drink for drink. But Jamal knew he was ahead of her because he'd gotten started in his hotel room by drinking half the bottle of whiskey. He'd had the mind to tell her that her ex-husband must be stupid to let her get away, but he suddenly thought about his own ex, the *filet mignon,* so he abruptly erased the cognition.

"Another round!" Jamal yelled as a waiter approached their table. "Hell, I'm going to Mississippi to cover the murder trial of the two men who killed Emmett Till. I hope they fry their asses in the electric chair." Speaking the words had somewhat of a sobering effect on Jamal.

A man at the next table said, "Hell, more than half the Negroes in Chicago are from Mississippi. Why do you think we're up here and that it's so many blues singers in this city? White people gave Negroes lots of blues in Mississippi. They ain't gonna do nothin to those men. White men been gettin away with killin Negroes forever and it ain't gonna stop with Emmett Till. I bet'cha! And if yah never been to Mississippi, yah better be careful yourself or else they'll find your body underneath a bridge or someplace."

"Amen, brother!"

"He's sho' tellin it like it is."

"Damn right!"

"Yah better believe it."

"You sure better be careful."

Chapter Nine

The Mississippi Delta

White people in the Delta – particularly in LeFlore and Tallahatchie counties – were spitting fire and incensed about all the national attention that Emmett Till's death was receiving, which prompted the state of Mississippi to appoint a special prosecutor and to file charges against Roy Bryant and J.W. Milam. The federal indictment accused the defendants of willfully, unlawfully, feloniously, and of their malice of forethought, killed and murdered Emmett Till, a human being.

White Mississippians vented wide spread scorn about Roy Bryant and J.W. Milam being put on trial for their lives. The white citizens' disdain was toward the boy from Chicago who, in their collective opinion, came to Mississippi and caused trouble. And a lot of cynicism was expressed that cached into very crude jokes such as, "Ain't that like a nigger to try to swim across the Tallahatchie River with a cotton gin fan tied to his neck."

Members of the media interviewed both white and black people and got comments such as:

> *White man: "I can't understand how a civilized mother could put a dead body of her child on public display."*
>
> *White woman: "I'm almost convinced that the very beginning of this was by a communist front."*
>
> *White man: "I'll tell yah right now, if J.W. Milam and Roy Bryant get justice that jury will turn 'em loose. That's what I would do if I was on the grand jury."*

Reporters found that there was outright fear among the Negroes in the Delta when they tried to interview them. It was most apparent that the message to the Negro population was to hide what they knew or consider the consequences. Some Negroes spoke when given an assurance of anonymity.

One reporter found a young Negro schoolgirl more candid and who worked for a well-to-do white woman in Tallahatchie County. The young girl provided the following account:

> *"I was finishing up the dinner dishes and placing them in a cabinet when Mrs. Benjamin entered the kitchen. She asked me if I heard about the fourteen-year-old Negro boy from Chicago who was killed. I said no ma'am I hadn't heard as I almost choked on my words. She then asked if I knew why he was killed. I didn't answer because I had no answer. She went on to tell me that he was killed because he got out of his place with a white woman. She said a boy from Mississippi would've known better and said Negroes from up North had no respect for people. I knew she meant white people. She said Negroes from up North think they*

can get away with anything and that the boy who got killed came to Mississippi and put a lot of notions in the Negro boys' heads who live here and stirred up a lot of trouble. Then she asked me how old I was. I told her I was fourteen and she said, 'See, that boy was just fourteen too. It's a shame he had to die so young.' Her face looked as red as fire when she said it. When she left the kitchen, I sat there with my mouth wide open. I told myself to just do my work like I don't know nothing and I started washing dishes again. I went home shaking like a leaf. And for the first time out of all the times she'd tried, Mrs. Benjamin made me feel like filthy garbage. She had tried many times before to put fear in me but had given up. But when she talked about Emmett Till there was something in her voice that sent cold chills and fear all over me like nothing I never knew before. Before Emmett Till's murder, I'd known the fear of hunger, hell, and the Devil. But now there was a new fear known to me, which was the fear of being killed just because I was a Negro and that was the worst of my fears. I knew once I got food, the fear of starving to death would leave. I also was told that if I was a good girl, I wouldn't have to fear the Devil or hell. But I didn't know what a person had to do or not do as a Negro not to get killed. Probably just being a Negro period was enough, I thought...."

Three days before Roy Bryant's and J.W. Milam's murder trial, the Delta White Citizens Council met at the Grenada Township Hall. Members of the Council were sympathetic with the Ku Klux Klan in regard to issues of race, but many Council members felt uncomfortable with the Klan's overt viciousness. The Council was thought to be a more fitting and refined alternative in regard to dealing with racial issues, protecting the rights of white people, and maintaining a Southern way of life they felt entitled to. Aside from the trial, its president, Fagan McCormack, had two other matters of concern on the agenda that had white citizens up in arms: school desegregation and nonsense about coloreds registering to vote.

Since the 1954 *Brown vs. Board of Education* decision rendered by the United States Supreme Court declaring school segregation unconstitutional, white citizens were venomously upset and race relationships in the Mississippi Delta deteriorated. Whites were more resentful of Negroes and vocally defiant of the court order to desegregate schools. White citizens were bemoaning the decision and saying things like "Over my dead body!", "To hell with the Supreme Court", "I'd rather see my child go to school with monkeys than to sit next to niggas", and so on it went. And white citizens vented their dissatisfaction about matters at this evening's meeting.

President McCormick, a tall, heavy, balding man in his sixties, stood at a podium in front of an expansive audience without an empty seat in the hall. It was standing room only. He said, "In regard to the coloreds registering to vote, what we'll have is a repeat of *A Birth of a Nation* when northern carpetbaggers invaded the South after the Civil War during a period referred to as *Reconstruction.*" He stopped, cleared his voice, took a sip of water from a cup and continued. "Reconstruction is what northerners called it and how it's written in the history books, but we know that period to be more like *black-destruction.*" He received applause and shouts of confirmation from the audience.

"Yes, *black-destruction* is surely what it was when they gave Negroes the right to vote and to hold office. The whole thing resulted in making a mockery of how our government was run and functioned because the black imbeciles in office couldn't read a single sentence in the constitution and no less understand it and make any rational decisions regarding the construction of laws. And nothing has much changed in regard to Negroes. Yeah, they've got a few nigga preachers running around in suits who got as much education as white children in grade school, but what do they know about government and yet along governing? I say they don't know anymore than they knew in the film *A Birth of a Nation.*" He waited again while he lavished in the cheering and hand clapping resounding in the room.

"*So*me of these Negro preachers are putting a bunch of foolishness in the heads of Negroes and encouraging them to register to vote. But we'll have none of this. We will not accept it nor tolerate it. We white citizens need to defend our heritage, customs, and way of life and not allow outside agitators stir of Negroes and undermine the rights of white people."

The auditorium thundered with applause.

He continued. "The banks will be callin in the mortgages of the Negroes who try to register to vote and those of y'all who have Negro workers have already warned them that they'll be taking bread off their tables and clothes off their backs if they register to vote. And those of y'all who don't have Negro workers, have already passed the word that it'd be dangerous for any Negro to register to vote. And I'm sure you didn't have to explain what dangerous meant."

"We sure didn't! " someone in the audience shouted.

"And dangerous is what it's gonna be if Negro preachers don't stop feeding other Negroes this voter registration bullcrap. All this nigga foolishness brings me to our last topic – the trial of Roy Bryant and J.W. Milam who have been accused of killing a sassy, disrespectful nigga boy from Chicago who insulted Roy Bryant's wife by asking her for a date and whistling at her. Any white man would've been offended and upset about this. Roy Bryant and J.W. Milam say they ain't guilty of the boy's murder and just went to teach him a lesson, then let him go. We have to believe and support these men because they are each one of us and we can't allow the federal government, northern liberals, and those influenced by communistic views to come to Mississippi and dictate how we should live our lives and manage our affairs."

There was more applause and verbal approval.

President McCormick sipped from his cup and placed it on a near table. He said, "We have to band together against these northern intruders and other meddling folks who threaten our way of life. And I'm proud to announce that our campaign to raise money for Roy Bryant and J.W. Milam's defense has come in at a bit over ten thousand dollars."

Applauses erupted.

"And not only that", said President McCormick, " I'm also pleased to inform you that every white lawyer in LeFlore and Tallahatchie counties has agreed to aid in the men's defense."

All the people in the room, except the decrepit and those wheelchair-bound, stood, cheered, and gave a rousing ovation.

President McCormick ended the white citizen's council meeting by stating, "We're gonna circle the wagons and defend the rights of white people."

The meeting ended with loud applauding, chattering, and hooting.

* * *

Later the same evening, twenty-one members of the John Brown Christian Society met at the Masolt Homestead, which was formerly an old plantation near Sumner that was situated on thirty acres and built on Greek revival style architecture. The number of members of the Society was purposefully limited to twenty-one individuals, which correlated with the number of people in *John Brown's Provisional Army* that staged and mounted a raid on the federal arsenal at Harper's Ferry, Virginia in 1859 for the purpose of securing arms to liberate slaves. And the composition of the twenty-one members was just as it was in regard to the *Provisional Army*, consisting of sixteen white men and five Negroes. Just like John Brown, "The Liberator" and abolitionist, the Society members were dedicated to the principle of non-violence and equality of man. Their motto was fashioned from a quote of one of John Brown's sons:

> *It is better to be in a place and suffer wrong*
> *than to do wrong.*

Reverend Joseph Masolt, a Lutheran minister and distance cousin of John Brown, was a tall and distinguish looking man with gray at the temples of his otherwise dark hair. He was the leader of the Society and the inheritor of the homestead that he purposefully refused to call a plantation. He'd called the meeting this evening to determine the members' overall success in identifying people to testify against Roy Bryant and J.W. Milam. Meetings of the Society were very secretive and mostly conducted under the cover of darkness because its members were most aware of the danger if the powers-that-be discovered its deeds and purpose.

Reverend Masolt understood that the Society's work was counter to the bitter racial attitudes harbored by most white citizens in the Mississippi Delta. Meetings of the Society were informal. No official records were kept in order to avoid knowledge of its dealings inadvertently falling in the hands of the wrong people. Consensus was the general method of making decisions.

"Let's call the meeting to order," said Reverend Masolt upon acknowledging full attendance and the eagerness in the members assembled.

The members met in a large parlor accented with Victoria décor and with a large gold-plated chandelier hanging above a long, rectangular oak wood table in the center of the room. The members sat in large, high-back chairs. Reverend Masolt sat at the head of the table. He assessed the somber expressions of the members, which conveyed to him the measure of success they'd had in identifying witnesses to testify at the Emmett Till murder trial. He wasn't optimistic, knowing the climate of intimidation and fear that white citizens created for Negroes in the Delta and particularly about coming forward to help convict Roy Bryant and J.W. Milam.

"How many witnesses do we have?" Reverend Masolt asked.

"Two definite and one pending," said the member known as Brother Justice Two, who was second in command.

"Who's pending?" asked the reverend.

"Levy Collins, known as Too-Tight. He worked for J.W. Milam," Brother Justice Two responded.

"Okay, bring in Mr. Collins first and let's hear what he has to say," said the reverend.

Two black members of the Society escorted Levy 'Too-Tight' Collins into the parlor. "This is 'Too-Tight'," said the member to Too-Tight's right.

"Have a seat Mr. Collins," said the reverend as he observed how nervous and fidgety the man was. "Do you prefer Levy or Too-Tight?" the reverend asked.

"Too-Tight. Dats what most people call me," he responded in a low, shaky voice.

"Too-Tight, you don't have to be nervous. We're here to assist you and other Negroes who are victims of cruelty and injustices in the Delta. We're your friends."

Too-Tight looked around the room at the faces of the men sitting around the table, thinking that he'd never been in a room with so many white men at one time and for certain not around white men who wanted to help him. He felt uptight and suspicious, even with five Negroes present, and two who'd convinced him to come this evening by greasing his palm with a few dollars.

The reverend said, "Too-Tight it was explained to you that we needed to blindfold you in order that our location would be kept secret. I will introduce myself as Brother Justice One. We don't use our legal names for reasons of security and protection. We are a very secretive organization. Relax. You are amongst friends. We understand that you might have some information regarding the murder of Emmett Till. Will you please share it with us?"

Too-Tight, a large man with dark complexion and in his twenties cleared his throat, looked toward the reverend, but not directly into his face because of being accustomed of not looking white men in the eyes. He said, " Me and Henry Lee wuz with Mr. Bryant, Mr. Milam, and another white man when they went to Moses Wright's house to get the boy from Chicago and took him to the Clint Sheridan Plantation. Me and Henry Lee didn't see 'em do anything to the boy, but we heard all the noise comin from a shed. The noise sounded like somebody bein beat real bad. We knowed da wuz beatin dat boy 'cause we could hear him screamin, cryin, and beggin. Afterwhile all the noise stopped and the men left in Mr. Milam's truck. They took Henry Lee with 'em."

"Do you know what happened to Henry Lee Loggins?" the reverend asked.

"No, suh. I never saw Henry Lee after dat night."

"Did you see anything else?"

"No, suh."

"Are you afraid to testify in court?"

"Yessuh. Mr. Milam is a real mean man and I still don't know what happened to Henry Lee."

The reverend said, "I understand the reason you're afraid, but if you testify at the trial about what you saw and heard we'll protect you."

"How yah gonna do dat?"

"We'll identify someone to escort you to the trial, then we'll send you North like we've done with some other Negroes who had trouble and were threatened. We'll pay for your transportation, give you some money, and arrange a job for you in Chicago, Detroit, Philadelphia, or New York where we have contacts. How does that sound?"

Too-Tight looked around at all the faces in the room, bowed his head for a moment, then said, " I don't know. Need to thank 'bout it."

"That's fair," said the reverend. "Can you give us an answer by tomorrow so we can make proper arrangements for both the trial and getting you North?"

"Yessuh."

"Okay, Too-Tight. We'll get you back home and be in touch tomorrow, early. Is that okay?"

"Yessuh."

After Levy "Too-Tight" Collins left the room, Reverend Masolt and his members listened to two other men who had information regarding Emmett Till. Moses Wright, Emmett Till's great-uncle, stated that he had been present the night that Roy Bryant and J.W. Milam came to his home and took Emmett away.

Willie Reed, eighteen-years-old, stated that he was in the field picking cotton when he looked across the field and saw seven or eight white and black men coming toward him and questioned him as to whether he saw anything, which he denied. But he told the present gathering that he'd seen Roy Bryant, J.W. Milam, and another white man with Emmett early Sunday morning on the day of his disappearance and that he'd heard sounds of a beating coming from a shed at the Clint Sheridan Plantation.

Both Moses Wright and Willie Reed had been threatened to keep quiet. They were nervous, but agreed to testify at the trial, along with the promise that the John Brown Christian Society would provide them and their families sanctuary and safe passage North after the trial.

The members reassembled in the parlor after Moses Wright and Willie Reed were dismissed.

Brother Justice One said, "Brothers, we have our work cut out. The tension is thick and lives are surely at stake. Let us pray.

The members knelled in prayer and then stood.

Brother Justice One said, "May God, justice, love, and peace be with us."

The members all recited the words back in unison.

* * *

Roy Bryant sat on his porch under the stars. The approaching murder trial as well as the condition of his health weighed on his mind. He possessed an ill feeling in his stomach, which had been diagnosed as ulcers. His doctor had given him some medication to comfort the ailment, but had no clue in regard to the source of the red rash on the palm of his hands. His doctor diagnosed it to be some type of infection and stated that he hadn't seen a case like his during the twenty years he'd been practicing medicine. Roy contemplated that the ointment he'd been prescribed to apply on his hands hadn't done much good. His hands didn't pain but he didn't like the sight of them and the reason he wore gloves a lot or kept his hands stuck in his pockets. And too, he mulled that the incessant clanging in his head late at night – always after midnight -- was nearly driving him crazy.

Roy read the time on his wristwatch. It was 11:45 p.m. He went inside the house to secure earplugs and a pillow before the midnight hour. He looked down at the floor and saw a puddle of water and a bubble gum wrapper. He couldn't make sense of the mess. He went to the bedroom and saw his wife, Caroline, still asleep. He walked back in the living room, looked for a glass that maybe was accidentally knocked over in order to account for the puddle of water. He saw no glass. He looked up at the ceiling for a leak. No leak. And why would there be, he thought. It hadn't rained in days. Then how, he wondered to himself, as to how the water came to be on the floor along with the gum wrapper.

Clang, clang, clang, clang, splash... Roy knew it was midnight as a result of the noise and sound. He left the puddle of water and the gum wrapper on the floor and hurried back to his bedroom to secure the earplugs from a dresser drawer. He stuck the earplugs inside his ears, undressed, got in bed and buried himself under covers, although it was a hot Mississippi night. He pressed a pillow firmly against the sides of his head and over his ears. He felt a sharp pain in his stomach. He got out of bed to take his stomach medication. He heard *clang, clang, clang, clang, splash*....

* * *

The upcoming trial festered in J.W. Milam's mind, which made it difficult for him to sleep. All the strange and haunting images that he'd witnessed at night during the past few weeks had him feeling jittery and dumbfounded. He sat out in his truck behind the steering wheel smoking a cigar and watching the moon. He thought that he'd done a satisfactory enough job on Too-Tight Collins and Henry Lee to scare them from testifying about what they saw. He was comfortable in believing that both Too-Tight and Henry would rather jump off the Tallahatchie Bridge than testify at his and Roy's trial.

J.W. drew a puff from his cigar and blew smoke out the window of his truck. He heard rattling inside the barn where his truck was parked near. He couldn't imagine what in the hell was making the noise, then contemplated that maybe some animal had gotten inside the barn. He secured his twenty-gage shotgun and a flashlight from behind the seat and left the truck to investigate. He quietly opened the door to the barn and something wet and sticky dropped on him when he stepped inside. The substance was red and appeared to him to be blood. "Shit!" he bellowed. He stepped back, shined his flashlight up to the rafters of the barn and saw a large, dead rat hanging from a noose. The sight appalled him. He ran out of the barn breathing like he'd just run a marathon. He fell to his hands and knees and vomited. He found himself knelling in a puddle of water and saw a bubble gum wrapper next to both his hands.

Chapter Ten

"You work out finances, household bills, schedules, and a lot of other things in a marriage, but you don't work out infidelity."

Francine's statement was indelibly etched in Jamal's mind. All during his train ride to Mississippi her statement stuck in his head. He'd called Francine before leaving Chicago and asked to speak with Thurgood, although he really wanted to speak with his son, he also wanted to hear Francine's voice and to take the opportunity to make another appeal for reconciliation. But to his disappointment, Francine wasn't receptive and told him that he wasn't going to change and that the two of them needed to get on with their lives without the other, except for where their son was concerned.

Jamal couldn't deny still loving Francine. He knew her to be a good woman who'd been faithful to him all during their marriage. He remembered their first meeting when they were sophomores at the University of Detroit: Francine majoring in education and he in journalism. He recalled meeting Francine at a party on campus that her sorority, Alpha Kappa Alpha, sponsored. He'd recently pledged to Kappa Alpha Psi Fraternity. He remembered seeing this fine coed with a face that rivaled Dorothy Dandridge and with legs as pretty as *The Beige Beauts Dancers* who performed at the Flame Show Bar in the *Black Bottom* section of Detroit. He recalled it was love as first sight on his part and he ended up pinning her two weeks after they'd met. But even though he was in love with her, he remembered cheating on her while they dated in college and having had some close calls in regard to her discovering his philandering. He didn't feel proud of himself for cheating and more than once thought that he was suffering from sexual addiction. He enjoyed the hunt, staking out the women, and capturing them. But Francine was the only woman he'd wanted to marry. He knew that if ever he could win her back, he would need to somehow prove to her that he'd changed. He missed sleeping next to her and feeling her warm, supple body next to his even when they weren't sexually intimate, which he considered was much more than he could say about other women he'd slept with. He thought Francine had a quality about her that he hadn't discovered in other women. His thoughts were causing him pain and much regret, so he forced himself to close out his reminiscence and to concentrate on something else – like breakfast and his scheduled interview with Mamie Till this afternoon.

Jamal gathered himself and rolled out of bed. He stretched out his arms and yawned as he moved slowly toward the bedroom window at Mettie Coates Boarding House in Sumner, which was the only real decent place Negroes from out of town could stay, unless they went to Clarksdale, Grenada, Greenwood, or Mound Bayou. But like other Negroes who were in Sumner covering the murder trial, he wanted to be close to the action. And he was pleasantly surprised to run into Detroit Congressman Charles Diggs who'd also come for the trial and was staying at the boarding home.

As Jamal looked out the window, he saw a few people out on the street. He noticed how the Negro men would move off the sidewalk when they approached white women and would bow their heads. He remembered his Negro cab driver, a pleasant young man in his twenties, giving him a crash course on how to conduct himself around white people while in Mississippi. Jamal recalled that the young man had simply introduced himself as J.D., who edified him that it was custom to vacate the sidewalk to a white woman, don't look directly at her, and for God's sake don't ever smile at her; and don't look white men directly in their eyes. The most salient thing he remembered J.D. telling him was that if he comported to custom that he'd live to return to Detroit.

As Jamal peered out the window he saw J.D.'s cab, which was easy to recognize because the 1948 Ford he drove had cruelly hand-painted, white lettering that spelled *Colored Taxi* on both front doors. The sign on the cab immediately caught his attention when he disembarked the train upon arriving in Mississippi, along with ubiquitously posted signs that read *Coloreds Only and Whites Only*.

Jamal shed his pajamas, took a bath, got dressed in a casual shirt and slacks. He bounded downstairs to the lobby where he witnessed a couple of Negro men toting commercial cameras, men decked in suits, women with well-groomed tresses, two young men hawking guests to carry their luggage, and Negro domestics scurrying about. Jamal surmised that some of the Negroes in the lobby were church-people in town for a revival that coincided with the trial. He left to walk across the street to a restaurant named Sadie's Southern Cooking and where last night he'd dined on Southern fried chicken, fried okra and tomatoes, mashed potatoes smothered with chicken gravy, cornbread that melted in his mouth, and Southern peach cobbler to top off his meal. Jamal eagerly anticipated breakfast.

Inside Sadie's, Jamal was kindly greeted and escorted toward the back of the restaurant. He was seated alone at a table for two. He was handed a menu by a young, countrified Negro woman whose Southern droll was thought by Jamal to be as thick as molasses. She supplied him with ice water in a Mason jar, poured him a cup of hot coffee, and left. He clinched his thirst with the water, checked his wristwatch, and marveled at how busy the restaurant was at 6:45 a.m. He settled back and observed the patrons: all Negroes. He conjectured that some of the people were local folks because they seemed more familiar with the workers and ordered without menus. The rest of the people he thought to be from out of town like himself who asked many questions about the items on the menu and about this or that.

A short Negro woman with frilly hair, in her forties, and wearing a white apron came to his table and asked if he decided what he wanted for breakfast. He ordered the house special consisting of fried catfish, scrambled eggs, and buttered grits. The woman thanked him and left the table after recording his order in her memory. Jamal retrieved a folder from his briefcase, laid it down on the table, and took a sip from his coffee cup. He noticed an older, tall, thin man with a thick mustache and fairly light complexion looking toward him from a table occupied by three other men. Jamal refocused his sight to the folder on the table and opened it. He lifted his head to drink from the Mason jar and saw all four men at the table now looking his way. Jamal looked behind him to determine if there was something or someone behind him that the men's attention might be drawn to, but there was no one behind him, nor was there anything that he discerned to be on any particular interest. He wondered why the men might be interested in him. He focused his attention back to the information inside the manila colored folder until his waitress returned with his order. He thanked the woman. She left. Jamal peered over at the table that the four men occupied. He saw them talking amongst themselves and focusing on each other.

Jamal finished his breakfast and left to use the restroom. He returned and was surprised to see one of the men he'd observed sitting at his table. He was a tall, thin man, and fortyish. The man stood up and said, "I apologize Mr. Peterson for the invasion of your space. My name is Brother Justice Fourteen. There's a very important matter related to the Emmett Till murder case that I would like to speak with you about, if you'd be so kind to permit me an audience and a little of your time."

Jamal felt pleasantly surprised, thinking hell-yes that he wanted to discuss any matters associated with the murder trial. The cliché *don't look a gift-horse in the mouth* entered Jamal's mind. "Please, have a seat," Jamal said, then asked, "How did you know my name?"

"Through some investigation, Mr. Peterson. We knew there'd be some Negroes from the media down here to cover the murder trial and we needed to find someone we could trust."

"Trust with what?" Jamal asked.

"Important information."

"What did you say your name was again?"

"Brother Justice Fourteen. It's not my birthed name, but one I've taken on in regard to the society I belong to. I can't give you the name of our society, but suffice it to say that it has been in existence for better than thirty years. White and black men belong to our society and we believe in nonviolence and justice for all men regardless of race. We've been effective in protecting Negroes from harm and danger and getting some relocated north for their safety. We have been able to accomplish this by infiltrating the Klan and white citizen councils and getting a heads-up on some things that would prove adverse to Negroes. We have to be very secretive in regard to our name, membership, existence, and purpose for reasons that obviously a man of your intellect and sophistication could understand."

"Of course I understand," Jamal responded.

"So, please, Mr. Peterson, don't even write a single word about what I just shared with you or else you stand to put the Society, its members, and our mission in danger."

"I understand," said Jamal. "And I promise not to write a word about any of what you told me. But you said something about investigating me and deciding whether you could trust me. So, how did that decision come about?"

"Like I said, we knew a few Negroes from the media would be coming and would need to find accommodations in Negro owned boarding houses or motels. We figured they'd wanna be relatively close to Sumner, so we asked questions, scouted around, and came up with several names, including yours and someone from Jet magazine, but decided on you as our first choice because you are a freelance journalist who doesn't have any particular allegiance. In other words, you're your own man."

Jamal liked how "You're your own man" sounded. Brother Justice Fourteen had his attention. Jamal asked, "How did you come about the name Brother Justice Fourteen?"

"We have twenty-one members that belong to our society, sixteen white and five Negroes. And as I mentioned, we're for justice for all people – thus the justice reference in our names. Our numbers range from one through twenty-one. And because I'm number fourteen and Emmett Till was fourteen-years-old when he was murdered, I was selected for this mission with you."

"I'm not understanding what you mean by a mission, particularly as it relates to me," Jamal stated.

"The mission, Mr. Peterson, should you accept it, would be to inform the prosecutor that there are two witnesses under protection. We would like for you to provide their names and see to it that they get escorted safely to the courthouse. We also request that you work with us to get these men safe passage out of Mississippi once they testify. These men's lives won't be worth a fly's if they testify and remain in Mississippi. And the fact that you're from the media will provide a needed measure of protection."

* * *

After interviewing Mamie Till, writing reports and wiring the information to the National News Association, Jamal hobnobbed with some media colleagues for a while, returned to his room, and relaxed with a bottle of whiskey. He listened to the radio and read both local and regional newspapers such as the *Sumner Sentinel, Jackson Daily News,* and the *Memphis Commercial Appeal.* He was particularly interested in the pre-trial coverage of the Emmett Till case. He gleaned that Mississippi reporters and editors covered the pending trial in a much different perspective than the northern media. Northern coverage embodied references to *murder, civil rights violations, brutality, inequality, humanity, and justice;* southern coverage applied words such as *meddling, instigation, communism, right-wing plotting, and state rights.*

After reading the newspapers and taking a nap, Jamal hankered for some nightlife. He poured some whiskey in a glass, mixed it with coke, and stirred his cocktail with his index finger. He recalled that J.D, the colored cab driver, had apprised him of a Negro club in the all black town named Mound Bayou. He remembered being apprised that at the club they sold hot fish sandwiches, fried chicken, shredded barbecue pork on a bun, pig feet, pig tails, boiled eggs, and also served up some mighty good music and singing. The place was called *The Blues Shack* and which sounded like someplace Jamal wanted to be, so he convinced a fellow Negro reporter who had a rented car with Mississippi car tags to drive to Mound Bayou, along with another Negro reporter.

* * *

Jamal and his companions discovered crowded parking when they arrived at The Blues Shack. Yards away, they could hear a gravelly voice man coarsely wailing the blues. The aroma of southern cooking was thick and saturated every molecule of air, causing Jamal and his cohorts' mouths to salivate. They paid a one-dollar cover charge, entered the club and found the place jumping as patrons whooped, hands thundered, and feet pounded the stained, wooden floor. Jamal thought the Negroes in the place were rejoicing as though they'd just learned about the Emancipation Proclamation and felt liberated.

Jamal and his buddies fought through a throng of bodies and took seats near a back wall, close to the kitchen where two hefty size Negro women were cooking with sweat streaming down their ebony faces. They witnessed waitresses carrying orders and circulating back and forth as rapidly as the twirling blades of the fans that were strategically placed throughout the sweltering joint.

The club was furnished with long tables and chairs, a crude looking bar, a stage and not much more. Jamal and his reporter friend Bernard ordered setups that consisted of a large cup of ice and a coke to complement the liquor they were permitted to bring in because the club didn't have a license to sell spirits. The other reporter, Tony, declared himself to be a teetotaler and ordered a RC cola. Bernard had a bottle of scotch. Jamal produced a bottle of whiskey from a brown paper bag and plopped it on the table; eager to get in the same, merry mood as the other Negroes in the club who were more gleeful than he'd seen any Negro since he arrived in Mississippi. Their waitress returned with their setups and took their food orders. She hurried off like someone was chasing her.

Jamal had his cup beaming to the brim with whiskey and coke and was about to place it to his mouth when the music stopped. A short, stocky dark complexion man in a rumpled suit came to the stage, took command of the microphone and said, "Now ladies and gentlemen and others, it's my pleasure to bring to the stage a lovely, young woman who's goin places other than the cotton fields."

Laughter resounded.

The man with the microphone said, "She's sho' goin places'cause she has God-given talent. This young lady can sing the blues, scat like Elli Fitzgerald, and musically seduce you like Billie Holiday. Give it up for the Delta's own lovely and talented Vera Franklin."

When Vera Franklin walked on stage, Jamal nearly spilled his drink. "Damn she's fine!" he shamelessly pronounced. He sat spellbound, as did Bernard and Tony. Jamal thought that he'd never seen a woman any lovelier as he admired her chocolate, unblemished complexion, long, sweeping jet-black hair, and a figure to die for, he thought. His female radar was targeted and locked in. He surmised that she must have been poured into the satin, low-cut, blue dress she wore that fell above her knees.

The band began playing softly in the background as Vera took the microphone. She said, "Thank you so kindly ladies and gentlemen for that most warm reception. I'm gonna perform some Elli Fitzgerald and Billie Holiday tunes for you this evening and throw in something by Nina Simone. But first we're gonna continue with the blues for a moment and sing a song that was recently written by our piano player, David Mack. The tune is titled *Delta Blues*. Give it a listen and see how you like it.

Jamal was thoroughly enjoying Vera Franklin's performance and also plotting to meet her.

Bingo! He had it. He grabbed a napkin off the table and began writing a note with his pen. When the waitress returned to the table to remove the trash and checked to see if they needed anything else, Jamal beckoned to the woman with his finger. She walked over to him. Jamal whispered in her ear and handed her the note he'd written along with two dollars. Tony and Bernard were checking out Jamal. They smiled his way as they imagined what he was up to. Jamal returned their smile. The men focused their attention back on Vera Franklin who was masterly singing the Billie Holiday song *I Get a Kick Out of You*. Jamal tied a white handkerchief around his whiskey bottle while Tony and Bernard weren't paying him any attention.

"At this time folks, we're gonna take a little break, but don't go no where. I hope you've enjoyed my performance up to this point. Continue to eat, drink, and be merry."

There were thunderous applause and hooting.

Vera said, "I love y'all" and then strutted off the stage, shook lots of hand, spoke with a few folks, and made her way toward the back of the club.

Jamal, Tony, and Bernard had their eyes on the beautiful songstress as she glided closer to their table. Their eyes were lit up and sparkling like Roman candles. They each drank from their cups. Teetotaler Tony asked Bernard to pour some liquor in his cup. Vera arrived at their table with a bright smile. The three men smiled like lottery winners. Vera said, "You must be Jamal Peterson from the National News Association."

"How would you know that?" Bernard asked. "There are three of us sitting here."

Vera smiled and said, "But only one of you have a white handkerchief, or for that matter, any handkerchief tied around a bottle."

Tony said, "I wondered why Jamal had a handkerchief tied around his whiskey bottle. I thought it was a Detroit thing."

Everybody laughed.

Vera extended her dainty hand with well-manicured nails to each of the men. She introduced herself, then said, "I hope you fellas enjoyed the first half of my show."

The men unabashedly talked over each other, telling Vera how great they thought she was. Jamal moved over to an empty seat and offered Vera a seat between him and Bernard, which she accepted.

"So, Mr. Peterson, I'm interested in what you wrote in your note about wanting to interview me for national publication. Do you think a small town girl like me is worthy of national attention? I must admit that I'm flattered, nonetheless."

Jamal said, "In my work I travel a lot and been many places, including big cities, small towns, and even abroad. In my travels I've been to a many nightclubs and concert halls and have heard the best. I want to tell you Miss Franklin... Sorry. Is it Miss or Mrs.?"

Vera smiled and said, "It's Miss and please call me Vera."

"What I was saying, Vera, is that I've heard singers across the United States and abroad and you can sing with the best of them. And you're prettier than all them. You're lovelier than an Hawaiian sunset."

Vera smiled and blushed on the inside. Her complexion was too dark for the men to witness her blushing. She said, "That's real sweet of you to say. You're gonna swell my head talking like that. So, Jamal, have you really ever seen an Hawaiian sunset?"

"Yes I have. I went to Hawaii on my honeymoon. But I'm divorced now," he quickly added.

"Sorry to hear that."

"Well sometimes that's how the cookie crumbles. How come a lovely woman such as yourself isn't married?"

"I haven't found anyone I want to marry and certainly not here in the Delta. I want to go to a big city like Atlanta or Memphis or maybe north to Chicago or Detroit."

"Vera, I'm telling you that with your talents and looks, I think you can make it big."

Vera smiled and said, "Think so, huh?"

"I truly do," said Jamal. "I truly do. Let me interview you, but not tonight because I know you're working and we need to get back to Sumner before it gets too late. We have a murder trial to cover."

"So you fellas are down here for the Emmett Till murder trial?" Vera asked.

"Yes, we are. It was a most human tragedy in regard to what Roy Bryant and J.W. Milam did to Emmett Till," Jamal said.

For the first time since she arrived at the table, Vera smile vanished. A somber expression graced her face, which didn't go unnoticed.

"Is something wrong?" Jamal asked.

Vera perked herself up and said, "It just pains me whenever I think of what happened to Emmett Till. I plan to attend the murder trial."

"Well good," Jamal said. "Then if you're gonna be in Sumner for the trial, let's get together and have dinner and I can interview you then. How does that sound?"

"Sounds good," Vera agreed. "Give me your phone number and I'll give you a call. I need to get back up on stage. Too bad you fellas can't stay around for the second half of my show, but I understand you need to get back. Nice meeting you guys and I'll give you a call, Jamal."

"Please do. And nice meeting you. I'll be expecting your call."

As Vera got up and left, Jamal picked up his cup of liquor and drank it. He emitted a smile.

Bernard said, "Man, you're smooth."

Tony said, "I can take lessons from you, brother."

Jamal's smile grew larger.

Chapter Eleven

First Day of the Murder Trial
September 19, 1955

Jamal felt nervous now that the time had arrived. He realized that he could be putting his life in great danger for what he'd committed to. He thought of the Mississippi Delta as a giant guillotine for Negroes. He pondered that he wasn't a damn hero and conjectured that his role in getting the Negro witnesses to the courthouse to testify against white men in Mississippi should at least earn him the *Negro Medal of Honor,* if there were such a thing. He wasn't about to throw caution to the wind. He knew he had to be most careful.

The *Colored Taxi* pulled up in front of Mettie Coates Boarding House as planned and on schedule. Jamal checked the time. It was 5:00 a.m. He opened the door to the taxi and settled on the front passenger seat next to J.D. who was driving and whom Jamal now knew to be Brother Justice Twenty-one. The two men greeted each other with stony-faced visages, both understanding the importance of their early morning trek. The previous day Jamal had carried out the first part of his charge by providing the special prosecutor with the names of the witnesses. He understood that secretly gathering up the witnesses and getting them safely to the courthouse wasn't going to be easy by no means.

Jamal's stomach began knotting. He was tense. His mind was full. He shut his eyes in an attempt to relax. He said a silent prayer beyond those he'd already sent to the Lord back in his room at the boarding house. He visualized the horrid photo of Emmett Till lying in his casket, which provided Jamal with a reinforcement of purpose to hold steadfast to his mission.

Jamal and J.D. took back, country roads in the direction of the Masolt Homestead. The plan was to meet at a secret location near the homestead, pick up the two witnesses, and transport them in the trunk of the taxi to Sumner for the trial later this morning. As they rode in silence, Jamal surveyed the landscape consisting of low hills and sweeping terrain that was as flat as a pancake. He saw shacks, large plantations, and expansive cotton fields. Five miles farther down the road, Jamal saw a heavy-set, white man wearing a large straw hat and coveralls step out of a woody tract and looked in both directions down the road. The man stuck out a long stick with a piece of red cloth attached at the end. He waved the stick for J.D. to pull over. Two men, one white and the other a Negro, opened a camouflaged gate covered with vegetation. They closed the gate behind the taxi after it entered. In unison the men mouthed, "May God, justice, love, and peace be with you."

J.D. cited the phrase back. It was the first time Jamal had heard J.D. utter a word since leaving Sumner.

The man Jamal knew as Brother Justice Fourteen appeared from out of the bush along with two Negro men who looked haggard and frightened. One of the men was young and the other was considerably older.

Brother Justice Fourteen approached the taxi on the passenger side along with the two men and said, "Greetings Mr. Peterson. The Society is indebted to you for your assistance. May God, justice, peace, and love be with you. These are the two gentlemen who are witnesses. This here is Moses Wright (acknowledging the older man), Emmett Till's great-uncle. And this is Willie Reed."

Jamal said "Hello".

The two men acknowledged his greetings with a rigid bow of their heads and with frozen tongues.

Jamal detected fear in the men's eyes.

"All the details have been explained to Mr. Wright and Mr. Reed, so they're in your care at this point. We never could locate the third witness who goes by the handle of Too-Tight. He mysteriously disappeared, but we're still pursuing some leads and if we come up with something we'll contact you through Brother Justice Twenty-one. Hopefully, our two witnesses will be sufficient to get a conviction."

J.D. got out of the taxi and went to the back of it to open the trunk. The two men crawled in; J.D. closed the trunk, then returned to sit behind the steering wheel.

Brother Justice Fourteen handed Jamal a thick envelope and said, "Inside you will find money to purchase train tickets and to take care of other expenses we've discussed. Both men's destination is Chicago, where they will stay with relatives. And through our contacts the men will be provided employment. Take care of yourself Mr. Peterson and thanks so very much for your most appreciated assistance. Good luck to you and may we meet again under more auspicious circumstances."

Jamal and Brother Justice Fourteen shook hands. The taxi pulled out of the hideaway back onto the road after given clearance.

As they headed back to Sumner, the morning sun was a virgin in the sky. Jamal looked over at the cotton fields they passed and saw hordes of Negroes on plantations performing what he thought was backbreaking work by picking rows of cotton. The men in the fields wore loose fitting overalls and wide brim hats to protect them from what Jamal knew to be a blazing Mississippi sun. The women outfitted themselves in what looked to Jamal to be *Mother Hubbard* dresses. Their heads were wrapped with bandanas and some wore straw hats. Jamal recalled talking to a Negro man from Glendora who told him that plantation owners whipped Negro cotton pickers if for any reason they wouldn't or couldn't go out in the fields to pick, even if they were sick. Jamal pondered that it was the nineteen-fifties and that not much had changed on the plantations since slavery, except that Negroes weren't confined to the land and being officially bought and sold like livestock.

A truck with white men approached the taxi in the opposite direction. Jamal saw the driver stick his hand out the window and motioned for J.D. to stop. It was in Jamal's mind to tell J.D. to continue, realizing the danger if the men discovered the passengers in the trunk. But just as quickly, he knew his contemplation was crazy and irrational, understanding that there was no sanctuary for Negroes in the Delta who openly defied white men. Jamal could hear his heart pounding as J.D. slowed the taxi to a stop.

"Where yah boys headed? It's unusual to see a taxi out in these parts. Dat yah, J.D.?"

"Yes sir, boss. Jes' takin my passenger sightseeing. He wanted to see some plantations. He not from these parts."

The young, white man driving the truck asked, "Where yah from, boy?"

"Detroit."

The young driver snickered and emitted a grin. He turned to the other two white men in the truck and said, "Look what we got here, a nigga from Detroit. What y'all thank of dat? What's yer business down here, boy?"

Jamal knew he had to think fast. "Just here to get some flavor from the area. I've got relatives in Sumner and will be teaching in the Agriculture Department at Mississippi Valley State College in Itta Bena in the fall."

"Yah talkin 'bout that nigga college?"

"Yes sir."

"Yah sure y'all boys ain't picked up no nigga moonshine and got it hidden in the trunk?"

"No sir. Nothin of that sort, boss," J.D. assured.

"What y'all boys thank?" asked the driver as he looked toward his passengers.

Just then, the hood of the truck flew up and slammed with a mighty force against the truck's windshield. Glass shattered. Water gushed in the air from the truck's radiator and a large plum of smoke bellowed in the air. The men in the truck sat frightened and stunned.

J.D. said, "I'll head on down the road, boss, and stop at the next place to get y'all some help."

The taxi took off without nary a comment from the men in the truck who were sitting transfixed with their mouths open. A gust of wind blew a bubble gum wrapper inside the window of the truck.

* * *

Jamal had a self-imposed rule about drinking alcohol before noon, but was making an exception this morning after returning to his room and getting Moses Wright and Willie Reed safely consigned to a room at the boarding house. He thought J.D. and himself to be fortunate that the white men didn't look in the trunk of the taxi. He mulled how close he came to pissing in his pants. His legs felt as though he'd been out to sea on a boat when he got out the taxi after arriving back to Sumner. He thanked the Lord for having acknowledged his prayers, then poured himself a stiff whiskey and coke cocktail.

* * *

After eating breakfast and taking a quick nap, Jamal awoke and consulted his wristwatch. It was 7:40 a.m. and just enough time to freshen up and get downstairs to meet the other eleven Negro reporters who'd agreed to escort Moses Wright and Willie Reed to the courthouse. Jamal took a deep breath and muttered, "This is it." He got off the bed, went to the bathroom, splashed some cold water on his face and blotted his face dry with a towel. He looked himself over in the mirror, brushed his hair and mustache, and straightened his tie. He said a silent prayer, slid into his suit coat and left the room with his briefcase in tow.

When Jamal reached the lobby of the boarding house, he saw most of the Negro reporters already congregated. They earnestly greeted each other, realizing they were about to embark on matters of great significance as related to the murder trial, justice, and racial relations. In short order everyone was present. Mettie Coates led Jamal to a back room to retrieve Moses Wright and Willie Reed, where they were hidden and secured.

The Negro delegation left the boarding house like soldiers off to war. They marched the eight blocks to the courthouse under the watchful eyes of resentful whites. They needed to get to the courthouse early enough for the prosecutors to council with the witnesses they were escorting.

A large statue of a Confederate soldier stood prominent in front of the courthouse and reminded the delegation that they were in the South and where white men would put down their lives for their way of life and traditions. The Negro delegation was jeered by a mass of white people when they arrived at the courthouse and verbally assaulted with the cruelest of racial epithets.

The delegation encountered a milieu of hate that was more intense than anything they'd ever experienced or imagined. They found the scorn and hostility more stifling than the Delta heat and soon discovered that the malice and contempt wasn't confined outside the courthouse.

Inside the courtroom the delegation was confronted by Sheriff Clarence H. Strider who they discovered to be a big, fat plain talking man in charge of issuing press passes and who they assessed to be as mean as a cottonmouth snake. They also found the sheriff to be an obscene talking person who dutifully saw that the courtroom was segregated by race.

The sheriff said, "Listen up. We got twenty-two seats over here for you white men and four seats over there for you colored boys. We don't mix 'em down here and we ain't gonna start mixing 'em. And neither do we ever intend to. The coloreds ain't gonna be with the white folks and the white folks ain't gonna be with the coloreds. Some of y'all coloreds might think yah buddies with some of the whites, but it ain't gonna be no love fest with black and white folks up in this courtroom. That's how we do things down here."

The sheriff raised his gun-belt that had slid below his large belly and walked off.

The white reporters took their assigned seats. Jamal and two other Negro reporters, along with Congressman Charles Diggs Jr., took the four seats around a rough, unfinished table with splinters that tore into their clothes and scratched their hands and arms. The table was located in a far, back corner. The remaining Negro reporters parked their derrieres on the tile floor near the table or stood against the wall.

The courtroom was filled to the rafters. Jamal estimated there was well over three hundred people crowded in the courtroom. White people were let in first, then Negroes were allowed to occupy about fifty seats in the rear. Jamal mused that if admission was charged that the courtroom still would be packed; at least with white people.

Jamal thought it incredulous that both Roy Bryant and J.W. Milam had their young boys on their laps and playing with them before the trial began. Anguish built up inside Jamal as he watched the defendants smoke cigars and frolic with their kids and as though they didn't have a worry.

The court bailiff said, "...Presiding is Judge Curtis Swango. All may now be seated. Court is now in session."

Word got out among the press corps that Judge Swango had named a jury consisting of all white men (ten farmers, an insurance man, and a carpenter) who resided in Tallahatchie County where Roy Bryant and J.W. Milam lived. They'd been selected from a pool of one hundred twenty white men.

The Negro press corps smelled a rat.

Sitting at the table with Congressman Charles Diggs and two other Negro reporters, Jamal mumbled, "Disciples of the Devil." A *Jet/Ebony magazine* reporter at the table whispered, "What?"

Jamal said, "I'm referring to the all-white, male jury from Tallahatchie County. I can't help but think of them as the Devil's disciples."

The men's smiles underpinned Jamal's remark. They looked and saw Sheriff Strider glaring at them. Jamal looked and saw Mamie Till appearing somber but alert as she sat erect with her shoulders squared.

Spectators were fanning themselves as fans stirred the tepid air in the courtroom. To Jamal's surprise he watched vendors selling soft drinks, but only to the white spectators. Jamal conjectured that a profit was being made off Emmett Till's murder.

Judge Swango apprised the audience about proper decorum in his courtroom and rebuked several photographers for snapping pictures while court was in session. He directed the legal council to make their opening remarks, starting with the prosecution that consisted of Gerald Chatham, the lead prosecutor, and Robert Smith, both white men. Prosecutor Chatham rose from his seat, wearing his tie loose. He approached the snarling jurors whom all appeared to Jamal to have just sucked lemons.

Prosecutor Chatham remarked, "Men of the jury, the State will prove beyond any reasonable doubt that Roy Bryant and J.W. Milam did in fact go to the home of Moses Wright on the early morning of August twenty-eight and by force spirited away the young, Negro boy Emmett Till. We have a witness to attest to such and, in fact, Mr. Bryant and Mr. Milam have already admitted such to the authorities. Furthermore, we will produce a witness whom will testify under oath that Emmett Till was seen transported in a truck driven by J.W. Milam with Roy Bryant a passenger. The witness will testify that he was picking cotton in a field at the time he saw Roy Bryant and J.W. Milam. He will further state that he heard sounds of a beating along with pleading cries from a male voice that came from a shed on the Clint Sheridan Plantation. And it so happens that Leslie Milam, the brother of J.W. Milam and the half-brother of Roy Bryant, manages this plantation. In addition, the witness will state that the pleading cries from the shed grew silent and that moments later Roy Bryant and J.W. Milam emerged from the shed. And after emerging from the shed, these two men were seen leaving in a truck and that the bed was covered with a tarpaulin and that Emmett Till, who was seen earlier in the bed of the truck, was not visible. We will further establish motive by proving that Roy Bryant and his half-brother J.W. Milam with malice and forethought did set out to harm Emmett Till for allegedly wolf-whistling at Caroline Bryant, the wife of Roy Bryant."

There was jeering and hissing in the courtroom, coming from the white sections. The judge rapped his gavel and called for order.

Following the pause, Prosecutor Chatham said, "After all the evidence is entered into record we believe this jury will find the defendants guilty of murdering Emmett Till at the young age of fourteen, whose life had merely begun. And this vicious act has deprived Mrs. Mamie Till of the love and affection of her only child. Thank you, gentlemen of the jury."

Prosecutor Chatham took his seat. Jamal looked over at Mamie Till dabbing her eyes with a handkerchief.

The lead, defense attorney, Sidney Carlton, a gray-headed man of average height and weight, stood and strolled toward the suddenly transformed and benign looking jurors. Jamal witnessed four attorneys at the table for the defense. The lead attorney approached with his head slightly bowed and as though he was in deep contemplation. He looked into the jury box and with a southern drawl said, "This case is built as a murder case and as the State of Mississippi versus Roy Bryant and J.W. Milam. But the defense intends to prove to the astute members of the jury that Mr. Bryant and Mr. Milam did not commit the crime of murder as the prosecution contends. We'll prove that outside pressure and influence is the only reason that our clients have been charged in this case. We'll also prove that a juvenile delinquent boy from Chicago by the name of Emmett Till came to Mississippi and insulted Carolyn Bryant, the wife of Roy Bryant. Roy Bryant and J.W. Milam merely went to the home of Moses Wright on the morning of August twenty-eight to talk to the fresh-mouth boy. We'll also establish that Moses Wright gave our clients permission to take Emmett Till away from his home in order to have a talk with the boy because Moses Wright understood that what his great nephew did was improper. Moses Wright realized that Mr. Bryant had a right to be upset; just like any white man in this courtroom would've been if the same thing had happened to them. In fact, it was Moses Wright who suggested to our clients that Roy Bryant give the boy a beating for his transgression. The defense will additionally prove that the body pulled from the Tallahatchie River was not that of Emmett Till and which the sheriff of Tallahatchie County, Sheriff Herbert Strider, will attest to. Furthermore, you will discover that a murder weapon has not been produced as evidence against our clients. We trust, gentlemen, that after we give y'all the evidence that y'all will indeed find our clients not guilty of the charge brought forth by the prosecutors for the purpose of appeasing the liberal northern press that doesn't have any appreciation of the southern way of life. Thank you."

The defense attorney returned to his seat, sat back, and crossed his legs.

The judge asked the prosecution to call its first witness.

Jamal watched as Moses Wright walked slowly to the witness stand. He had to push his way through the huddled courtroom. All eyes were focused on him. He sat on the edge of a cane chair. He looked about as comfortable as a rabbit in the midst of wolves. Jamal discerned the hostile glare of the white spectators. He could tell Moses was feeling the pressure and heat of the situation. He wondered if Moses could weather it.

Prosecutor Chatham asked Moses if he could identify the men who came to his home and took Emmett Till away. Moses stood and said, "Thar 'em," as he pointed to Roy Bryant and J.W. Milam. He then sat back hard on the chair as though the gravity in the courtroom had thinned.

> Jamal wrote on a sheet of paper: *History has just been made with a poor, Negro sharecropper accusing white men of a crime in Mississippi, daring to send them to the gas chamber for murdering a Negro.*

Jamal knew everyone in the courtroom understood both the nature and the magnitude of what Moses had done by pointing out the defendants. .

Willie Reed appeared nervous on the stand when it came time for him to testify. Jamal observed him looking down at the floor, fiddling with his hands, and speaking in a whisper. Several times the judge instructed him to speak up.

Jamal and all the reporters in the courthouse perked up when the prosecutor brought Mamie Till to the stand. She confirmed that she'd indeed identified her son's body. After a few more questions the prosecutor rested.

The lead defense attorney approached Mamie for cross-examination. He wasted no time. He stated, "Ain't it a fact Mamie that the body pulled out of the Tallahatchie River wasn't that of your son, but was another body and that the NAACP in Chicago encouraged you to say that the body was your son's? And ain't it also a fact that your son, Emmett, is alive in Detroit living with an uncle?"

Suddenly lights in the courtroom flickered, except for the lights in the back where the Negro spectators were seated. A large chandelier hanging from the ceiling of the commodious courtroom shook and as though breached by a strong wind. The fans in the courtroom became silent. A water pipe burst and accounted for water pouring down upon the table of the defense. The lead defense attorney stumbled backwards and fell on the floor as water streamed on him and caused a red piece of paper in his shirt pocket to bleed through and give the appearance of blood.

Roy Bryant coughed up blood and bent over in pain and agony.

A leg of the chair that J.W. Milam sat on broke and caused him to fall backward as his head pounded the floor and bled, inducing him to wince and grimace in pain.

Judge Swanson, though in awe, had the presence of mind to pound his gavel and call for a recess.

The courtroom was vacated. Maintenance workers came to attend to the damage and was amazed to see more than a dozen bubble gum wrappers floating in water on the floor that'd turned red.

* * *

During the break in the trial, Brother Justice Twenty-one (a.k.a. J.D, the taxi driver) sought out Jamal and handed him a note that read: *Our sources have revealed that Levy "Too-Tight" Collins is in the Tallahatchie County Jail. Please provide this information to the prosecutor inasmuch as Too-Tight's testimony is critical to the case.*

"Damn!" Jamal muttered to himself, thinking that he was in a quagmire. He contemplated that if Too-Tight was in Sheriff's Strider's jailhouse, then obviously the sheriff was intentionally suppressing evidence against Roy Bryant and J.W. Milam. Jamal saw it as an obvious conspiracy and considered that the sheriff had testified for the defense, which was most unusual in the people's case against the defendants. Jamal contemplated that justice in this case was about as blind as an eagle with binoculars. Still, Jamal knew he couldn't ignore the importance of Too-Tight's testimony but, then too, he was wary about personally providing the prosecutor with the information that would identify him as the source and knowing full well that the prosecutor would have to confront Sheriff Strider with the information. And Jamal didn't want any encounters with the sheriff if he could in any way avoid it. He considered the sheriff's wrath to be far-reaching.

There were no chairs at their table when Jamal and his cohorts returned after the morning recess. Someone had taken them.

As the trial was about to reconvene, Sheriff Strider strolled to the *colored table* and said, "How yah niggas doin?" He grinned and walked off smirking.

* * *

Jamal witnessed no bombshells in the afternoon of the trial. At the end of the session, he hurried to the Western Union desk that was situated in the hallway of the courthouse. Many local people who couldn't get into the courtroom milled around the open phones and listened to the reporters call in their stories on special wires that were set up.

After sending his story to the National News Association office, Jamal noticed evil expressions of white people who were standing near. He realized they'd heard every word he'd reported. He tried to ignore them and closed his briefcase. He thought about having dinner this evening with Vera Franklin around six-thirty as they'd agreed to and which was the most pleasant thought he'd had all day. He made his way through a hostile, white crowd and back to the boarding house. He relaxed for a while, freshened up, and went across the street to meet Vera at Sadie's Southern Cooking.

* * *

After having dinner with Jamal, Vera Franklin hurried back to her place in Money. Her mind was full as she drove. She thought about the trial, which she understood was a farce. She knew Roy and J.W. to be guilty of killing Emmett Till because she'd heard with her own ears Roy confess. The thought of Roy and J.W. getting away with murdering the young, boy from Chicago bothered her to no end. She smiled as she recalled Roy throwing up blood at the trial, which she knew had much to do with the rat poisoning she'd been adding to his food a little at a time. She mused that justice would be served on Roy by her means. She wished that she could somehow get to J.W. in a similar manner.

Vera arrived at the small house where Roy Bryant was putting her up in exchange for her black licorice, female favors. She parked her car and unlocked the front door to the house. She was startled to see Roy slouched on the sofa in the small room off the kitchen area. She wasn't surprised that he'd gotten inside since he had a key, but was astonished that he was there at all since he was involved with the trial. She figured his car was parked out back.

"You black bitch, where you been?"

"I'm not a bitch. My parents were humans."

"Who in the hell you think you talkin to, black bitch? Have you forgotten I'm a white man? I'm not that nigga reporter you were seen talkin to today."

"And I suppose now you're a famous white man accused of killing a young, defenseless black boy. Do you want me to applaud?"

"Bitch, I'll kill you!"

"Like you did Emmett Till? Are you gonna throw my body in the Tallahatchie River, too."

Roy stood up from the sofa with his fist clinched and approached Vera. She cowered and stepped back. Roy grabbed both her arms and shook her violently. He said, "You black bitch you better keep yer fuckin mouth shut before I close it for good, along with your nigga reporter friend who I saw you with today during the trial's recess. What was you talkin to him about?"

"About doing an interview."

"What kinda interview, bitch?"

"I told you I ain't a bitch!"

Roy shook Vera and said, " Yer anything I say you are. If I say you a dog, you better get down on the floor and bark. Got that?"

Vera turned her head away from Roy and closed her eyes without responding.

Roy shook her again and said, "Did you here what I said, bitch. Yer whatever I say you are and nothin more. Is that understood?"

"Yeah, Roy. It's understood. Let me go. You're hurting me."

"Bitch, you don't know what hurt is yet. Now tell me about this fuckin interview."

"Jamal wanted to interview me about my singing. He heard me sing the other night at the club in Mound Bayou.

He said that he wanted to do a story about me, so we met and had dinner today after the trial."

"You had dinner with that nigga? Did you sleep with him, too?"

"No, I didn't sleep with him. We just had dinner."

"Yah probably plan to sleep with him. What name did you call that nigga?"

"I'm not telling. I don't want you bothering him."

Roy let go of Vera's arms and slapped her with so much force that blood squirted from her mouth and nose. Her head rotated forty-five degrees. She fell to the floor. Roy stood over her as she sobbed. He said, "You black, nigga-bitch, don't you ever insult me by tellin me what you ain't gonna do. Do you understand me?"

Roy started experiencing convulsions. He gagged and blood poured from his mouth. He fell to his knees, then rolled over in a fetal position. When the pain subsided and Roy struggled to his feet, he found himself standing in a puddle of water and saw bubble gum wrappers that were in a path from where he stood to the front door. He also discovered Vera gone.

* * *

Jamal read the note again: *Nigger -- you better pack your bags and get back to Detroit and leave in 24 hours or else start writing your obituary.*

He recollected having received the missive in an envelope while having dinner with Vera. The waitress told him that a white man left it for him, but she could only describe the man in vague terms. He shared the message with his Negro colleagues who all agreed that it would be foolhardy to assume that the threat was idle, especially when directed to a Negro from a white man in Mississippi.

Concerned about Jamal's welfare, one of the Negro reporters brought a loaded .38 Smith and Wesson pistol to his room for him to keep for protection. Jamal sat behind the locked door thinking that he'd come to Mississippi to cover a murder trial and to do his job, but by doing so his own life was being threatened. The rumination fueled his anger but couldn't dispel the fear he harbored. He heard a knock at the door but wasn't expecting anyone. He picked up the pistol from off the bed, walked to the door and asked, "Who is it?"

"Vera Franklin!"

Jamal placed the pistol in the waistband at the back of his pants and opened the door. He saw blood smeared on Vera's face and her holding two suitcases. Jamal stepped aside with his eyes bulging and said, "Come in!" He closed the door and asked, "What happened?"

"Roy Bryant hit me. He was angry about you interviewing me and me talking back to him." She sat her luggage on the floor.

Jamal stood gaping at Vera with his jaw dropped. He waited momentarily to allow her comment to fully register in his mind, then asked, "How do you know Roy Bryant?"

Vera took a deep breath, blew it out her mouth and said, "I slept with the bastard, which I'm ashamed to admit."

"What?"

"You heard me right. I slept with Roy Bryant. He was my white Sugar Daddy and I was his mistress."

Jamal stood like a statue in the middle of the floor as he froze his sight on Vera.

"Please don't look at me that way," Vera appealed. "It was a mistake; a big mistake. But please don't judge me and think badly of me. Please! I need your help. I've got to get outta Mississippi in a hurry. Roy Bryant will kill me if he finds me."

Jamal stood there thinking they both needed to leave the Magnolia State and that maybe they could run off together. Then quickly he considered he must be losing his mind and that the heat and hate in Mississippi had made him delirious. He began to think that as fine as a woman Vera was that he could never love her and for starters he understood that if ever he made love to her that he would always visualize Roy Bryant, Emmett Till's murderer, doing the same. He found the thought repugnant. And besides, Jamal had already come to grips with the fact that his love for Francine was undying and that he wanted her back in his life. But then he had to contend with the prospect of his life being cut short in Mississippi. He wasn't sure if he would ever see Francine and his son, Thurgood, again. The situation was proving more ominous to him.

Chapter Twelve

Jamal stayed up most the night guarding Vera Franklin and himself with a pistol inside his room while trying to reach Brother Justice Twenty-one, which he achieved around four o'clock this morning.

After considerable efforts, Jamal and Brother Justice Twenty-one were able to get Vera safe passage under the cover of darkness to Columbus, Mississippi to catch a train to Chicago. Jamal couldn't get over the fact that a white racist such as Roy Bryant had kept Vera as his mistress. And he found irony in discovering that Roy could lie down with a Negro woman but kill a young Negro boy for allegedly whistling at his white wife. Jamal's musing was short-lived, understanding that his own life was yet in danger.

* * *

As Jamal took his seat in the courthouse for the second day of the trial, he was both tired and pissed off. He was fatigued from staying up late last night, hardly getting any rest. And he was upset after learning from Prosecutor Chatham that someone from his office had inadvertently informed Sheriff Strider that he had provided the information that claimed that the witness Levy "Too-Tight" Collins was in the Tallahatchie County Jail. He was told that his name wasn't specifically referenced, but that the person from his office had mentioned the Negro reporter from the National News Association. "Duh!" Jamal muttered in disgust. He now knew why he was sent the note threatening his life. He thought to himself that white people's screw-ups were going to get him killed.

Jamal forced his thinking away from the contemplation of death until he looked and saw Sheriff Strider gazing toward him with a menacing scowl. He also observed Roy Bryant staring at him. Jamal felt fortunate that he'd decided not to rent a car for the trial, thinking that he didn't want to take the chance of law enforcement personnel in the Delta stopping and arresting him in regard to some contrived traffic violation, which he'd heard happening to other Negroes. And sometimes the Negroes would simply disappear. Jamal figured the blatantly racist sheriff was upset and itching to find him in violation of something in order to arrest him, so he knew he'd better not jaywalk or spit on the sidewalk.

After a few legal proceedings, Prosecutor Chatham said, "Judge, it recently came to my attention that a material witness by the name of Levy "Too-Tight" Collins is thought to be lodged in the Tallahatchie County Jail. I spoke with Sheriff Strider about this and he denies that the witness is incarcerated in his jail. But because this matter has been brought to my attention by a member of the media, I think it would be prudent to allow the media an opportunity to visit the county jail in order to determine if, in fact, Mr. Collins is lodged there."

Judge Swango called a recess until the next morning in order to permit the prosecution to produce Mr. Collins or any other witnesses. Jamal betted other Negro reporters that Levy "Too-Tight" Collins had probably been in Sheriff Strider's jail but by now had been removed or gotten rid of in some manner. He thought the trial had been a circus and that the only things missing were elephants, popcorn, and cotton candy.

When Jamal arrived back at the boarding house, Mrs. Coates, the proprietor, handed him an envelope. She informed him that a young, white boy had delivered it. Jamal opened it. The message inside stated: *Nigger – your 24 hours are about to expire and so are you. Dead niggers make good fertilizer in Mississippi.*

After learning about the second threat to Jamal, all the members of the Negro media banded together for protection for the duration of the trial. Mrs. Coates allowed them to stay in two sleeping rooms at the boarding house. And where one went they all went.

Chapter Thirteen

Last Day of the Trial

On Friday, September twenty-ninth, claps of thunder jolted the Delta. Lightning bolted through dark clouds as a heavy rain fell, but didn't stop spectators from crowding into the courtroom for the trial's summations.

Jamal thought God and nature were sending a message in the form of the storm as he sat at the *colored table* wondering about what became of Levy "Too-Tight" Collins who seemed to have disappeared like a coin in a magician's hand. Jamal mused that he would bet a dollar to a dime that the big, fat, flat-footed, bad teeth, stinking breath, racist-ass Sheriff Strider was behind Too-Tight's mysterious disappearance. He loathed the sheriff for all he stood for and was convinced that Negroes would never get justice in Tallahatchie County with such a detestable human wearing a law badge.

Jamal wondered if Too-Tight's disappearance had anything to do with him not receiving another threatening message since the second one. No matter, he had no intention of letting his guards down until he left Mississippi. He sat in the courtroom thinking that since he'd been in Mississippi, he'd seen the worst of humanity. But then too, he thought, he'd also seen the good in regard to the human efforts of members of the Society, which was a rumination he pledged to take away from Mississippi, no matter the outcome of the trial.

Jamal ruminated about how the jury had been stacked with all white men who were of Roy Bryant and J.W. Milam's ilk. He thought that if the dozen white men the judge chose to serve as jurors were unbiased or dispassionate, then he, himself, stood a good chance of being elected the governor of Mississippi.

Judge Swango said, "The court is prepared to hear summations from both the prosecution and defense."

Jamal ended his meditation in order to concentrate on the closing statements. He anticipated no surprises in regard to the lawyers' summations. He watched as the prosecutor approached the irksome-looking jurors and purported that Moses Wright and Willie Reed's testimonies were proof enough that Roy Bryant and J.W. Milam abducted Emmett Till and killed him. He urged the jurors to remember Willie Reed's testimony about hearing a beating and the agonizing screams heard coming from the shed on the night of August twenty-eight.

"...And last but not least, honorable men of the jury, recall that Emmett Till's body was recovered from the murky water of the Tallahatchie River and though badly beaten and greatly disfigured, his body was positively identified by Mamie Till, the victim's mother. And who best can identify a child's body better than the mother?" He quoted from the twenty-eight chapter of Proverbs, thanked the jurors, and then took his seat.

The quiet in the courtroom was broached by a few coughs and some throats being cleared. Jamal watched the lead defense attorney rise from his seat and encountered members of the jury whose visages were now friendly.

The attorney said, "Positively identified is what the prosecutor has said to you, but you've heard differently. You heard from Sheriff Strider stating that the body pulled from the Tallahatchie River could not be positively identified. Mamie Till stated that the body was that of her son, but the most substantial evidence she cited was that of a ring with the initials L.T. Now how can any one on the jury be certain that Mamie Till did not arrange to have someone to slip that ring on the finger of the corpse?"

The defense attorney looked up at the ceiling, as did Roy Bryant, J.W. Milam, the sheriff, and the judge. Jamal knew they were looking to see if any disturbance was about to come from above like on the first day of the trial.

The attorney continued and said, "Moses Wright's testimony did not refute that he gave Roy Bryant and J.W. Milan authorization to take Emmett Till from his home on the morning of August twenty-eight, so it was not an abduction. And in regard to the testimony of Willie Reed, I think he was adequately established to be a liar and someone who was encouraged to manufacture a story about what he saw and heard. But the main thing is that our clients can not be found guilty of murdering someone when the corpse can not be positively identified. In this case justice will be served by finding our clients not guilty. Furthermore, honorable men of the jury, your ancestors would turn over in their graves if these men are found guilty."

The attorney walked back to his seat after extending his gratitude to the jury.

Judge Swango dismissed the jury for deliberations and called a recess. All the reporters rushed to the Western Union center in the hallway to wire reports. After sending his report, Jamal walked down the hallway and congregated with other news people who were standing near the jury room. They could hear laughing but were unable to make out what the jurors were saying.

* * *

The jury foreman smiled and asked, "Does anyone think Roy Bryant and J.W. Milam are guilty?"

"No!"

"I don't."

"Not me."

"Me either."

And so the comments went with all twelve jurors.

"They couldn't prove that the body was that of that boy's. Could've been any nigger's body. If Sheriff Strider says the body was unidentifiable, then who is anybody else to say different? Hell, they could've planted that ring on the finger of the dead body like it was said."

"You're right."

The foreman assessed that all the jurors were in support of an acquittal and said, "Well, we can't just rush back into the courtroom with a not guilty verdict with all those reporters hanging around like vultures. We have to make it look good. Let's give it an hour at least. What about some sodas? Anybody thirsty?"

"So what do you think happened to that Emmett Till boy?" a juror asked.

"Hell, Roy Bryant and J.W. Milam probably scared the bejesus outta that nigga and he ran off and jumped in the Tallahatchie on his own."

Everyone laughed.

"I believe the defense attorney's statement that the boy is in Detroit with relatives and that the NAACP is trying to stir up trouble for white people in Mississippi."

"Can't blame Roy Bryant for being angry. Anyone of us would've been upset enough to at least beat some respect in that niggah for insulting our woman."

"Yah think Roy and J.W. are nervous about our decision?"

"Hell, those boys should know we ain't about to cause our ancestors to roll over in their graves on account of some disrespectful nigger from Chicago."

* * *

Word circulated that the jury had made a decision and was about to return to the courtroom. All the reporters rushed back to their stations. The court was brought back into session.

The all white, male jurors filed into the room.

Jamal looked at his watch and assessed that the jury had been out about sixty-seven minutes.

Judge Swango asked if the jury had arrived at a verdict.

The jury foreman rose from his chair and said, "Yes we have, Your Honor."

"Then what say you?"

"We, the members of the jury, find defendants Roy Bryant and J.W. Milam not guilty."

Pandemonium erupted in the white only sections of the courtroom. Roy Bryant and J.W. Milam sprang from their seats, hugged each other, and patted their lawyers on their backs. They lit cigars. Photographers flashed their cameras to capture the scene. Reporters sprinted from their stations to wire the verdict across the nation and abroad.

The *not guilty* verdict caused Jamal to feel ill to the point of almost vomiting. Not guilty? Can a pig shave? Do cows fly? Is water dry? Will the Devil pray?

"They can eat shit!" Jamal mumbled, convinced that the verdict smelled like manure. He contemplated throwing a roll of toilet paper in the jury box so the white men could wipe their asses for shitting on justice and on top of Emmett Till's grave. He examined the Negroes in the back of the courtroom sitting and standing silently with their demeanor consistent with his – gloomy and defeated. Jamal mused that all along he'd hoped for the best but prepared for the worst and now understood that the latter had occurred. He watched the white spectators to a person celebrate the verdict. Tears formed in the corners of his eyes.

Mamie Till applied her handkerchief to her damp eyes as she watched and heard the jubilation going on inside the courtroom. She was most sadden by the verdict but not surprised – not in Mississippi and especially in the Delta. She mused that she would've been surprised if Bryant and Milam had been found guilty by their peers of mean, bitterly prejudice white men who'd been carefully selected to serve as jurors. She knew the men were guilty of killing her son – but not only them. She understood that at least six other people that witnesses mentioned were also involved but never brought to justice. She also blamed thousands of others for aiding and abetting the murder of her child: Powerful and influential white people and a dominant culture that condoned hate crimes as opposed to condemning them. She felt very grieved but not the least surprised.

Judge Swango thanked the jurors for performing an important civic duty, which Jamal discerned that the jurors felt proud of. He was convinced that some of the jurors were likely members of the Ku Klux Klan and the White Citizens Council who were yet bitter about the school desegregation ruling. He would bet that everyday of the trial that the jurors likely thought of the Brown versus Board of Education ruling and fumed about the prospect of black and white children attending the same schools. Jamal was convinced that the trial had more to do with white people maintaining *The Southern Way of Life,* which meant that Negroes had to be put in their place and victimized if need be.

* * *

After the trial, strange occurrences began to happen. Upon leaving the courthouse, the jury foreman slipped on a bubble gum wrapper, fell down twelve flights of stairs, struck his head several times, and was taken to the hospital in a coma. Sheriff Strider went to his office and was removing his service revolver when it suddenly discharged; shooting himself in the groin and finding himself bleeding on several bubble gum wrappers that were on the floor.

Negroes in the Delta hadn't forgotten about what happened in the courtroom when the lights flickered, the chandelier shook, the fans stopped, a water pipe broke, the lead defense attorney fell to the floor, Roy Bryant coughed up blood, and J.W. Milam fell and received a concussion. Word of all the bizarre happenings traveled faster through the black community than an acute case of diarrhea is how people assessed it.

On the night of the not guilty verdict, dark clouds blanketed the sky and turned the night as black as one thousand midnights as a Negro woman was heard to say. Negroes raised the specter that Emmett Till's ghost was behind the strange events. They whispered their belief throughout the Delta and particularly for the edification of white people. White people dismissed the notion of Emmett Till's ghost as simply black superstition, nonsense, and ignorance. Nonetheless, many white people became spooked when they heard church bells ringing at unattended churches and eerie sounds emanating from the Tallahatchie River. And the next morning, Leslie Milam, the owner of the Clint Sheridan Plantation, reported sighting blood on cotton in his fields.

Chapter Fourteen

The morning after the trial, Jamal left Mississippi as though there was a gold rush to Michigan. He was happy to still be alive. He conjectured that the Mississippi Delta was the most oppressive place in America for Negroes – a living hell.

Jamal peered out the window of the coach as the train traveled north and would stop in Chicago and points in between before he changed trains to arrive back in Detroit. He watched the Delta landscape pass by as the train sped down the tracks. He saw herds of Negroes stooping over cotton plants and going about their labor like human robots. He leaned back against his seat, shut his eyes, and took a deep breath. He pondered that never returning to Mississippi would be too soon.

As the train headed for Chicago, Jamal remembered being edified by the man in the London House who pontificated that the reason there were lots of blues singers in Chi-Town was because white people in Mississippi gave Negroes much cause to sing the blues. He recalled the song *The Delta Blues* that Vera Franklin sang at the juke joint in Mounds Bayou.

"The blues indeed," Jamal mumbled under his breath. He opened his briefcase and began working on his editorial for the *Michigan Gazette*, which was to be syndicated to other Negro newspapers across the country. He wrote:

The Delta Blues and Hate

By Jamal Peterson

On September 16, 1955, I left Chicago to travel by train to the Mississippi Delta in order to cover the Emmett Till murder trial. In case some readers have been living underneath a rock or perhaps just recently recovered from a coma, I will briefly enlighten that Emmett Till was a fourteen-year-old teenager from Chicago who was savagely murdered for allegedly whistling at a white woman while on vacation in Money, Mississippi. Roy Bryant and J.W. Milam were arrested for the young man's murder and placed on trial.

Before departing for Mississippi to cover the trial, I passed time on the night before by patronizing a Chicago night club called the London House, where on that evening, renowned jazz-pianist Dorothy Donegan delighted a captivated audience, including myself. Toward the end of the night I mentioned to some patrons that I was going to Mississippi to report on the Emmett Till murder trial. My heralding induced a gentleman sitting nearby to portend that Chicago came to have many noted blues singers because a great number of them migrated from Mississippi, where white people gave Negroes plenty to sing the blues about.

By happenstance, or I might say that serendipitously, I came across a promising talent in the Mississippi Delta by the name of Vera Franklin, who is as physically beautiful as she is talented. I found her to be a lovely blossom existing in the milieu of human thorns and thickets. I further discovered her voice to be as sweet as molasses and sinfully appealing. Miss Franklin sings various genres of songs and I had the distinct pleasure of listening to her as she sang a song titled

'The Delta Blues'. Hence, I left Mississippi with a personal and explicit understanding of what causes Negroes to inherit the blues in the delta of Mississippi. And in a word it is "hate" – unadulterated hate – and which I found to be as searing as the Mississippi sun at high noon in August. The hate translates to squalor and inhumane living conditions for Negroes that one might see in a Third World nation. The hate converts to white plantation overseers physically abusing Negro cotton-pickers that, for any reason, can not labor in the fields as demanded. And, no less, the hate destroys jurisprudence for Negroes and therewith causes justice for Negroes in the criminal justice system in Mississippi to be no more of a reality than the Tooth Fairy.

This writer left Mississippi with a solid case of the Delta Blues. In fact, my life was threatened because I was basically doing my job. Any Negro who sat in the Tallahatchie County Courthouse and endured the circus of a trial and the carnival atmosphere had to be imbued by the blues. And if anything caused Negroes to acquire an acute case of the blues it was the "not guilty" verdict that the white, male jury rendered. If justice was imparted in the Emmett Till murder case, then people in the South will never again fly the Confederate flag or drink mint juleps, which is as likely as seeing a Negro soon elected the governor of Mississippi.

I don't envision racial hatred in Mississippi vanishing any time soon. In fact, I predict that man will land on the moon first. But for certain, Negroes will continue to migrate north from Mississippi seeking a better life and some like Vera Franklin will land in Chicago and sing the blues.

The blues are striving in Mississippi and so is hate. Before Emmett Till's murder there were five hundred lynchings of Negroes in the State of Mississippi since 1882. It is high time that the President of the United States spoke forcibly, clearly, and uncompromisingly against lynchings. It is pass time for Congress to enact legislature that would make murder by lynchings a federal crime, which would impede states like Mississippi from protecting the lynchers under state law by frequently allowing the murderers to go unpunished. Lynching is a scourge to a civilized society, and I personally discovered that civility is trampled over and mutilated in Mississippi, and that acts of cruelty against Negroes are commonplace.

This nation has been rudely awaken by the murder of Emmett Till, but the white citizens of Mississippi have buried their heads in the sand. Emmett is buried, but not forgotten, and we must not allow him to be forgotten. Because if we do, then we will turn our backs on a heinous human atrocity, which, as a result, would both compromise and weaken our souls as human beings. So, let not Emmett Till be forgotten. Let us stand together against racism and injustice no matter where it occurs. Let Emmett's death be a lightning rod for justice and a ramrod against oppression and injustice everywhere. Remember Emmett!

* * *

Mamie Till sat silently in a coach of the northern-bound Illinois Central train heading back home to Chicago. She, relatives, and other Negroes on the train wore somber facial expressions. The trial had prevailed upon them that *Lady Justice* had peeped from behind her blindfold in Judge Curtis Swango's courtroom and protected the men who killed Emmett Louis Till.

Mamie felt mentally exhausted and hollow on the inside. The trial had mutilated her heart and soul. The *not guilty* verdict had penetrated her heart like a dull scalpel. She was struggling not to hate and to cling to Pastor William's spiritual counseling to not hate the perpetrators but only their deeds. She found it most difficult to separate the men from their deeds. She saw them as a whole with no division or demarcation. She despised the men who had been on trial for killing her son. She loathed the judge. She abhorred the sheriff. She detested the defense attorney and his gall to question her veracity in regard to identifying her own dead son. She scorned the jury. She possessed contempt for the people who cheered the verdict.

Tears filled Mamie's red eyes like every time the harrowing ruminations of the trial came to her mind and which was often.

"Not guilty." She knew those two words would forever pain her.

Mamie used a handkerchief to sponge the tears on her face. She squeezed her eyes shut, balled her hands, and summoned her heart and soul for internal strength. She opened her eyes, stood up, looked above, and pledged, "I swear to God and as long as I have a voice that I won't let the world forget what happened to Emmett!"

Chapter Fifteen

Jamal felt elated to be back home in Detroit in the comfort of his west-side two-bedroom apartment on West Grand Boulevard. He'd arrived home around two in the afternoon after detraining at the Michigan Central Depot and retrieving his four-door Ford Victoria from the parking structure.

He contemplated that the sound of traffic outside his living room window with roaring car engines and honking horns was a vast departure from the time he'd spent in Sumner, Mississippi. He turned on the radio and tapped his bare feet as Chuck Berry strummed his acoustical guitar and sang the hit song *Maybellene*.

Jamal had a few people to call and wanted to make good on his promise to call Tessie Robinson as soon as he arrived back in town. He pondered that he hadn't had sex since he went to bed with Tessie before leaving for Chicago and Mississippi. He recalled being sexual with Stephanie Parker from Cleveland whom he'd met at the London House in Chicago, but things didn't go any further because she had to leave that evening with relatives. And, besides, he knew he'd been too intoxicated to pleasure her in bed, even if he'd had the opportunity. But he did have her telephone number.

And he'd desired to make love to Vera Franklin, imagining looking down into her lovely face and her groaning in carnal pleasure. He still couldn't get over her telling him that the racist-murderer Roy Bryant had gone to bed with her. And it troubled him to no end that the racist bastard who killed Emmett Till had had the pleasure of making love to a beautiful black woman like Vera. He yet felt repulsed by the thought. He suddenly brooded over whether Francine had shared a bed with another man since their divorce, which was a cogitation he found most troublesome. He forgot about Tessie, Stephanie, and Vera as he picked up the handset of the phone and dialed.

"Hello."

"Hello. Francine this is Jamal. How are you doing? And how's Thurgood?"

"We're both fine. I had to take Thurgood to the hospital for stitches."

"Stitches! What for?"

"Thurgood fell while playing baseball. He cut his chin and needed eight stitches. But he's doing fine. He misses you? How did it go in Mississippi? I heard they acquitted the men accused of killing Emmett Till. I bet his mother is more distraught than she was before the trial. I feel so badly for her."

"She took the verdict real hard, which was to be expected. I even got my life threatened."

" You did? By whom and what for?"

"By white people who didn't appreciate me giving the prosecutor information about additional witnesses. It's a long story," Jamal said as he sighed.

"I'm glad you're all right."

"Thanks. Babycakes, I really miss you and Thurgood. I want us to be a family again."

There was silence. Francine didn't respond.

Jamal said, "Babycakes, I really do miss you and it's no jive. I really mean it. I love you very much. I know I royally messed up our marriage, which I'm truly sorry about. But, I've always loved you."

"Jamal, you had a family and a loving wife when you were gallivanting around town and sticking your dick in every piece of pussy you could find. How can you say you loved me when you were doing things like that?"

"Babycakes, I did love you. It's hard to explain why I did what I did. I was stupid, but I never stopped loving you. I swear. I truly do love you, Francine."

"Jamal, I really don't think you know what love is. Love wouldn't have had you out at all times of the night. Love would've brought your ass home at a decent hour. Love would have made you honor your wedding vows like I did. I loved you, Jamal. I really did. I was a faithful wife and had a child for us. I wanted our marriage to work and you screwed everything up."

She began to sniffle and said, "Damn, Jamal! You don't know how much you hurt me. And another thing, stop calling me Babycakes. I can't stand it now when you refer to me as Babycakes. I used to love you calling me Babycakes. It sounded so sweet and endearing, but now when I hear you calling me Babycakes, I think of you being with other women then coming home to me and still calling me that. So, Jamal, if you really care about me, I ask you please not to refer to me as Babycakes anymore. Please! Do you want to talk to Thurgood? I need to get off the phone."

Francine's soft sobbing pained Jamal. He said, "Yes, I want to speak with our son, but, Francine, please don't go. Give me another minute or two. Please, Francine."

"Jamal, it's not going to work between us. I told you that I don't think I can ever trust you again, and trust is very important in a relationship."

"I know, Babycakes. Sorry. I mean Francine. I agree with everything you said. But, I'm gonna change. I really am. I'm gonna change for you and Thurgood and for us. I promise with all my heart that I'll change if you just give me another chance. You're a real good woman, Francine. I consider you a treasure. I know I didn't treat you like a treasure before. But if you give me another chance I'll honor and cherish you as my woman and never cheat on you again. Francine, if you want me to beg, I will. I'll get down on my hands and knees if that what it'd take. Please reconsider. Think about it, Francine. Please! I'll do anything for us to be a family again. I want you to be my wife again. I want and need you in my life. I'll do whatever it takes; go to church and get counseling from the pastor; any and everything. Just tell me what you want me to do. I'll be the best husband in the world to you, Francine. I promise."

"Jamal, I'm not interested in making you beg. And you're assuming that I'm not seeing someone else. What makes you think that I would drop a relationship with someone else to take a chance on you again after all you did? I'm not like you, Jamal, I don't gamble with love."

Jamal got silent. Francine's statement *"I don't gamble with love"* tore into his heart. And he knew she was right because he had gambled – that he would admit. He couldn't deny it because he realized that he'd rolled the dice and came up snake eyes. He contemplated that he'd rather wagered and lost a fortune in money as opposed to losing Francine.

He didn't want to think of the prospect that Francine was seeing another man. It was too painful. But he realized that it was pretentious of him to presume that she wasn't seeing someone new. He realized other men would find her attractive – perhaps a treasure. He had to know. He asked, "Are you seeing someone else?" He held his breath and braced himself.

Chapter Sixteen

Thursday, December 1, 1955

Rosa Parks felt exhausted from her work as a seamstress at the downtown Montgomery Fair department store as she left to go home late in the afternoon. She donned a full-length wool coat against the cool, overcast weather. She crossed the street to a drugstore to purchase a few items then headed for the bus stop to wait for the Cleveland Avenue bus. She stood at the bus stop, removed her eyeglasses, cleaned them with a handkerchief from her purse and placed them back on her face. Just then the city bus arrived. She routinely paid the bus driver her fare, got back off the bus and boarded again from the rear, which was the procedure for Negroes. She saw that the *reserved seats* for white people were partially filled and that the seats just behind them were vacant and where she took a seat. She felt good to relax for it'd been a most busy day with all she'd had to accomplish on her job before the Christmas holiday. She watched as the bus began to fill with Negro and white passengers. She heard the bus driver say, "You hav'ta give up the seat." She looked up and saw the driver focusing his attention on her.

"This is not the reserved section," Rosa replied.

"Reserved section or not, you hav'ta give the seat up to this gentleman," the bus driver insisted.

Rosa observed that the man who the bus driver was referring to stood silently and looked very healthy. She weighed in her mind that the white, male passenger was standing next to the driver like an anointed king. She thought about the two white men accused of killing Emmett Till, which gave her both the will and fortitude to say, "No! I'm not going to get up. I'm tired. I'm a woman, he's a healthy man, and I have a right to sit here."

"If you don't get outta that seat right now I'll call the police!"

"Go on and have me arrested. I'm not moving."

The bus driver summoned the police and within a matter of minutes Rosa Parks, a middle-aged, civic and religious worker, cultured and soft-spoken, was arrested. She maintained her decorum and poise as the white policemen placed her in a squad car and took her to jail.

* * *

The vocal bulletin of Rosa Parks' arrest spread through the Negro community in Montgomery faster than Jackie Robinson stealing third base. Telephones jangled and Negroes gathered in homes and on street corners. They talked incessantly about Rosa's arrest. Rumor of a bus boycott crept in the Negro community, creating much tension and anxiety. Negroes waited for someone to do something.

On Monday, December 5, the day that Rosa Parks was to go on trial, the Women's Political Council printed tens of thousands of leaflets throughout the Negro community with the message:

Another Negro woman has been arrested and thrown in jail because she refused to get up out of her seat on the bus for a white person to sit down. It is the second time since the

Claudette Colvin case that a Negro woman has been arrested for the same thing. This has to be stopped. Negroes have rights, too, for if Negroes did not ride the buses, they could not operate. Three-fourths of the riders are Negroes, yet we are arrested, or have to stand over empty seats. If we do not do something to stop these arrests, they will continue. The next time it may be you, or your daughter, or mother. This woman's case will come up on Monday. We are, therefore, asking every Negro to stay off the buses Monday in protest of the arrest and trial. Don't ride the buses to work, to town, to school, or anywhere on Monday. You can afford to stay out of town for one day. If you work, take a cab, or walk. But please, children and grown-ups, don't ride the bus at all on Monday. Please stay off all buses on Monday.

The Women's Political Council got the message out to the Negro community by printing and distributing over fifty thousand handbills encouraging the bus boycott. The Negro ministers were impressed and realized that it was time for them to step forward in support. Baptist, Methodist, Catholic, Congregational, other ministers, and leaders of various organizations came together and created the *Montgomery Improvement Association (MIA),* designed to mount Christian, non-violent, legal protest. The ministers pledged themselves and their congregations to remain off the city buses until legal steps were taken to assure fair, unbiased, and equal treatment of all bus passengers. A committee was appointed to draft resolutions and make proposals to be presented to the bus company's officials.

On the first Monday of the boycott, **Dr. Martin Luther King Jr.** was elected president of the MIA. A mass meeting consisting of several thousand Negroes was called and held at Holt Street Baptist Church, the largest Negro church in Montgomery. Those in attendance crowded the auditorium, the balcony, the basement, the aisles, the steps, and the churchyard. For three blocks up and down Holt Street, people sat in cars with windows rolled down. Many stood close enough to hear from loudspeakers what was being said inside the two-story, brick church. There was a police presence and more than once the cops warned that the volume of the loudspeakers be turned down, but to avail.

White journalists from Montgomery, including the city editor of the *Montgomery Advertiser* newspaper, as well as white reporters from nearby locations, were present to cover the news of the boycott. Cameras flashed continuously and took pictures of the thousands gathered at the church.

Dr. Martin Luther King Jr. stood at the microphone. His deep, melodious voice exploded through the loudspeakers. He said, "…Since Emmett Till's tragic death I've been carrying a picture in my wallet of the young man who was brutally murdered at the hands of vicious racists in Mississippi. His death should stand as a wakeup call for every Negro gathered here this evening and throughout America. And not only that, but the nature and circumstances of his death should also sound like Gabriel's trumpet in the conscience of every decent-hearted white person in American as well as around the world."

The audience applauded and voiced affirmation.

Dr. King raised his hand for quiet. The peopled settled down. He said, "I spoke with Mrs. Rosa Park at her home the other day after she was bonded out of jail. Those of us who know Mrs. Park know her to be a quiet, dignified, well-respected, unassuming, Christian woman. She was not looking for trouble when she refused to give up her seat to a white man on a Montgomery public bus. But what she was looking for was dignity and the right to be treated with respect and equality as a human being. She said she thought about Emmett Till and just couldn't relent to giving up her seat that day like she'd done many times before."

One of the Negro women, a member of the Women Political Council, in the audience had read Jamal Peterson's editorial titled *The Delta Blues and Hate* and recalled the last two words of his article. She shouted, "Remember Emmett!"

Negroes in the auditorium took up the mantra and started shouting, "Remember Emmett!" People in the balcony, in the basement, outside on the lawn, as well as Negroes standing along the streets and sitting in cars echoed, "Remember Emmett!"

After the audience sufficiently quieted down, Dr. King said, "I've been encouraged by my distinguished clergy in the pulpit and by what we've just heard here this evening, to announce that we will officially use the slogan 'Remember Emmett!' during the duration of the bus boycott..."

* * *

Requests for Mamie Till to speak before audiences flowed in and it was as though the dam of human intolerance had spilled over in reference to the death of her son. And there wasn't the proverbial little Dutch boy to plug the dam is how one writer put it.

Mamie stood before an audience at a predominantly white high school in Ohio, where she had been invited to speak about the death of her son and race relations. Her recount of her son's brutal murder caused some students to gasp, some to shed tears, and some to possess a feeling of horror. But it wasn't only the student body exhibiting such emotions, for some of the faculty mirrored similar compassion.

Mamie said, "...I'm often asked if I hate white people because of what happened to my son. I tell people that not all white people killed my son and that some white people were just as enraged as Negroes in regard to what happened to Emmett. Love and civility aren't manifested in the human soul and spirit according to race or the color of one's skin, but by individual human compassion. So to answer the question: No, I do not hate white people. For me to hate white people would be no less wrong than anyone else who hates another person because of race or skin color. We are all God's creatures, so if I hate any of his creation then I am questioning the wisdom of God and his judgement. I don't hate the men who killed Emmett. What I do hate is their cruel deeds. To hate the men who murdered my child would cast me in the same light as these men who hated my son because he was a Negro. I choose not to be cast in the same light as these men by God. I choose to be spiritually and humanely better. Hate is a debilitating emotion that robs the hater of his soul, civility, humanity, and, I might add, his Christianity. Hate causes the hater to become withered like a scrub. People who love are nourished and blossom as human beings. Hate is like a desert. Love is an oasis. Emmett was a loving child. I believe that righteous people stand on solid ground, while evildoers stand on sinking sand. I chose to stand on solid ground and I hope all in this place will do the same. Emmett stood on solid ground. I taught Emmett at a young age to be respectful of all people and not to think that any person was better than he was. And young people – like I told Emmett – you first have to love yourself, but not in a selfish way. When you love yourself, you will respect yourself. When you respect yourself, you will demand respect from others and walk tall with confidence. Emmett was a confident child. I know Emmett is in Heaven. The men who murdered him are hell-bound. I told Emmett to look up to God and not to man and that God is the only one who can really look down on you, and God does so with mercy, compassion, and love. They killed Emmett, but I'm certain that they didn't kill his spirit. Thank you."

An arousing applause echoed throughout the auditorium. People outside the school could hear the reverberation. The noise awakened a janitor who thought he would catch a catnap while all was in the assembly. A white faculty member shouted, "Remember Emmett!" And rapidly everyone in the auditorium was shrieking the same.

Chapter Seventeen

The Mississippi Delta

Roy Bryant's friends and supporters didn't have the heart to tell him, but some thought it and others whispered it behind his back. Their concern and observation was that Roy was beginning to live like a sharecropper or worse. No one said it, but it was obvious that Roy's reversal of fortune was due to the fact that Negroes had started boycotting his grocery and meat market after he was acquitted for murdering Emmett Till.

The boycott wasn't planned or organized, but, rather, happened as a natural order of events because Negroes understood that white people could force them to do a lot of things in the Delta, but couldn't compel them to spend their hard-earned money as they pleased. So, they went about the business of avoiding Roy Bryant's store in Money and denying him the income to make a living.

Some Negroes thought Emmett Till's ghost had taken up residence at Bryant's grocery store in regard to the weird things some of them had seen and all of them had heard. They spoke of the mysterious red stains on the counters and

147

walls, and bubble gum wrappers appearing on the floor each morning that the Bryants opened their store.

The strange occurrences were rumored throughout the Delta and caught sail after two more of the jurors in the Emmett Till murder case came upon misfortune. It was reported that two men who served on the jury fell off their motorboat into the Tallahatchie River one evening as the sun was setting and one got his arm severed by the blade of the motorboat engine and the other had a leg cleaved. They both lived, but the word was that white people were afraid to fish any longer in the Tallahatchie River, which left all the good fishing to Negroes. And Negroes in the Delta were dumbfounded to learn that some plantation owners had organized food pantries for cotton-pickers and offered second-hand clothing to Negro farmhands for free. Even Negro tenant farmers reported receiving a larger share of the return for their labor. But what took the cake, as some Negroes said, was when some plantation owners announced that the Negro laborers would get Christmas Eve and Christmas off and get paid for it.

Negroes became convinced that tales about Emmett Till's ghost had given cause for white people suddenly becoming benevolent to their Negro farmhands.

* * *

It was Christmas Eve, but Roy Bryant was as close to possessing the Christmas spirit as the Mississippi Delta was in proximity to the Vatican. After closing his store early, he drove home in his truck as he pondered that his finances had sunk like lead and understood that business at his grocery store had been reduced to a trickle. He wished that nigger boy from Chicago had stayed up North because he knew if he had, then everything would be normal. Roy didn't feel at all contrite about killing the boy because he was convinced he'd deserved what he got. He truly believed that he did what any respectful white man would've done when it came to a nigger getting fresh with a white woman. The fact that white people in the Delta had treated him like a hero was proof enough to Roy that he'd done the honorable thing. Regardless, he realized that closing his store for good was practically inevitable.

Roy told himself that he wasn't going to be taken in by all the ghost stories that'd been circulating in the Delta. He refused to think much about it, although he was still hearing the strange, loud, aquatic sounds late at night that didn't seem to be audible to anyone else. On top of his financial problems, he was experiencing poor health, but was feeling better after his doctor alerted him that he'd ingested poison and gave him medication to counteract the ailment. And after some discussion with his doctor, and considering those who would have the opportunity to poison him, he eliminated his wife and deduced that the culprit had to be the nigger-bitch Vera Franklin. He vowed that if ever he saw her again that he'd do far worst to her than he did to Emmett Till.

* * *

J.W. Milam – like his half-brother Roy Bryant – was experiencing a cash-flow problem in regard to the several businesses he owned due to a significant decrease in Negro patronage. Unlike Roy, he was of the mind that killing Emmett Till wasn't such a good idea. No matter that they'd been found not guilty. He had heard the scuttlebutt about Emmett Till's ghost, which Negroes were attributing to Sheriff Strider shooting himself, the jury foreman lying in a coma, and two jurors crippled for life from a boating accident. And he was aware that the other nine jurors – though claiming not to believe in ghosts – were nonetheless concerned about their own well-being.

J.W. went out the backdoor of his house to get some firewood. He carried his ruminations with him as he thought about his problems with insomnia as well as frequent visions of silhouetted, misty, and foggy human forms that sometimes animated life. He filled his arms with wood and walked back to the house. Suddenly a large owl swooped down from a branch of a nearby tree and clawed him across his forehead. He dropped the wood. Blood ran down into his eyes, blinding him. He stumbled over a bench and fell to the ground, which resulted in a one-inch nail in a board impelling his forehead.

* * *

On Christmas Eve, Mamie Till returned home from church service, which was a tradition with her since the death of her husband. She understood that without Emmett Christmas wouldn't be the same. She closed the door behind her, locked it, and began removing her overcoat. She pondered that this would be the first Christmas she'd spent without Emmett. She felt most appreciative of the kind words of support, the outpouring of love, and all the prayers she'd received from her church family this evening, but still her heart was heavy with grief. She missed Emmett and felt weak behind closed doors and out of the view of the public when she was alone with her thoughts. But then she remembered what Pastor Harem Williams told her about not being alone. He imparted to her that God was always present, even in her darkest hours.

Mamie deposited her overcoat on the arm of the sofa in her living room and knelt on her knees. She leaned on the sofa with her elbows and formed her hands into a steeple. "God All-Mighty," she prayed, "please help me to be strong. I am in my darkest hours, although I know you're taking care of my child. God, in the name of Jesus my Savior, I know you understand a mother's love and hurt. I'm simply a mortal soul, dear Lord, and I'm hurting. I'm hurting like

I never hurt before. Please Lord, give me strength to carry on...."

Mamie got off her knees with tears in her eyes. She cut the lights off in the living room and prepared herself for bed. She heard a stub. The sound seemed to come from Emmett's bedroom. She went to investigate, turned on the lights in Emmett's bedroom and saw that a bible had fallen off the dresser onto the floor. She picked up the bible and saw a piece of paper protruding from it in Emmett's handwriting. The message read: *Today in Sunday school the teacher said we should honor our mother and father and she explained what the word honor means. My father is dead so I can only honor his memory. My mama is alive and I honor her everyday because she takes care of me, tell me to be good, cook my favorite food, and every night before I go to sleep she tells me that she love me. I think I have the best mama in the world and I will always honor her.*

Tears fell from Mamie's eyes and dampened the note. She said, "And Emmett you were the best son in the world."

She moved toward the bed, fluffed the pillow, and said, "Goodnight, Emmett. I love you, son." She looked up and said, "Thank you, Lord. Thank you."

Chapter Eighteen

Sunday Morning, December 26, 1955

"The present temperature in Detroit is twenty-two degrees. Today will be overcast with no precipitation expected and with a high of thirty-one degrees..."

Jamal turned down the volume of his car radio. He was happy to have gotten beyond Christmas Eve and Christmas. His Christmas spirit had been as damp as a whale's belly. It was unlike past holidays when Francine, Thurgood, and he were a family. He'd spent the holidays virtually alone with the exception of bringing over his son's presents on Christmas Eve and chatting. Beyond that he'd had a bottle of whiskey for company.

Jamal pulled into the driveway on the westside — about five miles from his apartment — to pick up Francine and Thurgood to make the long journey with him to New York City by car. After beseeching Francine, Jamal was most elated that she'd agreed to make the trip to the National Negro Press Association Awards at the Drake Hotel in Harlem. At Francine's insistence, he'd promised to get two sleeping rooms: one for Francine and Thurgood and the other for himself.

Jamal understood that Francine had made it clear that she was treating the trip as a vacation during the holidays before Thurgood had to return to school and she to her teaching job at Wayne County College, where she was an associate professor of mathematics. And, besides, she'd never been to New York is what she told Jamal.

Jamal had summoned both the courage and inspiration to ask Francine to attend the awards ceremony after she'd informed him that she wasn't seeing someone. However, he also understood that she'd made it clear that the reason she wasn't involved with someone new was because of her busy schedule that consisted of her job, taking care of Thurgood, and working on her doctoral degree in education, but not because she hadn't been approached. She'd also informed him that she wasn't ready for a new relationship because she was still hurt by him and not trusting of men.

* * *

It was evening and prior to the early winter darkness when Jamal, Francine, and Thurgood arrived at the Drake Hotel on 125th Street in Harlem on the island of Manhattan in New York City. Seeing all the Negroes in Harlem reminded Jamal of Detroit's Paradise Valley, but on a much grander scale.

Thurgood was all smiles, which didn't go unnoticed by Jamal nor Francine. They understood that their son was joyful to see his parents together. Francine was pleased that Thurgood was happy, but was concerned about sending him and Jamal the wrong message in regard to her agreeing to make the trip. She didn't want to give Thurgood the impression that his father and she were back together. And she didn't want to suggest to Jamal that she was relenting toward reconciling.

Jamal understood that Francine had told him that their trip was merely a time for her and Thurgood to get away on vacation. But yet he desired that it would turn out to be more. He hoped to romance and court Francine and to convince her that he'd changed the perspective of his life. He wanted to prove to her that he truly had grown to understand what really matters in a relationship. He desired to let her know that he'd learned to appreciate the importance of a family.

Jamal pondered that it'd been a pleasant drive. And now that they'd arrived in New York, he wanted to spend some time alone with Francine and talk; just the two of them. He figured he would mix business with pleasure. Tomorrow he would go to the National News Association's headquarters to discuss future assignments and contracts and then later Francine, Thurgood, and he would take in some sights and catch the Broadway musical *House of Flowers*, starting Pearl Bailey and Diahann Carroll.

* * *

The following day after sightseeing and taking in the Broadway play, Jamal, Francine, and Thurgood ate dinner at Marlene's Kitchen on Lennox Avenue. They later returned to the Drake Hotel. Jamal was in his room relaxing on the bed, reading the Negro novelist John Oliver Killens' book *Youngblood* that told a story of a Negro family's struggle with racism in the south. He also had the radio quietly playing, listening to jazz by Charlie Parker, Thelonious Monk, Miles Davis, Dizzy Gillespie and the likes.

Jamal looked at the clock on the nightstand. It was ten past ten. He thought Thurgood was probably asleep. He wondered if Francine was still awake and what she was doing. But mostly he wanted to know what thoughts were in her head. He pondered if she'd enjoyed the trip thus far. He deliberated if she was beginning to see him in a different light. He mused if she was in her room thinking about him like he was thinking about her.

Jamal twisted his body off the bed, placed his feet on the floor, and picked up the handset of the telephone.

"Hello."

"Hello. Francine it's me, Jamal. Is Thurgood asleep?"

"Yes. He's knocked out. It's been a long day for him. Thank you for everything. I want to give you some money to help cover the expenses since this is a vacation for me."

"Francine, I told you that the trip is on me and to consider it as a Christmas present for both you and Thurgood."

"I know what you told me, but New York is expensive and I want to help out. I can afford it."

"I know you can, Francine. But please allow me to do this. What were you doing before I called?"

"Reading and now I'm getting ready for bed."

"Francine, I would like for us to talk. I could come to your room, but don't want to awaken Thurgood, so will you come to my room so we can talk?"

"No, Jamal. I'm not coming to your room. It's not a good idea and I thought we had that understanding before I agreed to come on this trip."

"Francine, we did. I wasn't suggesting anything more than just us talking."

"I'm not coming to your room, Jamal. You can forget it."

"Then what about us going downstairs to the hotel's lounge so we can talk?"

"I don't know, Jamal. It's late. I'm tired and what about Thurgood? It might not be a good idea to leave him in the room alone. We can talk tomorrow."

"Francine, please. I'd really like for us to talk alone tonight; just thirty minutes is all I'm asking. Please, Francine. Thurgood will be okay for thirty minutes. You know he sleeps like a rock when he's tired. And you said yourself that he was knocked out. Come on. Francine, thirty minutes won't hurt. And that's all it'll be. Just thirty minutes. Please?"

There was silence followed by Francine saying, "Okay, Jamal. Thirty minutes is all. Give me ten minutes and I'll tap on your door. We'll go downstairs, but for only thirty minutes and I'm serious, Jamal."

"Okay. See you in ten. Bye."

"Bye, Jamal."

Jamal hopped off the bed, put on his shoes and a shirt, then went to the bathroom to brush and comb his hair. He splashed on some after-shave. He heard a tap on the door to his room and went to answer it. He saw Francine standing in the hallway wearing a purple blouse and black pants. Her hair was down to her shoulders. He smiled at her. She said, "Thirty minutes, Jamal and I mean it."

Jamal and Francine witnessed about twenty or so patrons in the lounge when they walked in. The song *Ain't It A Shame,* recorded by Fats Domino, was playing on the jukebox. Jamal pulled out a chair at a table for Francine to sit. He occupied a seat across from her at the small, oval-shaped table. A waitress came over to take their order. Francine ordered a ginger ale. Jamal requested a double shot of Johnny Walker Black with coke.

Francine said, "You always liked your liquor, which was one big problem in our marriage."

Francine's comment caught Jamal off guard. He'd expected to initiate their topic of discussion, knowing that he had only thirty minutes with her. He said, "I know, Francine. I will quit drinking as a condition of our getting back together if that's what you would like."

"Jamal, I'm not asking you to give up anything for me. You need to live your life like you please. I'm not your mother and never tried or wanted to be your mother. I only wanted to be a good, loving, and supportive wife and I think I held up my end."

"Francine, I don't want us to argue."

"I don't want to argue either. Why do you consider my stating fact as an argument?"

"You're right, Francine. It is fact. You were a loving, supportive, and faithful wife. When I was out in the street messing around, I wasn't looking for anyone to replace you because no one can. I was just plain selfish and stupid. I know I was the one who was wrong and that my drinking had much to do with how I behaved in our marriage. I haven't had a drink since returning from Mississippi. I just felt like having a drink tonight, but I'll give up drinking on my own accord if we can get back together. That didn't sound right. I know my drinking is a problem, which I'll own up to, so I plan to do something about it whether or not we get back together."

Francine said, "Self-awareness is a good thing, Jamal. I'm pleased to hear you say that."

"I'm very pleased to hear you say that you're pleased to hear me say anything," Jamal said with a smile.

Francine smiled back, which warmed Jamal on the inside like hot chocolate on a cold night.

The waitress brought their drinks to the table and left. The song *Only You* by the Platters was playing on the jukebox.

Jamal asked Francine to dance. She accepted. He escorted her to the dance floor and cradled Francine in his arms. He said, "I love this song and I always think of you when I hear it. We've never gotten the opportunity to dance on it because we were divorced when it came out."

Francine nestled her head on Jamal's chest. She was quiet and introspective. Jamal held her close and gently. And though he had his eyes closed tight, he saw visions of Francine and him back together, needing each other, wanting each other, and forever loving one another.

Francine suddenly pushed away from Jamal. She said, "I'm going back to my room." She bowed her head so Jamal couldn't see the tears forming in her eyes.

"Why are you leaving? I thought we'd agreed to talk."

"I'm not in the mood to talk," said Francine as she walked off.

"Wait, I'll walk you back to your room."

"No, Jamal. I'm very capable of finding my room. Just stay here and enjoy your drink. Maybe you'll find a woman this evening in the bar to share your bed with tonight." She walked away quickly, leaving Jamal stunned.

* * *

After fretting most of the night, tossing and turning, Jamal called Francine's room, but there was no answer. He surmised that Francine was avoiding him or else she and Thurgood had gone to breakfast. But what he absolutely knew for certain was that he'd hurt the woman he truly loved by carousing and being unfaithful. Last night he'd felt Francine's hurt for the first time, but he wasn't going to stop trying to win her back, no matter how long it took or whatever it took. And he now really understood not missing your water until your well runs dry. He felt like the world's biggest fool.

Jamal wrote a note to slip under Francine's door. He took a shower, got dressed, ate breakfast, then drove to the National News Association's headquarters to take care of some business and later to do an interview with Adam Clayton Powell Jr., a former columnist and editor of Negro newspapers who was now a U.S. Congressman from New York. Jamal thought Congressman Powell to be a powerful and courageous Negro for having organized boycotts to compel white merchants in Harlem to hire Negroes and urged Congress to allow Negro journalists to sit in the congressional press galleries. And he appreciated the Congressman for lambasting Mississippi in regard to leading the nation in illiteracy and lynchings.

Francine returned to her room with Thurgood in tow. She figured Jamal had left the hotel by now. She unlocked the door and saw an envelope on the floor with her name on it. She assumed it had been slipped underneath the door. She picked it up, opened it, and saw that the missive was from Jamal. Its contents read:

> *Dearest Francine,*
>
> *Last night after you left and returned to your room, I truly felt that I understood how much I've hurt you. There's not enough time in my lifetime to apologize to you for all the hurt, pain, and disappointment I've caused you. I was sincere about doing whatever it takes to be with you again. But if you never forgive me, I will understand and I know that I have no one but myself to blame. I hope you haven't changed your mind about attending the award ceremony with Thurgood and me this evening. I would love to have you both there. I love you with all my heart. I truly do. And I'm so very much disappointed in myself for what I've done to you and us.*
> *Always Loving You,*
> *Jamal*

* * *

"Ladies and Gentlemen, it's my privilege to introduce the winner of the *1955 Ida B. Wells Editorial Award*. There are three necessary criteria to be met in order to be considered as a nominee for this award: One, the editorial must be cutting edge. Next, the writer must engage a subject of broad human interest relative to the lives of Negroes. And thirdly, the contents of the article must stir or move people to action. The *Ida B. Wells Editorial Award* is named after a courageous, gifted, and talented woman who was co-owner and editor of the *Freedom Speech* Negro weekly newspaper in Memphis, Tennessee. She was also a founding member of the NAACP, active in the anti-lynching campaign, and she once refused to give up her seat on a railroad car designated for whites only. Rings of what recently happened with Rosa Parks in Montgomery, does it? This year's recipient wrote the syndicated editorial *The Delta Blues and Hate*, which appeared in Negro publications across the nation and even in a few so-called mainstream newspapers. *The Delta Blues and Hate* editorial met all the criteria for this award and has certainly stirred people to action inasmuch as activists in the Civil Rights movement have been heard to use the slogan 'Remember Emmett!' as this journalist put forth in his editorial. It is my pleasure on behalf of the National Negro Press Association to present this year's *Ida B. Wells Editorial Award* to Jamal Peterson. His bio is featured in your program."

Jamal proudly approached the rostrum smiling as a thunderous ovation engulfed the ballroom. He raised the microphone to accommodate his height and waited for the audience to settle down. He said, "Thank you so very much. Thank you. I, of course, feel most honored to be presented an award named after such a courageous person as Ida. B. Wells whom was a skilled journalist and a pioneer for civil rights. I want to thank the Association for this distinction and honor. Indeed it's an honor and one I will always cherish. My parents aren't here this evening because they both have passed and I'm an only child. But I have two special people here his evening whom I would like to recognize: my son, Thurgood, and his lovely mother and the love of my life, Francine Peterson."

Francine and Thurgood stood up at their table to receive the applause rendered by the large audience. They resumed their seats.

Jamal said, "When I was writing my editorial, I thought about a few things some people tend to take for granted, such as a fair trial, our children living longer than us, others fighting on our behalf for civil rights, we'll see the next day, et cetera. I've had the opportunity to examine myself and have concluded that I took the love of a good woman for granted in the person of my ex-wife and thus the reason she is designated my ex. This award is very special to me, but the most special thing I've ever had in my life was the love of Francine Peterson. I wanted to say that this evening on this occasion and in front of all of you and the world if it could be my audience. I thank the Association for this prestigious award and thank you, Francine, for the best years of my life."

Chapter Nineteen

Roy Bryant had to close his grocery and meat market after Negro customers continued their de facto boycott. His white patrons had heard the rumor of Emmett Till's ghost hanging out at the store, although they wouldn't admit that talk of Emmett's apparition was the reason for them avoiding patronizing his store. They used other excuses instead or just avoided Roy, period.

J.W. Milam wasn't fairing any better in regard to his business enterprises. His income had sputtered like an engine running on fumes.

Both men were in acute need of revenue, so the four thousand dollars offer from *Look magazine* was most appealing for the purpose of confessing to murdering Emmett Till. And, too, their lawyers had informed them that they couldn't legally be tried again for the murder due to the Fifth Amendment's *Double Jeopardy Clause* of the U.S. Constitution that protected them from a second prosecution for the same offense after acquittal. However, they were warned of the possible social and personal consequences. But neither one was concerned about the potential backlash. The money was more important.

Bryant and Milam agreed to meet journalist William Bradford Huie from *Look magazine* in the company of their lawyers at the Clint Sheridan Plantation in Sunflower County. The men assembled in a parlor.

Mr. Huie said, "Well, let's get started, gentlemen. We all know the reason we're here. Roy Bryant did you murder Emmett Louis Till?'

"Yes, I did and for cause."

"J.W. Milam did you help murder Emmett Louis Till?"

"I certainly did."

"Were any other people involved?"

Bryant said, "Other people were involved in regard to goin to talk to the boy, but they didn't help kill him. Hell, we could've brought a bus load of folks for what that nigga did."

"Who were the other people who went to Moses Wright home the night Emmett Till was abducted?"

"Our lawyers advised us not to implicate anyone else. Me and J.W. will only talk about ourselves and our involvement," Bryant responded.

"Fair enough. For what reason did you murder Emmett Louis Till?"

Milam nodded to Bryant to begin.

Bryant said, "What it boiled down to was that I was infuriated with the fact that that nigga molested my wife and which is no less than any white man worth livin would've been. I was outta town when it happened and my wife never informed me 'bout the incident until a colored fella told me and then I asked around and found that others had heard the same thing and were wonderin what I was gonna do about it."

"Why didn't your wife tell you about the incident at your store?"

"She said that she knew I would be angry enough to hurt that nigga real bad and didn't want no trouble, so she decided to let it go. But she told me all that happened once I caught wind of it. She said the nigga touched her, too. So, hell yeah I was spittin mad. We don't behold to such nigga foolishness down here. If I'd let it go, no white woman would've been safe. And we ain't havin no such goin-on in these parts."

"After you heard about the incident, you went to Moses Wright's home and what happened then?" Mr. Huie asked.

"J.W. and me went to Moses Wright's house late at night, around two in the morning, knocked on the door, and Moses came to the door after I announced who I was. I told him that we were lookin for the boy from Chicago who'd gotten fresh with my wife. Moses led us to a back bedroom where three boys were sleepin. I told him to point out the one who'd molested my wife. And after he did, we made the boy get dress and took him with us with the intent of teachin him a lesson. Moses said the boy didn't know better 'bout want he'd done 'cause he was from up North. He begged us not to take the boy, but to jes' whip him and let it be. But that wasn't good enough for me. We wanted to really scare the nigga, but he never showed that he was scared and that really made us mad. He kept saying that he wasn't afraid of us and that he was jes' as good as we were. It was obvious that northern rabble-rousers had filled the boy's mind full of poison. He was hopeless, so we drove him to Leslie Milam's plantation. We dragged him in a shed and commenced pistol-whippin the nigga on his face and head. The nigga hollered and cried like a baby, but he still insisted that he was jes' as good as we were. That nigga was a lost cause and jes' hopeless."

Milam interjected and said, "Like Roy said, the nigger was hopeless. He had to be seriously dealt with. What else could we do? Because of what that Chicago boy did, I thought we had to remind the coloreds down here as to what'd happen for assaulting a white woman. I said,

'Chicago boy, I'm tired of 'em sending your kind down here to stir up trouble. Goddamn you, I'm gonna make an example of you just so everybody can know how me and my folks stand.'"

The lights in the parlor flickered. Blood poured from Byant's nose. Milam felt a sharp pain in his head and winced as a cigar fell from his mouth onto his lap and burned a hole in his pants, causing him to spring up in pain as he ferociously patted the burn.

Mr. Huie and the men's lawyer were awed by what was happening. Bryant grabbed some tissues to sponge the blood running from his nose. Milam stomped the burning cigar that was igniting the carpet. He pressed his palms against his head in an attempt to subdue his excruciating headache. Milam took the aspirins produced by Leslie Milam.

After the situation quieted, Mr. Huie asked, "Are you okay to continue?"

Bryant and Milam consented and the interview persisted.

"Was Emmett Louis Till killed in the shed?" Mr. Huie queried.

"No he wasn't," Bryant responded as he held fresh tissue to his nose. "We beat him good in the shed and hung him by the neck until he gagged. We wanted to scare him real bad, but we didn't kill him there. We made him load a cotton gin fan into the bed of the truck, then made him get in the truck. We then drove him to a remote location on the Tallahatchie River. It was about seven o'clock Sunday morning. We ordered the boy to get outta the truck and take his pants and shoes off."

Milam said, "Then I stuck my .45 to the nigger's head and said, 'You still as good as I am? He said, 'Yeah.' I then shot him in the head. We used barbwire to attach the cotton gin fan around his neck and threw his body into the river."

A window in the parlor shattered. A picture of Confederate General Jefferson Davis fell hard on the floor off the wall. A flower vase tumbled off a table and dumped suddenly wilted flowers on the floor. Water from the vase soaked into the red carpet. Blood gushed from Bryant's nostrils and fell upon his hands. Milam's headache returned and magnified. A red rash encircled his thick neck. A strange and eerie sound – like an animal dying – transmitted from the shed outside. The lawyers gathered up their briefcases, excused themselves, and trampled upon bubble gum wrappers as they left the plantation in less than a liar's minute.

Mr. Huie sat spellbound.

* * *

William Bradford Huie's interview with Roy Bryant and J.W. Milam was published by *Look magazine* and appeared in its January 24, 1956 issue under the heading *The Shocking Story of Approved Killing in Mississippi.* The article incensed Negroes and whites throughout the country and abroad.

Most Southern whites who had defended Roy Bryant and J.W. Milam withdrew their support for them after the article appeared. The men ceased being considered heroes and were looked upon as *nobodies* who managed to tarnish their supporters and the state of Mississippi. White citizens in the Magnolia State felt disgraced. Roy Bryant and J.W. Milam were urged to leave Mississippi.

Negroes in the Delta were not surprised by the confession because they knew all along that Bryant and Milam were guilty. Negroes had discussed among themselves how it'd taken the death of a Negro boy from up North to really bring attention to the racial injustice in Mississippi.

* * *

After friends, relatives, church members, and neighbors dropped by or called to express their outrage in regard to the confession of Emmett Till's murder in *Look magazine,* Mamie Till was finally alone. She sat on Emmett's bed in the late evening with a photo of him in one hand and the *Freedom Soil* jar clutched in the other. The magazine article wasn't a shock to her and she mused that any reasonable, civil, and justice-loving person knew all along that Roy Bryant and J.W. Milam had killed her son and gotten away with his murder. She pondered that the two murderers had had a number of confederates in the persons of Sheriff Strider, the all-white, male jurors, and prominent officials and citizens.

It pained Mamie to read the sordid details of how Emmett was killed. She couldn't believe that her son had done all that was said in regard to offending Roy Bryant's wife because she had sat him down and explained southern ways to him before he left for Mississippi. She found it difficult to accept that Emmett had been fresh with Bryant's wife.

Mamie reminisced as to how smug and confident Bryant and Milam appeared all during the trial and as though they felt all along that they wouldn't be convicted. The fact that the two men had become brazen about getting away with murder and having gotten paid for their confession was most upsetting to Mamie. It required all her faith in God to not hate the men. She held on to the words that Pastor Williams left with her this evening when he said, "…The men will experience God's wrath and will be duly punished. Man's justice can be porous and subjective, but God's justice is solid and precise. So, let God be your shining light, strength, and armor. God will deal with the men in His own way."

Mamie experienced a quiet peace to come over her. The *Freedom Soil* jar in her hand felt thermal and transmitted an energy that imbued her body with a feeling of warmth and comfort. She felt as though she was bundled in a wool blanket. She experienced a divine comforting.

Chapter Twenty

Montgomery, Alabama
"Cradle of the Confederacy"

Jamal hailed a Negro taxicab driver at Union Station in downtown Montgomery. He checked the time on his wristwatch as the driver placed his two pieces of luggage in the trunk. It was 3:38 p.m. and a cool, overcast day.

"Where to?"

"The Ben Moore Hotel," Jamal responded.

"A nice hotel owned by Negroes," the driver said as he closed the trunk. The driver adjusted his side-view mirror after he and Jamal settled into the cab. The driver pulled aggressively into traffic, then asked, "You here for business or pleasure?"

"Business," Jamal confirmed. "I'm here to cover the bus boycott and would like to accomplish interviews with Dr. Martin Luther King Jr. and Rosa Parks. I'm a freelance journalist. Not long ago I was in Mississippi to cover the Emmett Till murder trial."

The driver took his eyes momentarily off the road, looked in the rear-view mirror to check out Jamal and said,

"No kiddin? Bet that was interestin. Jes' read the confessions in *Look magazine* of the two white men who killed that boy. Gees, that was somethin. Never heard told of anyone confessin to a murder after found not guilty. I bet they got paid real good for their confession."

"They did. Four thousand dollars," said Jamal.

"Ump, white people can kill Negroes and then get paid for it. This is hellava country."

"Yes it is," Jamal lamented.

"So, you saw in person the men who killed Emmett Till?"

"Yeah, I did. They were two hateful, mean, bona fide, and cocky rednecks."

"What do you think causes some folks to hate that way?"

"Acclimation."

"What's that? You've gotta break it down to me, brother. I'm jes' a cab driver. I didn't go to college. Had to work all my life since I was eight-years-old picking cotton."

Jamal said, "People who hate like that are oriented or taught to hate. No one is born into this world hating any one. Hate has to be taught and learned. People are conditioned to hate."

"Well, there's enough hate here in Montgomery, especially with the bus boycott goin on. They don't refer to Montgomery as the cradle of the Confederacy for nothin. I tell yah some white folks are sho' hating Negroes in Montgomery. They ain't killed no Negroes yet over the bus boycott, but I suspect it jes' a matter of time. Welcome to Montgomery: the state capital, the first capital of the Confederacy, the home of the first electric streetcar, and might I add, home of the bus boycott."

Jamal said, "I didn't know all that about Montgomery."

"Before they give us a taxicab permit, we have to learn that information and more and tell it to our outta town customers. There's more I could tell you about Montgomery but I thought I would spare you. You seem like a man with a lot of his mind."

Jamal chucked and said, "In fact, I do have a lot on my mind." He peered out the window of the cab and saw a group of Negroes huddled on the side of the street and shouting what sounded like "Remember Emmett!"

Jamal asked, "What are they saying?"

They're saying, "Remember Emmett! They been sayin that since the bus boycott started. Some even wear T-shirts that say 'Remember Emmett!' They got that sayin from an article some Negro reporter wrote."

Jamal smiled, realizing that the driver was referring to his editorial *The Delta Blues and Hate.*

The driver said, "Everybody wants to interview Dr. King and Mrs. Parks, which I have nothin against, but the engine behind the bus boycott is a man by the name of E.D. Nixon. He's a powerful Negro in this town. He's the one who got Rosa Parks outta jail; and it's said that he handpicked Dr. King to be the president of the Montgomery Improvement Association to lead the bus boycott."

"You say his name is E.D. Nixon?"

"Yeah. He's a good man. Negroes listen to him in this city."

"Thanks. I will try to contact Mr. Nixon while I'm here."

The cab pulled in front of the Ben Moore Hotel on the corner of High and Jackson Street in a Negro section of town known as Centennial Hill, an affluent Negro middle-class neighborhood. The cab driver informed Jamal that Dr. Martin Luther King Jr. lived in the Dexter Street Baptist Church parsonage located there and just a half-block from Alabama State College for Negroes.

Jamal gave the cab driver a tip to remember before entering the hotel.

* * *

Jamal asked around about E.D. Nixon. He discovered that Mr. Nixon was indeed an important man who had the respect of both Negroes and white people, not only in the city of Montgomery, but also in the county and much of the state of Alabama as well. Jamal did his homework and further discovered that Mr. Nixon had been president of the Progressive Democratic Association, which was an organization of Negro leaders. He'd also served as president of the local and state branches of the NAACP and was an official for the Brotherhood of Sleeping Car Porters, the first successful Negro labor union in America that advocated for better working conditions for Negro porters. Mr. Nixon was a man who Jamal was eager to meet.

* * *

Early the next morning after a restful night, Jamal called the office of the Montgomery Improvement Association to make an appointment with E.D. Nixon, which he had no problem achieving after stating his occupation and credentials and identifying himself as the author of the *Delta Blues and Hate* editorial.

Jamal decided to spend the biggest portion of the day on the streets interviewing ordinary Negroes who were involved in the boycott. He saw a group of Negroes walking toward him and at the same time an automobile occupied by four white men approached and yelled out the window, "Walk niggers, walk!" He stopped to speak with some Negroes congregated in a parking lot waiting for rides. While he spoke to them, a carload of young, white teenagers drove up, tossed balloons out the car windows, causing liquid to spatter on several of the Negroes in the lot. The culprits sped off. It was obvious to Jamal from the stench that the substance inside the balloons was urine and a tactic he learned that was common – including tossing eggs as well as rotten potatoes and tomatoes.

* * *

Jamal felt emotionally fatigued when he returned to his room at the hotel. All day he'd observed police harassing Negroes and arresting some on trumped up and bogus charges in an attempt to break the backs and spirit of the boycotters. He also heard accounts of Negroes being fired by white bosses who were angry about the boycott. He met college students who hadn't gone back to school because they were essential to the cadre of drivers used to transport people in lieu of them using the public buses.

Jamal discerned that Negroes from every spectra and social status were making sacrifices on behalf of the boycott that was now in its fifty-fourth day. It'd been a busy day. He looked forward to meeting with E.D. Nixon later in the evening.

* * *

After meeting with E.D. Nixon at his home in Centennial Hill and returning to the Ben Moore Hotel, Jamal felt captivated. He was infatuated with Mr. Nixon's involvement in civil rights as well as his impact on the Montgomery Improvement Association, Dr. Martin Luther King Jr., and the bus boycott. Jamal recalled Mr. Nixon telling him that he'd gotten his second wind in the struggle for civil rights after the death of Emmett Till. He'd also enlightened Jamal that Dr. King carried a picture of Emmett Till lying in his coffin in his wallet. What Jamal found most interesting upon meeting with Mr. Nixon was learning that he was asked to be the president of the Montgomery Improvement Association but offered Dr. King's name instead.

Jamal had had a full day but was looking forward to attending a mass meeting in regard to the boycott and was thankful for the invitation from Mr. Nixon, a man he'd grown to appreciate and admire.

* * *

The next evening, Jamal drove his rental car to the Holt Street Baptist church to attend a mass meeting scheduled by the Montgomery Improvement Association. He was told to arrive early in order to get a good seat because a lot of people would be in attendance. As Jamal sat waiting for the meeting to begin he watched several hundred Negroes – young and old, male and female, healthy and decrepit – flow into the church as though money was being given away. He marveled at the people piling into the church. He heard someone shout "Remember Emmett!" and soon the chant filled the church and filtered outdoors where people on the street could hear; and they, too, took up the recitation. Jamal was in awe of the spirit around him.

Soon after the crowd settled into the church, Jamal witnessed a group of Negro men wearing dark suits and ties march in and took seats in the pulpit. He recognized E.D. Nixon and Dr. Martin Luther King Jr. whom he kept his eyes on as he conceived how young he was but appeared as mature and dignified as the older Negro men around him.

The men in the pulpit took turns coming to the microphone to address the assembled mass. A minister by the name of Ralph Abernathy took the mike and said, "God hears our prayers, and in His own good time He will acknowledge our prayers and deliver us. So, I ask you not to tarry, lose hope, and give up for when the time comes, God will make the rough ways smooth and the crooked ways straight. We're gonna win this thing with the will of God...."

Jamal sat more erect in his seat when Dr. King approached the microphone.

Dr. King greeted the large gathering with enthusiasm and with what Jamal thought was a voice gilded with gold and as powerful as a hurricane. He heard Dr. King say, "Now Mrs. Sadie you have been with us all along in this boycott, and you're getting up there in age, so now you can go ahead and start back to riding the bus because you're too old to keep walking."

There was a clamor of approval from the audience. Jamal clapped along with everyone else. He saw an elderly woman rise to her feet and say, "Oh no, Dr. King. Oh no. I'm gonna keep walkin jes' as long as everybody else. I'm gonna walk 'til it's over."

The audience responded with applause, shouts of amen, and exclaimed other spiritual incantations.

Dr. King smiled and asked, "But aren't your feet tired?"

The elderly woman said, "Yes, my feets is tired, but my soul is rested. Yessuh, Dr. King. My soul is rested."

The church was filled with joy, merriment, and a spirit Jamal had never before witnessed. He stood, clapped, and laughed as tears formed in his eyes. He understood then that Negroes in Montgomery would not rest until the bus boycott was settled in their favor.

After the mass meeting, Jamal hurried back to his hotel room. He shed his overcoat as soon as he crossed the threshold and tossed it on the bed. He fetched his briefcase, took out paper and pen, and began to write. Early the next morning he had completed to his satisfaction his next editorial.

My Soul Is Rested
By Jamal Peterson

A little more than four months ago, I was in Sumner, Mississippi covering the Emmett Till murder trial. The world now knows that the two men who ended Emmett Till's young life later confessed to his murder in an article written in

Look Magazine. I left Mississippi downhearted as a Negro and felt my body was fatigued and that my soul was even tired. And, I suppose, I wasn't the only Negro journalist who felt as I did who covered the murder trial. And I'm confident that a lot of Negroes in Mississippi and in other southern states where Jim Crow (segregation of the races) is the law are possessing tired bodies and souls.

I was recently in Montgomery, Alabama where the current bus boycott is going on because of segregated seating on public buses, which got started because Rosa Parks refused to relinquish her seat to a white man. Mrs. Parks was tired that day, I'm sure, after leaving her job as a seamstress. But I think she refused to give up her seat because she was not just physically fatigued, but, rather, because she was emotionally and perhaps spiritually tired of the injustice heaped upon her as a Negro woman. I believe Mrs. Parks' soul was rested when she demurred about vacating her seat on the bus.

In Montgomery I met a man by the name of E.D. Nixon who has been in the forefront of the civil rights struggle in the state of Alabama for years and has remained in the struggle because his soul hasn't tired. And it was Mr. Nixon who enlightened me about his mentor A. Phillip Randolph who long championed civil rights and was instrumental in creating the Brotherhood of Sleeping Car Porters, the first "successful" Negro labor union in the United States. Mr. Randolph also pressured two Unites States presidents to end racial discrimination in regard to federal government jobs and segregation in the armed forces. I suppose Mr. Randolph must have gotten weary along the way, but continued his gallant fight for civil rights and human dignity because his soul didn't tire.

At an invitation from Mr. E.D. Nixon, I attended a mass meeting of the Montgomery Improvement Association where Dr. Martin Luther King Jr. is the president. It was at this meeting when Dr. King told an elderly Negro woman that it was appreciated that she had supported the bus boycott as long as she had, but that she could start riding the bus again because of her age. Well, the little, gray-haired, up-in- years woman wouldn't have any of that. She stood tall –though she was short in statue – with her back as straight as a board in the midst of a standing room only audience inside a large Baptist church and told everyone that she was going to continue to walk until the bus boycott was over. She said that though her feet were tired, her soul was rested. Her soul was rested!

After listening to that little, old Negro woman, my overall disposition changed and suddenly my own soul felt rested. I knew that evening like I'm sure every single Negro in the church knew: The struggle for justice and liberty for the Negro masses must go on and we can't allow our souls to become enervated.

If anyone's soul was tired that night, I'm sure the words that little, old woman spoke resuscitated it. I felt both inspired and uplifted that evening, and I am certain every Negro in the audience felt. I'm confident the bus boycott in Montgomery, Alabama, the "Cradle of the Confederacy", will succeed because the collective spirit of Negroes in Montgomery has been buoyed by an old, Negro woman.

The souls of Negroes in Montgomery are revived and rested and these once weary souls know like Harriet Tubman, Nat Turner, Sojourner Truth, Frederick Douglas, W.E B. DuBois, Ida B. Wells, A. Phillip Randolph, and Mamie Till that their battle is just and humane. The struggle for civil rights forges ahead, and I repeat, "Remember Emmett!" But let not your soul become tired.

* * *

It was Monday, September thirtieth. Jamal thought he would complete his last evening in Montgomery by touring the Negro sections in order to get a better feel of things. He was leaving the campus of Alabama State College and heading down South Jackson Street in the Centennial Hill area when he heard a loud explosion. He saw a light-colored car with a white man inside speed past him. Jamal slowed his car and saw smoke emanating from the front of a house about three blocks away. He then saw Negroes coming out of their houses and running in the direction of the fumes rising toward the sky.

The street quickly filled with humanity. Jamal parked his car near the curve, got out, and joined the throng of people moving as an army battalion down the street, armed with anger and hostility. He heard someone yell in torment, "It's the Kings' house!"

"My God!" Jamal uttered as his heartbeat accelerated and his adrenaline induced his feet to move faster in concert with the mob of Negroes who were moving just as rapidly toward the explosion.

In a matter of minutes, Jamal estimated about as many as five hundred people – Negroes and white people – had converged on the block. He heard sirens wailing. Two white men arrived who were ushered through the crowd. Jamal heard someone identify them as Mayor Gayle and Commissioner Sellers.

Soon the police arrived in force and tried to take command of the situation by ordering people to move away from the bombed area. Their efforts proved to be in vain. The Negro congregate was stubborn and resolute, refusing to bulge, and angry, although the crowd was quiet. Jamal assessed the crowd to be dangerously silent and as though the people might explode and cause all-hell to break loose at any moment. He thought the tension was as thick as locusts.

A policeman vociferated, " Please go back to your homes people! No one is hurt! The situation is under control!"

No one moved. The crowd stayed intact, defiant, and eerily mute. Jamal could sense the fear of the white policemen who'd arrived on the scene. He likened the situation to dry kindling, realizing that it would only take a single spark to ignite the situation and create an inferno.

Negroes stood gathered in a angry hush and stared contemptuously at the white cops, the white mayor, and the white commissioner as the front porch of Dr. Martin Luther King Jr. and his family's home smothered from the explosion.

A white officer cleared his throat a couple of times to again give instructions to the crowd but said nothing, unable to form words in his mouth as he looked into the large gathering. Finally a white officer requested the crowd to disperse. A voice from the crowd said, "We'll move when you inform us as to which one of you bombed Dr. King's house!"

The officer attempted to ignore the statement and continued to plea with the people to leave the area, but not a single soul budged an inch.

Someone shouted, "It's Dr. King! He's here!"

Dr. King ran through the crowd with concern and worry plastered on his face like neon. He reached his home out of breath and was greeted by the mayor and police chief who accompanied him inside the house.

Jamal watched intensely until Dr. King appeared from his home and stood on the damaged porch. The air remained tense and volatile. Dr. King waved to the crowd for its attention and was joined on the porch by the mayor, several city commissioners, as well as the fire and police chiefs – all white men.

A reverential silence settled over the mass and the police halted their futile efforts to dissipate the people. In a calm and assuring tone, Dr. King said, "It is regrettable that this has happened, but we must remain peaceful, for we believe in law and order. Don't get panicky; don't get your weapons. He who lives by the sword will perish by the sword. We are not advocating violence. Love your enemies. I did not start this boycott. I was asked by you to serve as your spokesperson. I want it known the length and breadth of this land that if I am stopped, if I am killed, this movement will not stop, for what we are doing is right and just! God is with us and is on our side. Go home to your families and know that all of us are in the hands of God!"

* * *

Later that evening, after numerous visits and telephone calls from close friends, fellow-clergy, associates, and well-wishers, Dr. King retired to the solitude of his study, read from his bible, and knelt in prayer. He rose from his knees, took out his wallet, and removed the folded *Jet magazine* picture of Emmett Till. Dr. King spoke at the photo and said, "Emmett, there's a long, hard, and difficult battle ahead of us, but you won't be forgotten; not as long as I have breath in my body."

* * *

The following morning Jamal checked out of the Ben Moore Hotel and hired a taxicab to drive him to Union Station to catch a train back home to Detroit. As the taxi drove the city streets to the train station, Jamal rolled down his window to delight in the joy of hearing Negroes walking down streets chanting "Remember Emmett!"

The Negro taxicab driver said, "I supposed yah heard what happened to Dr. King yesterday? I hate to say it, but I think white people gonna kill him one day."

"I hope not," Jamal lamented. "Let's pray that never happens. I was at the scene of yesterday's bombing. I heard the explosion."

"No kiddin?"

"Yeah, I did. I tell you it was something. I think the crowd would've gone wild if Dr. King hadn't calmed the people. I tell you, the man is magnetic. I think he's gonna make a great difference in the civil rights efforts in this country."

"You probably right," said the cab driver. "But I bet those white folks, the police chief and all, won't ever find who bombed Dr. King's home. If they do, I'll eat my shoe and the Lord knows this my only pair."

Jamal laughed.

After arriving at the train depot, Jamal retrieved his luggage from the cab, paid and tipped the driver, and said to him, "You take care my brother and let not your soul be tired. Hang in there. Better days are coming. Remember Emmett!"

Chapter Twenty-One

The Mississippi Delta

Roy Bryant and J.W. Milam's popularity faded with the white people of Mississippi after their confession appeared in *Look magazine*. They were no longer considered heroes. White people felt betrayed because the confession had brought dishonor and disgrace to Mississippi. The White Citizens Council offered to pay Roy and Milam's passage out of the state.

The twelve jurors who'd rendered the "not guilty" verdict felt doubly betrayed by the confession. Several of them wondered if misfortune had befallen some of them on account of the verdict. But some other yet-unscathed jurors were not swayed that Emmett Till's ghost was haunting them as Negroes in the Delta rumored. No matter, both Negroes and white citizens alike thought it to be most peculiar that jurors for the Emmett Till murder trial were experiencing a rash of mishaps, and the latest being a bad automobile accident on the same day that the *Look magazine* article hit the stands. One victim was paralyzed; another lost vision in one eye, and the other had a foot amputated.

The casualties for the former jurors were mounting, which no one could deny and whether anyone believed it was the doing of Emmett Till's ghost or not.

In at least one Negro church during Sunday morning service after the automobile accident was reported, a Negro minister was heard to say, "The casualties for the jurors in the Emmett Till murder case are piling up. Proves that God don't like ugly."

Negroes in his congregation concurred with the pastor's pronouncement with shouts of "Amen!"

Negroes in the Delta joyously stirred tales of Emmett Till's ghost. They were keeping track of the victims: seven down, five to go. The more Negroes chronicled the existence of Emmett Till's ghost via the victims, the kinder they believed white people became. Negroes had no other explanation in regard to the reason that plantation owners and other white employers had announced that they were going to give their Negro cotton-pickers, field hands, and domestic laborers Labor Day off with pay.

* * *

Sheriff Clarence Strider sat at this desk in his office at the Tallahatchie County Jail glaring at the *Look magazine* on top his desk as he fumed about Roy and J.W.'s confessions. "Those goddamn stupid bastards!" the sheriff intoned as he reached to turn on the lamp on his desk. He walked over to the window and lowered the shade against the backdrop of the late evening darkness. He returned to his desk and chair, brushed his large, pale, freckled hands through his gray hair, then knocked the magazine off his desk onto the floor.

The sheriff deliberated that no other white citizen in the Delta could be any more bothered or chagrin about Roy and J.W.'s confession than him, considering all that he'd done to assist the bastards with an acquittal. He recalled hiding two key Negro witnesses in the persons of Levy

"Too-Tight" Collins and Henry Lee Loggins by arranging to have them confined in a jail in Charleston under false identities until the trial was over. He thought he was doing the right thing because of all the northern, liberal intrusion into white people's affairs in Mississippi that was thought to be threatening to southern traditions and life. But never did he remotely entertain that Roy and J.W. would sell their confessions.

Sheriff Strider reminisced about his testimony during the trial when he alleged that Emmett Till's body couldn't be identified because it was so badly mutilated and decomposed. But he knew all along that the corpse was that of the Chicago boy. He realized that if he hadn't falsely testified and hidden the witnesses that Roy Bryant and J. W. Milam would have likely been found guilty. But the very thought of two white men going to prison for killing a smart-mouth nigger from Chicago for something he had no business saying to a white woman was reason enough, he thought, to aid in getting Roy and J.W. off.

Sheriff Strider felt angry and fatigued. He placed some papers in a briefcase to take home. Turned off the lamp on his desk, closed his office door behind him, and said good night to the second shift crew. On his way out the building, he remembered needing to pick up some medication from the drugstore across the street. He headed across the dark street, tripped over something, and fell into the street just when a produce truck rounded the corner.

By the time the driver saw the man lying in the street it was too late. The truck's brakes squealed, followed by a loud thud and a guttural scream, resulting in the sheriff lying banged up and blooded in the street but still breathing as he watched a shadowy image fade into the darkness.

* * *

Misery kept perpetual company with Roy Bryant and J.W. Milam. Both men were the objects of scorn by their one-time supporters. They were ostracized by many white citizens in the Delta and treated like lepers for confessing to the murder of Emmett Till. And the situation was hard on their families.

Leslie Milam, J.W.'s blood brother and Roy's half-brother, was one of only a handful of individuals who had any empathy or contact with Roy and J.W. He invited them and their families to have dinner at his plantation this evening. After dinner and several cocktails that Roy and J.W. rapidly put away, Leslie invited the men to go for a horseback ride.

The three men saddled and mounted horses outside the barn, then rode off toward the east acres as the sun dipped low in the sky and cast a bright orange aura on the horizon. They rode on the edge of popular trees, laughing and enjoying their respite without having to witness accusatory stares and conspicuous whispers from people they encountered.

Suddenly they heard wolves howl, which spooked their mounts, throwing Roy hard to the ground in the company of a rattlesnake. J.W. looked back at Roy as his mount took off. A low hanging tree branch caught J.W. at his neck, knocking him off his horse into a bed of poison ivy. Leslie steadied his steed and watched the men sprawled in weeds with Roy screaming for help and J.W. groaning in pain and misery. The sound of the wolves as well as all of nature's living creatures quieted to the extent that all three men could hear their hearts pounding.

Leslie rubbed his eyes, half-believing he was seeing a misty, human-like silhouette drift through the trees and out of sight.

* * *

Reverend Joseph Masolt (a.k.a., Brother Justice One) had called together the members of the John Brown Christian Society. The meeting ended ten minutes ago. Reverend Masolt sat at his desk at the Mazolt Homestead to write a letter to Jamal Peterson as was decided at the meeting this evening. He contemplated that some things had gotten better in the Delta since Roy Bryant and J.W. Milam's confessions, considering that some plantation owners and other white folks were treating Negroes more humane as laborers. However, the members of the Society understood that nothing had changed in regard to white citizens' bitter attitudes, nasty dispositions, and collective inverse opinion regarding school integration and voting rights for Negroes. Because of the recent media coverage regarding the confessions to Emmett Till's murder, the Society thought the timing ideal to also shed media attention and scrutiny on the too often vicious opposition in Mississippi to legally sanction and enact voting rights for Negroes.

Reverend Mazolt ended his letter to Jamal Peterson by writing:

> *Mr. Peterson, we think the time is right to place media pressure on white citizens councils and white officials whom are obstinate against extending voting privileges to Negro citizens in the South. We think if national attention could be focused on the hostilities perpetrated against Negroes in Mississippi, and here in the Delta, then eventually the powers-that-be will relent and therewith Negroes in the South will garner the right to vote as a prerogative of their citizenship. We beseech you to use your contacts and influence with the Northern media to assist us with this endeavor. And we ask your personal*

189

involvement by returning to the Delta. May God, peace, love, and justice be with you. Sincerely, Brother Justice One

Chapter Twenty-Two

Sunflower County, Mississippi

Jamal Peterson was back in Mississippi and the Delta at the invitation of the John Brown Christian Society. He lay on top his bed at the Negro-owned Fairchild Hotel in Greenville, mapping in his mind his plans for today. He recalled thinking soon after the Emmett Till murder trial that if he never returned to Mississippi that it would be too soon. Jamal expelled an uneasy, surrendering smile, thinking how soon *never* had arrived.

Jamal pondered that when he was last in Mississippi, he'd seen Negroes labor for pittance, witnessed a circus of a trial that allowed the accused to eat ice cream cones and play with their kids while the trial was in session, and then get away with murder. And the fact that he'd had his life threatened was yet etched deeply in his mind. In spite of the unpleasant memories and negative reflections, Jamal had found it difficult to not honor the Society's invitation to return to the Magnolia State for the purpose of caring out some investigative reporting in regard to Negroes' plight to register to vote. He wrote down his itinerary: call the home-office before 5:00 p.m., call Francine, at 6:30 p.m. meet with Reverend Johnny McAfee, president of the Greenville branch of the NAACP; and tomorrow at 9:00 p.m., meet J.D. (a.k.a. Brother Justice Twenty-one) for an audience with members of the John Brown Christian Society.

* * *

After completing his call to the National News Association's home-office, Jamal called Francine.

"Hello."

"Hi, Francine, it's Jamal."

"Made it to Mississippi okay, I gather?"

"Yes, I did. Never thought I would return to this state, but here I am on another assignment."

"Thurgood misses you when you're away," said Francine.

"I know. I miss him too. He's growing up and I'm gonna make arrangements so I don't have to travel as much. I want to see my son grow up, and, Francie, I want to spend more time with you also if you'd let me. I've really changed, Francine. I really have. I haven't taken a drink since I was last in Mississippi. And I told you that the night I ordered that drink in the lounge at the hotel in Harlem that I left it untouched. I've stopped drinking, Francine. The only thing I ever want to get high on again is from loving you. I'm very serious. And I haven't been with any other woman in a long time and don't have a desire to be with anyone but you."

"Jamal, it's real good that you've quit drinking. And I know you love your son. You keep telling me how much you love and care about me, but you told me that before when you were messing around with other women. I can't forget that, Jamal. I don't think I ever will."

"Francine, I don't expect you to forget. I won't ever forget it, myself. I'm asking you to forgive me. Just find it in your heart to give me another chance so that Thurgood, you, and me can be a family again. I promise on my parents' graves that I will never, ever let you down again and will be faithful to you until the day I die. And I've never promised anything to anyone on my parents' graves."

Silence ensued before Francine said, "I'll think about it, Jamal. That's all I'll promise."

"That's good enough for me and probably more than I deserve. I really appreciate it, Francine, and I really do love you. I really do, Francine."

"You take care of yourself, Jamal. Be careful down there and we'll talk later. I'm going to put your son on the phone. Be careful, Jamal."

"Francine!"

"Yes?"

"One more thing before you leave the phone."

"What's that, Jamal?"

"I want you to know that if anything happens to me while I'm here in Mississippi that I have a rather nice life insurance policy with both you and Thurgood as the beneficiaries. I'm insured with Metropolitan Life, and a copy of my policy is in a desk drawer in my apartment."

* * *

An elderly Negro man in a crumpled dark suit, tall, slender, slow talking and walking, who introduced himself as Reverend Henderson, picked up Jamal at the Fairchild Hotel around six-ten in the evening to meet with Pastor McAfee and other representatives of the local NAACP.

On the drive down back, rural, dusty roads to the church where the meeting was to take place, Jamal listened to Reverend Henderson talk about being born in Mississippi to parents who were former slaves and who had six children. Jamal was enlightened about all the hardships the reverend's family endured as a result of poverty and racism – common to most Negroes in the rural South – and how it'd been religion that helped the family survive the oppression and hostilities fostered on them.

In about twenty-five minutes the men arrived at Shilo Baptist Church that was tucked in the woods in darkness, with the exception of a dim light emanating from the window of the church. Jamal didn't possess a clue as to where he was other than in Sunflower County and about a half-hour drive from the hotel.

Several cars were in the church parking lot when the men arrived. Jamal and Reverend Henderson entered the modest, wood-framed church and saw about a dozen men and women gathered in pews in the front of the church near the pulpit. They rose from their seats as Jamal and the reverend approached them.

"I'm Pastor McAfee," said a stout, dark-complexion, man of medium height and with thick, wooly hair. "Pleased that you agreed to meet with us Mr. Peterson."

After formal introductions, Pastor McAfee said, "We're gonna dismiss any further pleasantries and get right down to business. The reason we've asked you to meet with us, Mr. Peterson, is because we need your assistance, as well as that of any other open-minded journalists. We need people like you to frankly report on the great difficulty Negroes down here face in order to register to vote. We think it's gonna take a public outcry from people in the North and pressure from the federal government in order to make it possible for Negroes in Mississippi, as well as other states in the South, to be able to exercise the right to vote without hostilities. By the way, I enjoyed readin your column about *The Delta Blues and Hate.*"

Others present expressed their delight in regard to the column.

Jamal smiled and thanked them.

Pastor McAfee said, "I'm gonna let some people here this evening share some stories about the troubles they've faced and experienced in regard to registering to vote. Mrs. Hampton, why don't you start."

Mrs. Hampton, a matronly looking middle-aged woman said, "I wanted to vote, but they got this thang called a poll tax. How poor people like myself, and there a lot of us, gonna pay a poll tax? I hardly make 'nough money to keep a roof over my head and food on the table. It jes' ain't right. Poor people should be able to vote like everybody else."

"Mr. Cantrell, now you. Tell Mr. Peterson what happened with you," said Pastor McAfee.

"My boss man, Mr. Winters, threatened to fire me from my job if I tried to register to vote and I personally know of two Negroes he fired when they tried to vote. We poor Negroes got to have jobs to survive and white people know it, so lots of Negroes are afraid to register to vote even though they wanna 'cause da fear bein fired."

"Mr. Waters, you go next," the pastor instructed.

"I ain't had much schoolin jes' like most Negroes in the Delta 'cause we work on the plantations full-time and get jes' five months off to go to school. I'm almost fifty years old and been workin full-time in the fields since I was six. So, now, white people got what they call a *schoolin tax*."

"He means a *literacy tax*," Pastor McAfee corrected.

"Yeah, that what they call it. Hard for me to say that word, but the way they explained it to me, they jes' well call it a schoolin tax 'cause white people ask yah all these learnin questions before they let yah vote. And they know most Negroes ain't gone to school that much 'cause they be in the fields workin most the time like I said."

"Thank you, Mr. Waters," said Pastor McAfee, then added, "Now Mrs. Watkins here, she's got more education than a lot of Negroes in the Delta. She passed the literacy test and paid the poll tax, but tell Mr. Peterson what happened with you, Mrs. Watkins."

"Like Pastor McAfee said, I did pass the literacy test and scrapped up enough money to pay the poll tax, then they asked me to interpret a part of the constitution about *facto laws*. I knew as much about facto laws as I know about flying an airplane, so they wouldn't let me register."

"Mr. Nelson, tell what happened in your situation," Pastor McAfee requested.

"My wife and son went to register to vote and wuz told the office wuz closed, even though it wuz only three o'clock in the afternoon. Then that night some men rode by our home and fired gunshots into our house."

Jamal stopped taking notes and asked, "Was anyone in your family hurt?"

"No. But we understood they were warnin shots in regard to tryin to vote," Mr. Nelson answered.

Pastor McAfee said, "Another tactic they use to discourage Negroes from voting is that they make you travel to the county courthouse during hours when most Negroes are working in the fields. The county courthouse is the only place you can vote, which is a great distance for many poor people. And they don't allow registration on the weekend. Even with all these obstacles, Negroes still want to be able to vote, but white people are making it very difficult with the use of intimidation and the threat of violence. Sixty percent of the people who live in the Delta are Negroes, so white people are afraid about losing political control and dominance if Negroes are permitted to exercise the right to vote."

Jamal said, "I find all of this very disturbing and appalling. Negroes here are demonstrating lots of courage to pursue the right to vote. It's said that the pen is mightier than the sword. I promise you that I will wield my pen as a weapon in the battle to earn Negroes in Mississippi and other Southern states the right to vote. I promise my support and assistance."

All those present stood and cheered Jamal. He smiled, then said, "May I use the restroom?"

"Sure," said Reverend Coleman who had been introduced to Jamal as the pastor of Shilo Baptist Church. "The bathroom is out back. I will get a flashlight and show you."

"We'll wait for you gentlemen to return, then finish up our meeting and get Mr. Peterson back to his hotel," said Pastor McAfee.

Jamal and Reverend Coleman stepped out the back of the church and suddenly found themselves airborne, flying headfirst into the grass as a result of being propelled by a deafening explosion inside the church. They were showered by shards of broken glass, fragments of wood and rendered unconscious.

Jamal gradually roused from being knocked out. He heard Reverend Coleman moaning next to him and saw smoke and fire discharging from the church. The church was in ruins. Jamal struggled to his feet, entered the church, and dragged victims outside on the church grounds. He stood over the carnage sweating and half-believing. He saw Reverend Coleman appear from out of smoke and wobbled toward him like a drunken man. Both men cried at the sight. They triaged the victims by checking their pulses to determine who was alive and hauled their bodies to the car. Jamal and Reverend Coleman took off back to town, leaving road dust, the church rubble, and dead Negroes behind them.

* * *

Jamal experienced nightmares about the explosion that occurred at Shilo Baptist Church, which was now known to be intentional, although the local authorities hadn't made any arrests nor questioned any suspects. But such results on the part of white officials were hardly a revelation to Negroes in the Delta who knew such to be standard fare when it came to crimes against the descendants of Africans.

Negroes in the Delta understood that the church bombing was a reprisal against the NAACP's voter registration efforts. And they were as certain about the fact that white men committed the bombing as they were as sure that cotton is white. Negroes were furious about the bombing, which resulted in killing six Negroes, maiming four, and seriously injuring two, including Pastor McAfee and Mrs. Hazel Watkins.

Jamal found it difficult to sleep and contemplated packing his bags to leave Mississippi for good, but the promise he'd made in regard to using his pen in support of Negroes' efforts to vote had him committed. He thought it would be cowardice of him to hightail it back to Detroit and abandon the intrepid Negroes in the Delta and in the South who had not been deterred by all the violence that was common to them.

Jamal felt astounded to witness more resolved in the will of Negroes in the Delta. It seemed to him that the church bombing had encouraged Negroes instead of the opposite as though some spiritual presence was among them that bonded them. He reminded himself that it was he who'd stated in his editorials to "Remember Emmett!" and championed to readers to not let their souls tire in the struggle for human and civil rights. He began to feel shameful about his meditation to leave Mississippi at such a critical time when his assistance was requested and needed. He got angry with himself and his anger elevated his courage. He'd put it off for a couple of days in order to attend to his physical wounds and mental scarring, but now he was ready to honor an appointment with the John Brown Christian Society. He used the phone in his hotel room to call Brother Justice Twenty-one.

* * *

When Jamal arrived at the Masolt Homestead he was greeted by members of the John Brown Christian Society who expressed their elation that he wasn't hurt any worse than he was by the church bombing.

Brother Justice One said, "Mr. Peterson, we're most pleased that you accepted our invitation to return to Mississippi, although it wasn't our intent to place you in harm's way. As you've experienced, there are some hateful and Godless people in Mississippi who will go to any length to keep Negroes from voting and exercising their full rights of American citizenship. A lot of people's bitterness is fueled particularly by the school desegregation ruling."

Jamal said, "I feel like I'm in a war zone."

"It pains me to say, but you are in a war zone, Mr. Peterson. It's a battle for civil and human rights and the opposition is reinforced with hate, ignorance, intolerance, and might I add by the Devil himself. But we, the members of the Society, believe this war is winnable because eventually love will conquer hate, enlightenment will overcome ignorance, tolerance will outdistance intolerance, and our Lord and Savior will defeat the Devil. We will be victorious with your assistance. God, love, peace, and justice will prevail."

All the members shouted, "God, love, peace, and justice!"

One of the Society's members rushed into the parlor where the meeting was held. The man wore a somber expression. He approached Brother Justice One and whispered in his ear.

Brother Justice One's visage turned as dour as that of the messenger.

Jamal wondered what was going on, figuring it had to be something important and seemingly quite serious from the way the men were behaving.

Bother Justice One said, "A serious matter has come up. I would like brother justices five, ten, and fifteen to accompany me. Mr. Peterson I would also like for you to accompany us."

No one asked a question, so Jamal followed suit, not wanting to be contrary. He figured in due time he would know what was going on. He was blindfolded, led to a truck and assisted inside. He heard the engine start and felt the truck in motion. After what seemed like fifteen minutes, the blindfold was taken off Jamal. He rubbed his eyes and looked at his surroundings, but it was dark and he had no idea where he was or what was happening. The men rode in silence with nary a word passed between them. Likewise, Jamal kept his mouth closed, though he had questions galore.

The truck stopped in a heavily wooded area. Brother Justice One opened the front passenger side door and got out. Everyone followed his lead. Jamal trailed the men into the woods and through underbrush. He noticed the men walking as though they were stalking some type of prey by wending slowly, quietly, and deliberately. Jamal did the same, though not knowing why.

Voices were heard, which got louder as the men progressed through the woods and underbrush. They saw a glow ahead of them through the trees and distinguished men laughing, shouting, and carrying on as though they were having some type of celebration.

Jamal was dumbfounded, not understanding what was going on and why the need to trek and steal through the woods simply to come upon some type of gala.

Jamal saw a clearing with about thirty or forty men gathered around a bonfire. Brother Justice One signaled for his party to take cover in the brush. Everyone got down in the prong position. Jamal didn't have any understanding of anything that was happening. He heard a voice in the clearing shout, "Bring the niggers forward!"

Jamal eyes bulged as he watched two Negro men, both tattered, being pushed and pulled out in the opening with their hands tied behind their backs. Jamal thought the two men looked as frightened as deer in a hunter's den. He watched as two white men placed a noose over the head of each Negro and tightened them around their necks.

The men in the clearing howled their approval. Someone in the clearing said, "What we got here is two niggers who decided they wanted to register to vote after being warned. Somebody give me a voter registration card for these niggers."

Jamal watched a white man step from out of the gathering and handed something to the man doing the talking. The man doing the talking said, "Niggers, I'm gonna placed these voter registration cards in your pockets and when you get to hell you can register to vote with Satan himself."

Loud laughter and cheering came from the clearing. Jamal waited for Brother Justice One to say or do something, but no one in the brush said a word. He saw the men in the clearing parade the Negro men over to a tall tree where two white men were perched in the tree standing on thick branches. The ends of the ropes around the Negro men's necks were tossed up to the men situated in the tree.

Jamal said, "Aren't we gonna do something?"

"Quiet," Brother Justice One whispered. "There's nothing we can do."

"What do you mean? We can't just watch them lynch those men. Is this why we came out here? To watch men hanged to death?"

"I beg you, Mr. Peterson, to be quiet before you give our position away."

"The hell with our position. I'm not gonna lie here and do nothing."

"What do you recommend, Mr. Peterson," Brother Justice One muttered. "There's about forty of them and five of us and I'm sure some of them have guns."

"Damn it, nobody here has a gun?"

"We don't carry weapons. We don't believe in violence."

"So, what in the hell are we doing here. If you knew this was going on why didn't someone call the sheriff?" No sooner than Jamal made the statement, he mused that they were in Tallahatchie County, Sheriff Strider's jurisdiction, and the fat son-of-a –bitch who helped Roy Bryant and J.W. Milam to get off with murdering Emmett Till.

Jamal figured the sheriff probably never solved a murder of a Negro in his life. The situation felt hopeless to Jamal. He heard a voice in the clearing say, "Someone's in the woods. I heard a voice from over there."

The men in the clearing looked in the direction where one of the men was pointing. Brother Justice One rose up and began to run. Everyone in his entourage followed suit.

Jamal hearkened the statements, "They're runnin. Let's go after 'em. They're prob'bly niggers. Fix more of those nigger necklaces."

Jamal didn't know how far they'd walked into the woods, but was wishing they would reach the truck in time enough to get away safely. He heard gunshots. His heart was clapping against his chest cavity. He looked back and then tripped over a stump. He fell hard to the ground but wasn't injured. One of the Society members assisted him to his feet and they took off.

It sounded like a large mosquito whizzed passed Jamal's head, but logic caused him to understand that it was a bullet and too close for comfort. He saw the truck ahead and three of the society members reach it and got inside. He heard the engine, then felt a burning pain in his back that dropped him to his knees and into a prostrate position. His body felt hot and numb. He couldn't move. Two society members dragged him to the truck and hauled his body in the bed. The truck took off with the lights off until it was safe. Jamal lay in the back of the truck unconscious and bleeding profusely.

"Mr. Peterson has been shot! He needs a doctor in a hurry! He might not make it!"

"Hurry!" said Brother Justice One to the driver.

* * *

Francine Peterson flew into Thompson Field outside of Jackson, Mississippi after receiving a telephone call from Brother Justice One. She was met at the airport by two members of the John Brown Christian Society who drove and escorted her to the hospital in Greenville where Jamal was in critical condition from his gunshot wound.

Tears clouded Francine's eyes as she approached the hospital bed and saw Jamal lying there unconscious and unresponsive with a large bandage rapped around his upper torso, tubes attached to his static body, monitors humming, and saline fluid dripping into the arteries of his arm.

She occupied a chair next to his bed, deposited her purse on the floor, and gently stroked Jamal's forehead. She folded one of his hands into hers and whispered, "Don't you die on me, baby. I love you, Jamal."

Jamal lay still and incommunicable, but he could hear Francine's words as he felt life slowly seeping from his body as though it was turning flat like a punctured tire. He found himself suspended above his bed and looking down on his own body. He saw Francine by his bedside holding his hand with her forehead buried in the crook of her arm. She was crying. He saw her caring for him. Felt her loving him. Could hear her repeatedly saying, "Don't die Jamal. Please God don't let him die."

Jamal so much wanted to hold her, caress her, and comfort her. He wanted to return to consciousness to honor her, cherish her, protect her, devote his undying love to her, and never, ever again forsake and hurt her. All the while he discovered himself drifting toward a bright light, feeling warm and tranquil. Although the light was very bright, it wasn't blinding. To the contrary, it was the opposite. The brighter the light got, the better his vision became. He saw visions of his life. He saw the people he'd loved: his mother, his father, his fourth grade teacher, his high school coach, Francine and Thurgood. He saw things in his life that mattered and nothing more. His vision was focused only on those who cared about him and who he'd loved. Nothing else. His vision was strangely, immutable, and rewardingly focused on positive relationships and events that had occurred in his life. It was like a reel-to-reel movie of his life running in slow motion that he was watching unfold as he drifted closer and closer toward the brilliant, comforting, white glow.

Chapter Twenty-Three

Journalists across the nation learned that Jamal Peterson was barely clinging to life. They were incensed that something like this had happened to one of their colleagues. And after being edified of the reason Jamal was in Mississippi, many correspondents vowed to pick up on and continue to investigate the complaints of atrocities against Negroes in the South in regard to voter registration. Journalists – black and white -- flocked to Mississippi and other Southern states with a mission.

* * *

An emergency meeting of the Montgomery Improvement Association was called at the behest of E.D. Nixon who'd heard about Jamal Peterson's condition. The meeting was held at the Dexter Avenue Baptist Church, where the Reverend-Dr. Martin Luther King Jr. was pastor.

Mr. Nixon was most pleased that all the ministers who belonged to the Association were in attendance, especially after he'd asked them to drop and cancel everything in order to attend the meeting. And everyone was punctual.

Reverend Ralph Abernathy opened the meeting with a prayer, which was succeeded by a chorus of "Amen!"

Dr. King approached the podium and said, "We all know why we're here this evening. A dear friend of ours in the struggle for human rights lies mortally wounded in a Mississippi hospital as I speak. Mr. Jamal Peterson is the young man whom I'm speaking of and is a respected journalist who came to Montgomery just weeks ago to cover our story in regard to the bus boycott. Before coming to Montgomery, Mr. Peterson was in Mississippi covering the Emmett Till murder trial and had his life threatened there. But that did not deter Mr. Peterson, for he went on to write a column entitled *Mississippi Blues and Hate* in which he encouraged readers to remember Emmett Till. The 'Remember Emmett!' admonishment has been the rallying cry for we Negroes in Montgomery as we press forward with the bus boycott and fight for justice and dignity as a people."

Dr. King picked up a glass of water from the podium and sipped from it. The church was quiet, except for several coughs and the clearing of throats.

Dr. King continued. He remarked, "While Mr. Peterson was in Montgomery he wrote an editorial entitled *My Soul is Rested*. That editorial uplifted the spirits of every Negro in Montgomery, as well as the souls of people of all hues across this nation who read Mr. Peterson's article and believe in justice and equality for all people. The reason Mr. Peterson returned to Mississippi was to report on the harsh, degrading, and inhumane treatment of Negroes who clamor for the right to vote in Mississippi and throughout the South. There are mean and spiteful people in Mississippi, and we've seen them here in Montgomery, who didn't want Mr. Peterson to rock the boat in regard to the Southern way of life, which we know to be decades of cruelty toward the Negro. Well, my friends, Mr. E. D. Nixon and I have discussed it, so we are asking that the Montgomery Improvement Association draft a formal resolution to make the statement 'Remember

Emmett!' the official battle cry of the civil rights movement across this nation. And by so doing we will encourage all groups and organizations throughout this nation that fight for human rights to adopt this battle cry, and in so doing it will be a fitting tribute to both Emmett Till and our friend Jamal Peterson."

"I move adoption of the resolution, Dr. King."

"I support it."

Dr. King asked, "Are we ready for the vote? Any questions relative to the motion to adopt the resolution?" After surveying the room he said, "All in favor of the resolution let it be known by the verbal sign of aye."

The sanctuary reverberated with "Aye!"

In accordance with Robert's Rules of Order, Dr. King said, "All opposed, let it be known by the verbal sign of nay."

There was silence.

Dr. King ended the meeting by asking the ministers to encourage their congregations to pray for Mr. Peterson. On the following Sunday pastors in all the Negro churches did as Dr. King petitioned. Members of Negro congregations bombarded Heaven with prayers.

Chapter Twenty-Four

J.D., the Negro taxi driver, who was also cloaked as Brother Justice Twenty-one, was pleased to see so many reporters converge on the Delta to report on the conditions and circumstances that Negroes faced in regard to voter registration. He was incensed and fed-up about all the hostilities against Negroes and expressly angry that it was two of his kinfolk in the woods that night who the white men planned to lynch before members of the John Brown Christian Society came upon them.

J.D. learned that the men decided against lynching his kin because they weren't sure who'd been in the woods that night to witness what was going on, so instead they administered brutal beatings on the two Negro men, short of killing them and with nary an investigation from law enforcement.

Now that J.D. knew who the ringleader was in regard to the lynching, he'd made up his mind to seek revenge, no matter the danger or consequences. He sat in his taxicab in the early evening across the street from Salinger's Hardware Store in Sumner, observing, paying close attention, making an assessment, feeling hostile by the minute, and plotting as to when it would be best to strike. He felt nervous but yet determined to carry out his plan.

* * *

Reverend Joseph Masolt (a.k.a., Brother Justice One) sat alone in the study at the Masolt Homestead in the late evening. He possessed a heavy heart and felt guilty about placing Mr. Peterson in danger five nights previously when they went into the woods to investigate the lynchings. He was praying for Mr. Peterson to pull through, even though he'd been told that his chance of survival was less than twenty percent.

The reverend pondered the irony of the fact that Mr. Peterson had actually saved the lives of the two Negro men who were about to be lynched in the woods that night when he vociferously protested about doing nothing to aid them. Mr. Peterson was considered a hero, and all members of the Society were pulling for him to cheat death.

Mary Masolt, the reverend's wife, knocked on the door of the study. She walked in with Brother JusticeTwenty-one behind her. He looked like a man who'd survived a bad car wreck. The reverend could tell that something was amiss. He said, "Brother Twenty-one have a seat. Rest yourself. May I get you some water?"

"No thanks," said Brother Twenty-one as he paced.

The reverend dismissed his wife. She closed the door to the study behind her.

"Brother, you appear troubled. What's wrong?"

"Everything's wrong! The Delta's wrong! Mississippi is wrong! The United States is wrong! The world's wrong? And I'm beginnin to think that God's wrong!"

"Brother, what makes you say such about God. He's never wrong. It's obvious that you're deeply troubled, but God is our strength and our light. That's what all the brothers have held to as members of the Society. You confessed to be a man of Christian faith when you came to us, so why this reversal in regard to what you've spoken in reference to the All-Mighty?"

Brother Twenty-one continued to pace. He said, "Why does God let Negroes suffer so much and let white people get away with murder? Those were two of my kinfolk in the woods that night who those men were gonna hang. And ten years ago, white men hanged one of my uncles 'cause they said he sassed one of 'em. My daddy said Mr. Jack Salinger in Sumner, the man who owes the hardware store, was the man who claimed my uncle sassed him. And he's the one who came and got my cousins the other night to string 'em up because they tried to register to vote. And the rope they were using was probably rope from Mr. Salinger's hardware store and the same kinda rope he used to hang my uncle. Daddy told me he heard Mr. Salinger refer to the rope as a nigger necklace. Well, he ain't gonna be using any nigger necklace any more 'cause I killed him tonight. I shot him dead with a rifle when he came outta his store."

Reverend Masolt sat starring at Brother Twenty-one who was watching him and waiting to see and hear his reaction. The quietude in the room seemed to stretch the circumference of the Delta before the reverend rose from his chair and said, " This is a very grave matter, Brother Twenty-one; very grave. You're aware that violence is not condoned by the Society and once a member commits an act of violence against another human being, he is to be banished from the Society. The Society cannot approve of what you did by killing a man, no matter how vile or detestable he was."

"I know I've forsaken my membership and I'm prepared to be banished. I don't expect the Society to approve of what I did. All I'm askin is safe passage outta Mississippi, the same as the Society has done for other Negroes."

"How did you arrive here, brother?"

"I drove my taxi."

"Did anyone see you shoot Mr. Salinger?"

"No one saw me shoot him, but after the shot some white people gathered around and saw me drive my taxi outta town. So, they might be suspicious."

"Law enforcement will probably be looking for you," said the reverend.

"I'm sure."

"We need to get rid of your cab by disassembling it and burying the parts. I hope you haven't endangered the Society," said Reverend Masolt.

"I never intended to do anything to harm the Society," said Brother Twenty-one. "I was crazy with anger and mad at God. To me, Mr. Salinger was the Devil himself and if God punishes me for killin that devil, then so be it. But I'm not sorry for killin Mr. Salinger".

* * *

Negroes in the Delta secretly rooted for Emmett Till's ghost, shouting hallelujah, and everyday wondering when his phantom would show more signs of retribution. And they applauded the fact that Emmett's spirit wasn't letting up on Roy Bryant, J.W. Milam, and Sheriff Strider. Negro laborers and domestics believed Emmett's ghost to be better than a union steward because it was apparent that each time his ghost surfaced, white people made concessions. And the conviction of the Negroes was recently supported when just two days ago, two of the jurors in the Emmett Till murder trial had a roof of a barn collapse on top of them, crippling both men. That incident was followed by the rumor that plantation owners were going to offer free medical service to Negro workers.

Negroes kept count: nine jurors down, three to go. Some Negroes were betting that by the time Emmett Till's ghost got around to the last jurors that the plantation owners would be serving lemonade to Negroes on their breaks.

Chapter Twenty-Five

The day after Jack Salinger's murder, the Sumner White Citizens Council called an emergency meeting and had a full agenda planned. It was apparent to contrary white people that there was no stopping of the federal school desegregation order. Also in spite of all they'd done to discourage it, Negroes were still insisting on registering to vote. And it appeared that a Negro had resorted to killing a white man with the murder of Jack Salinger. Furthermore, rumors of Emmett Till's ghost haunting white people in the Delta had become more prevalent, which had some white citizens acting more benign toward Negroes than racially callous white people were pleased about. Some white people thought the situation to be downright disgusting and appalling and imagined that their forbears weren't resting in their graves.

Many white citizens were still bitter about Roy Bryant and J.W. Milam's confessions, which had caused things to become topsy-turvy in the Delta and throughout Mississippi because it appeared that the eyes of the world were focused on the Magnolia State.

Ray Bolden, president of the Sumner White Citizens Council, brought the meeting to order at the packed township hall.

"My fella citizens," he said, "this ain't a good time for the good white people of Mississippi who believe in southern tradition and the separation of the races. The federal government is ramming the integration of schools down our throats. State rights are in jeopardy. If Negroes start goin to school alongside white children there will surely be trouble with Negro boys wantin to date white girls and we ain't gonna stand for it."

"Not on my dead body!" a man in the audience blustered.

"We're not gonna have it!" shouted another man.

The uproar cascaded until Ray Bolden raised his hand for order. When the crowd quieted, he said, "White citizen councils throughout Mississippi are studying this matter and figuring out what to do. It might have to come to closing down some public schools and starting private ones."

There was a loud cheer of support.

Ray Bolden uttered, "Roy Bryant and J.W. Milam turned things upside down for the people of Mississippi by confessing to killing the Negro boy from Chicago. Now most of us understood why Roy and J.W. would wanna harm the boy and most of us supported 'em, so then what did they do? They went ahead and confessed to murder because of money and made it appear that every white person in Mississippi was a co-conspirator. Roy Bryant and J.W. Milam are traitors to the white people of Mississippi and don't deserve to live in this state any longer."

The building erupted with utterances of approval.

Bolden pronounced, "Tonight we're asking you to approve a resolution that will formally rebuke Roy Bryant and J.W. Milam as citizens of Tallahatchie County and the state of Mississippi. Furthermore, this resolution will be submitted to Roy and J.W. in writing, and we will therewith demand that they leave the county and state."

"I move adoption of the resolution!" a man yelled.

"I support!"

Bolden carried through the vote that was unanimously approved. He then said, "What we now have in Mississippi are Negroes who are emboldened to register to vote. And this has been fueled by Northerners who disagree with how we conduct our affairs and by the white liberal media people who think they can dictate to white people in the South how to live our lives. But it ain't gonna happen because we're gonna fight this thing with every breath in our bodies, every marrow of our bones, and every fiber of our beings."

The loud affirmation of the crowd flooded the hall.

Bolden said, "As you've heard, and one of the primary reasons we're here this evening, is that one of our fine and upstanding citizens, Jack Salinger, was murdered on yesterday. Gunned down as he left his store. And the suspect is a Negro taxi driver whose name is J.D. Henderson who was seen speeding out of Sumner right after the shooting and neither him or his taxicab has been seen since."

"Reckon the nigga drove his cab to Detroit or some place up North?" a man asked.

"Really don't know, but law enforcement is lookin for him. And somethin else of particular concern and interest has materialized. Just the other night when some of our good ol' boys had council with two niggers out in the woods, they chased some men who were hidin in the bushes. The men hidin were both white and Negroes, which means that there is a faction of white men in the Delta aiding Negroes and to what extent we don't know, but we plan to find out."

A man in the audience said, "I think we oughtta start with the Masolt Homestead because Negroes have been seen coming and going out there and there ain't no cotton picking going on. Reverend Masolt is a man who stays pretty much to himself, and we don't see much of him. Does anyone here know what really goes on at the Masolt Homestead?"

* * *

Reverend Gerald Myers (a.k.a., Brother Justice Twelve) left the white citizens council meeting early. He was a long-standing member of the John Brown Christian Society and one of sixteen white members of the Society who provided intelligence for the Society. He understood that the Society could now be in danger of being exposed if measures were not made to avoid detection. He rushed home to call Reverend Masolt.

As soon as Reverend Masolt got off the phone he put *Operation Cover-up* in action. Everyone knew their roles in regard to gathering up any thing that could expose the Society to interlopers. Things considered to be incriminating were stored in a secret vault. J.D. was concealed in a hideaway on the homestead. But the most troubling thing the reverend contemplated was the freshly dug hole, where the remnants of J.D.'s cab were buried, even though it was well camouflaged.

* * *

The next afternoon, Ray Bolden and other members of the Sumner White Citizens Council converged on the Masolt Homestead like storm troopers. The men were convinced that some sort of "monkey business" was going on at the homestead, for it was reported that Negroes employed at the homestead wore clean, neat clothing and that some lived in cabins on the property that were fit enough for white people.

When Ray Bolden and his associates arrived at the gate of the Masolt Homestead, they were provided entry by two Negro men who were as neatly dressed. That didn't settle well with the white men who came demanding to see Reverend Masolt.

Reverend Masolt received his brazen visitors on the covered porch of the mansion and said, "For what purpose am I favored by your men's visit?" He looked into the faces of about a dozen white men whose visages appeared most unfriendly.

Roy Bolden announced, "This ain't a social visit, reverend. We, the members of the white citizens council, are concerned about how Negroes are acting with all this voter registration nonsense. And just the other day, Jack Salinger was gunned down outside his store and the Negro cab driver J.D. was seen speeding away and not seen since."

"Sorry to learn about Jack Salinger, but what does any of this has to do with me?" Reverend Masolt asked.

"We don't rightfully know, but came to find out. What business goes on here? It's very unusual to see Negroes in a white man's employment that dress in the manner your niggers do. Hell, none of 'em look hardly dirty, and why don't you grow cotton out here like most plantation owners?"

"Well, first of all this isn't a plantation. It's my homestead. And as you can see, gentlemen, there are lots of greenhouses on this property. We grow and sell mostly orchids, which we also ship and sell abroad."

"Orchids?" Ray Bolden asked.

"Yes, orchids. It's a family tradition. My father and mother grew orchids and my father's people before him grew and sold orchids."

"What do niggers know about growin orchids?" a man asked.

"Not to offend you, but I choose not to refer to my Negro employees as niggers, but rather as Negroes. The Negroes in my employment have been well trained in the craft of growing orchids. Follow me."

Without protest, although the men appeared both amused and shocked, they followed Reverend Masolt who led them to a greenhouse. They entered and watched several Negroes going about the business of attending to orchids. The men watched a Negro employee turn potted plants upside down, which appeared strange and prompted the white men watching to think the Negro didn't know what he was doing, thus an assessment that Reverend Masolt discerned from the men's expressions. The reverend said to the Negro employee, "Clarence, explained to these men what you're doing."

"Yes, sir, reverend, gladly. Orchids grow slow and most like this kind need to be repotted about once every two years. The orchids need to be set in the pot with its roots spread out and then the pot is filled two-thirds with orchid potting medium consisting of orchid culture that provides support and lots of air spaces. Then more medium is packed tight around the plant to hold it in place. If the pot is packed right, then you should be able to turn the pot upside down without the orchids or medium falling out."

The reverend asked another Negro employee to explain her job. The Negro woman said, "I'm a temperature controller. My job is to be sure that the orchids grow in the proper temperature, depending on what kinda orchid it is. Cattleyas , Epidendrums, Oncidiums, and Laelias need a medium temperature. Cymbidiums, Odontoglossums, and Miltonias require a cool temperature. And Phalaenopsis, Paphiopedilums, Vandas, Rhynchostylus, and Dendrohiums need a warm temperature."

Reverend Masolt introduced the men to Negro employees who were water and humidity specialists, lighting technicians, and pest and diseases examiners. He said to the group of white men, "As you can see, growing orchids commercially is a very involved process that require expertise and diligence. There is well over twenty thousand species of orchids. Orchids are the most rapidly and genetically changing group of plants on earth."

Ray Bolden, not to feel outdone, cleared his throat and said, "This is all interesting, reverend, but we would like to look around inside your home and the rest of the property."

"I can't agree to you looking around inside my home, Mr. Bolden. The inside of my home is personal, and I would consider it a violation. I'm sure you wouldn't appreciate people snooping inside your home, and certainly that's what you're asking."

"Well, reverend, like I said, we didn't come all the way out here to pay a social visit. We had one of our fine citizens killed. We know some white men are aiding Negroes with this voter registration nonsense and God knows what else, so if you ain't got nothin to hide, then you would accommodate us."

"And if I refuse?"

" Well, let me put it to you like this, reverend. You're a man of the cloth and a white man, so we don't wanna harm you, but we think some white men are encouraging Negroes to defy our traditions; and we believe someone among 'em know the whereabouts of the nigger taxi driver, J.D., who we suspect killed Jack Salinger. So if you don't cooperate we will be forced to loosen the tongues of some of your nigger workers. And I think you very well know what I mean."

Reverend Masolt stood for a moment looking Ray Bolden directly in his eyes, then he observed Mr. Bolden's henchmen whose demeanors appeared to the reverend to be like that of vultures eyeing a carcass.

Reverend Masolt said, "I consent only under threat and may the good Lord have mercy on your men's souls."

The men searched inside the mansion but found nothing incriminating. Ray Bolden led his companions outside the mansion and directed them to fan out on the grounds to look for anything remotely suspicious.

Reverend Masolt possessed great concern, thinking that if the men discovered the fresh dirt from the hole they'd dug to bury sections of the taxicab that there would be hell to pay.

As the men spread across the grounds, something strange began to happen. Wolves howled. Never before had Reverend Masolt or any of his employees heard wolves yowl from the woods, nor had they ever seen one of the bushy-tail predators. The howling got louder and appeared to be closer. Trees in the woods began to shake. Tree branches broke. A miniature tornado-like funnel lurched from out of the woods, spewed dangerous debris, and swooped down upon the men who were investigating the property. The velocity of the wind flung the men violently to the ground and injured them.

Dazed and wounded, the men rose from the ground, hurried to their vehicles, and left the Masolt Homestead.

Reverend Masolt didn't know what to make of the bizarre happening, thinking that perhaps it was an intervention from God. But Negroes who saw what happened and those who'd heard what occurred were convinced that it was Emmett Till's ghost that drove the men off. And no one was any happier than J.D. Henderson (a.k.a., Brother Twenty-one) who was smuggled from the homestead to catch a train out of Jackson, Mississippi to Memphis, Tennessee.

* * *

Negroes in the Delta went out of their way to make sure white people heard the latest saga about Emmett Till's ghost, which got around as fast as the morning after a hangover. Shortly after, plantation owners established a free health clinic for their workers. And once again Negroes in the Delta were shouting "Hallelujah!" and waiting for Emmett Till's ghost to reveal itself again.

Chapter Twenty-Six

Francine held steadfast by Jamal's bedside, holding his hands, stroking his forehead, speaking softly to him although he was unresponsive. She kept whispering, "I love you, Jamal."

She didn't want him to die and thought it had to come to the point that Jamal was on his deathbed for her to openly admit her undying love for the father of her child. She'd had time to do a lot of thinking: Yes, Jamal's cheating had hurt her deeply, which there wasn't a question about. He had disappointed her to no end, and she thought all of it had made her stronger as a person and as a woman. She pondered that Jamal had all but gotten down on his knees to beg her to give him a second chance. She remembered spending the past Christmas Eve with him and Thurgood, which reminded her of how it was when they were still married – the joy, the laughter, the closeness, and the holiday merriment. She recalled their trip to New York and understood that she had masked her agreement to go as simply a vacation, but knew it'd been more than that, for she truly wanted to determine in her heart if there might be a chance for the two of them. She thought about how Jamal and she had danced on the evening when they were in Harlem staying at the hotel.

She felt good in his arms, comfortable, safe, and loved, but nevertheless, scared about being hurt again because she'd possessed all those good feelings for him before.

She knew that she'd never forget the note he left underneath her door at the hotel when he said that he really understood how much he'd hurt her. He also said he'd do whatever it took to be with her again, and that he loved her with all his heart. She remembered reading his note over and over and believing what he'd written, but then she wasn't sure whether she believed him because she wanted to or because she thought Jamal had really changed. Then how could she forget, she thought, when in front of a room filled with people – most of them strangers – Jamal confessed that he'd taken her love for granted and that the most special thing he'd had in his life was her love. She remembered falling back in love with Jamal that evening as opposed to simply loving him, but was afraid to let him know.

Francine had her head down and felt Jamal's hand clutching hers, something that hadn't happened since being by his side. She looked up and saw Jamal's eyes open. She saw him smiling. She heard him say, "I love you too, Babycakes. I always have."

Tears fell from Francine's eyes, understanding that Jamal had heard her voice and heard her telling him over and over that she loved him. He was going to live, so she cried tears of joy. She rose from her chair, held one of Jamal's hands in hers, placed a hand against the side of his face, bent over him and kissed him gently on the lips and said, "Oh, Jamal, baby, I do love you; I really do."

* * *

Jamal was given a clean bill of health by the attending doctors and released from the hospital, although a period of recovery was necessary. He and Francine were on a United Airline flight from Mississippi to Detroit. Francine looked over at Jamal and asked, "Are you okay? Is everything all right? You seem to be in deep thought."

"I'm fine. I was recalling dreaming about being suspended above my bed when I was in the hospital and looking down at my own body and at you by my side. I remember walking, more like floating, through a tunnel with bright lights and feeling so at peace. It was really weird."

Francine said, "I've heard talk of other people having similar experiences when they'd actually died but recovered. It's called an out-of-body experience when a person has legally died. That's what probably happened to you because the doctors said that for awhile you were technically dead until they revived you."

"All I can say is that it was a real weird feeling. I felt so tranquil but at the same time I wanted to get back into my body so I could touch you. I didn't wanna leave you behind and not be with you."

Francine reached for and held Jamal's hand. She said, "Baby, I'm happy you didn't die and glad you recovered, but don't you make me kill you, Jamal. I'm not playing, now. You better do right by me this time."

"I will, Babycakes; I will. I promise with all my heart and soul."

"You'd better. And when did I give you permission to start calling me *Babycakes* again?" She smiled.

"Can I call you Babycakes? I love calling you Babycakes."

"Yeah you can, but I repeat: Don't make me kill you."

"I won't and that I promise." He leaned over and kissed Francine.

* * *

Jamal recovered sufficiently enough to begin writing again. Back in Detroit and in his study he began to write an editorial in regard to his return to Mississippi.

W. James Richardson

Dying to Vote
By
Jamal Peterson

Not long ago, I returned to the state of Mississippi in order to investigate first-hand the problems, or might I say the atrocities, that Negroes encounter in regard to pursuing the right to vote. Negroes are literally dying for the right to vote and I saw first-hand the murder and mayhem on one evening when I attended a meeting at a small, rural, Negro church outside of Greenville, Mississippi when the church was bombed, killing four Negroes and seriously wounding eight others. My own life was spared because at the time I was on my way to an outhouse.

Intimidation, brutality, and murder are tactics used against Negroes in the South to discourage them from registering to vote. When these offenses are committed, very seldom if ever are they investigated and the perpetrators brought to justice. It is as though elected officials and law enforcement personnel in these states give tacit if not open approval for citizens of the fairer complexion to attack and victimize Negroes who dare seek justice, human rights, equal opportunities, and the full rights of citizenship.

I came within an inch of being killed in Mississippi. Twice I have been in the Magnolia State to be threatened, exposed to a firebomb, and eventually shot and not expected to live. Negroes who live in Mississippi and choose to exercise rights of citizenship constantly come under attack, and the sad thing is that there is no public outcry about such from the President and elected members of Congress. How many lives have to be lost before our Government comes forward and enact a federal voter registration law that will give every American citizen the right to vote and absent of prejudice and without consideration of race, color, ethnicity, gender or religion? It is not good enough to simply pass laws into legislation, but they have to as well be enforced. A case at hand is the passage of the federal school desegregation law that has yet been enforced. Hence, it seems to be business as usual as southern states use tactics to skirt the law.

What is so important about voting that Negroes find so determined about that some are willing to die for? I searched within myself answers to this question and came up with the following:

- *It is important for Negroes to vote in order to help determine their own destiny.*
- *It is important for Negroes to vote in order to possess the full rights of citizenship for which they are entitled.*
- *It is important for Negroes to vote in order that justice and equality can be more readily attained.*
- *It is important for Negroes to vote in order that their manhood and womanhood can be duly recognized in the world-theater of human dignity, worth, and value.*

This humble writer foresees a time when Negroes as a race will be granted the right to vote throughout the South and, as well, in every village and hamlet in the United States of America because brave souls will fight the battles for this precious right. However, my worse fear – and God I pray it doesn't happen -- is that there will come a time when Negroes begin to take the right to vote for granted and begin to display apathy and forget that Negroes died for their right to vote. If that day ever comes, it will certainly be a great tragedy and a time when the deeds of their ancestors will be desecrated. I pray that I will never see that day.

Across the country both Negro and white citizens read Jamal Peterson's editorial and began calling and writing their congressmen to enact a federal voter registration law. Jamal received numerous invitations from every region of the nation to speak about voter registration and civil rights.

Negroes who resided in states where they could vote began to register in record numbers.

Chapter Twenty-Seven

August 28, 1956

Negroes throughout the country, and particularly in the Mississippi Delta, remembered today's date as well as their own birthdays. Many white people in the Delta recalled the day as well, but none no more than the two remaining former jurors who'd contributed to the not guilty verdict in the Emmett Till murder trial but had so far been spared any retribution, unlike their fellow jurors.

All were aware that it was the anniversary of Emmett's abduction and subsequent murder.

The remaining two former jurors' minds were at ease, believing that the misfortune of the other jurors was coincidental; so they dismissed the rumor that Emmett Till's ghost was roaming the Delta seeking revenge. But yet they were mindful that Roy Bryant, J.W. Milam, and Sheriff Strider – all significant parties in the murder case – had experienced their share of affliction. Roy and J.W. were sporting various wounds from the injuries that befell them, their businesses had gone bust, and their blood money – as Negroes in the Delta described the currency the men received from their murder confession – had dried up. Roy and J.W. were receiving almost daily pressure from white people to vacate the state.

Clarence H. Strider was now the ex-sheriff of Tallahatchie County due to being confined to a wheelchair after being run over by the produce truck. His successor, who was formerly the deputy sheriff, claimed not to believe in ghosts but wasn't taking chances by being cruel and abusive to Negroes like his predecessor. As a result, Negroes experienced kinder and gentler law enforcement, which they credited Emmett Till's ghost for and shouted "Hallelujah!" upon Sheriff Strider's retirement.

* * *

Prompted by an article written by Jamal Peterson, most Negro churches as well as a few white churches outside the South, rang bells at 2:00 A.M, which was the approximate time of Emmett Till's kidnapping one year earlier. Church bells chimed in memorial to Emmett Till and sounded for fourteen seconds, which denoted Emmett's age at the time of his death.

In Detroit, Jamal and Francine listened together as the bells filtered throughout the city in the early morning hour as they embraced each other on a living room sofa at the home he, Francine, and Thurgood shared as a family. They hadn't remarried; although, Jamal had raised the subject of marriage with Francine, but she wanted to give their relationship time. She assured Jamal that it had nothing to do with her loving him because she did. He understood and was hopeful that remarriage was in their future.

* * *

After the bells tolled in the Mississippi Delta, the night grew eerily silent. A loud droning of locusts with their pulsating humming filled the exceptionally humid night air, then suddenly a storm brewed, pelting the delta with heavy wind-swept rain as thunder roared and lightening bolted through the darkness like neon spears. The storm was loud enough to arouse both men and beasts from sleep. Dogs barked, cows mooed, and farm animals contributed to a clamorous symphony of fright and misgiving.

Roy Bryant heard wolves howl through the thunder, which frightened him, for he was starkly reminded of the predicament he'd found himself in when last he heard the sound of the bushy-tail predators.

The house dog yelped. Goats bleated. Roy's wife and two sons were awake and beseeched him to check out the situation, which meant to Roy that he needed to go outside as opposed to merely peeping out the windows. He reluctantly donned rain gear and went out in the night where the storm was furious and unrelenting.

Roy struggled against the wind to close the back door of the house behind him. He went into the night and the driving storm. His rain gear fluttered from the gale. Lightening silhouetted his form. He used the back of his knotty hands to wipe rainwater from his eyes as he peered into the night and saw a dark contour flitting in the rain and wind like a giant fly. The sound of wolves appeared nearer. The goats continued to bleat. Roy heard the dog inside the house yipping like crazy. A wind vane atop the barn was made airborne by the storm. It flew across the yard and the sharp end of the vane became impaled into Roy's arm. He screamed in agony, fell to the ground, and bled like a slaughtered hog as the rain peppered his body and the thunder drowned out his cry for help.

J.W. Milam also heard the sound of wolves out in the night. He, too, felt concern as he looked out the window into the night while his wife and son huddled in bed together. Lightning intermittently illuminated the interior of their home. Window shuttles banged against the outside of the house. J.W. thought he saw something move across the yard but couldn't make out what it was. He saw it again, moving slowly and upright – like a bear standing on its rear legs or maybe even a man. J.W. didn't like the idea of a creature or human on his property at this time in the morning – storm or no storm. He fetched his twelve-gage shotgun from a closet and sat in a chair in the small living room with his finger on the trigger as the wind howled, the rain fell in sheets, the lightning crackled, the thunder boomed, and wolves bayed.

J.W. heard a noise at the front door. It appeared that something or someone was trying to enter. Sweat poured down his face. He stood up from the chair, pointed the shotgun, and stared at the door. "Who's there?" he asked. There was no answer as the door rattled. He said, "You better go away. I've got a twelve-gauge and about to use it."

Suddenly the door was breached and flew off the hinges into J.W., knocking him backward. His trigger finger reflexively fired the shotgun that was pointed down at his foot as he was propelled backward. Intense pain struck J.W. and shock invaded him as he lay on the floor helplessly watching the blood and his right foot blown off.

* * *

The storm wrecked havoc in the Mississippi Delta during the night and early morning. County officials felt fortunate that more damage wasn't done and that more people hadn't been injured than was reported. More people began to believe in Emmett Till's ghost after it was established that the only people harmed by the storm were associated with the Emmett Till murder case, which included Roy Bryant, J.W. Milan, and the remaining two former jurors who hitherto escaped any tragedy.

Roy's arm was operated on and put in a cast and sling. Doctors prognosticated that he wouldn't ever have more than thirty percent use of his arm. J.W.'s foot was amputated. One former juror had an ear severed by flying glass from a busted window that was caused by the storm. The last former juror received first-degree burns on his lower torso from a bolt of lightning when he went out into the night to secure a hatch on a cellar door.

* * *

Three months later, broke, maimed, decrepit, depressed, and despised by both white people and Negroes, Roy Bryant and J.W. Milam decided to take the cash collected and offered by white citizens councils for them to leave the state of Mississippi, although neither man felt any contrition for murdering Emmett Till. Nor did they appreciate being coerced to leave the state or understood why white people had turned against them when once they treated them like heroes.

Chapter Twenty-Eight

September 1956

Mamie Till was home alone, exhausted, and in a state of solitude. She'd completed a recent tour – one of many – speaking about her son's death. This evening she wasn't amongst throngs of people as when she toured. She felt despondent and depressed. She really missed Emmett. Her home felt empty. She experienced loneliness without him to share her life with. She appeared to be strong in public, and also when she was with friends, relatives, and around complete strangers, but she knew that the perceived strength disappeared whenever she was alone and encumbered with vivid images as to how Emmett died. She just couldn't get over that he was taken away from her at such a young age and died in the manner he did. She'd soliloquized hundreds of times that she would've given her own life to save his. She felt a deep void and realized that she hadn't had any true time to grieve and to release her pain and suffering because of the tours and speeches.

Mamie was enveloped with self-pity as she sat at a table in her living room. Without Emmett she felt that her life would never have any real joy. She mused that her greatest pleasure had been being a good, loving mother.

She heard a voice say, "End it all."

The inner voice was powerful and convincing. Her mind was made up. She would end it all as the voice directed, believing it was the answer in regard to how she felt – empty and alone.

She contemplated as how to end her pain and suffering. She considered leaping out a window from the second floor, but the thought of her dress flaring up as she descended and her body splattering on the ground ended that consideration.

She thought about slashing her wrist but knew she couldn't endure the self-inflicted pain. The sight of lots of blood made her nauseous.

Sleeping pills, lots of them, that she thought was her solution and felt that she could do. She planned it out in her head. She would take a hot bubble bath, apply a fragrant lotion over her body, attire herself in her best nightgown; and when they discovered her body, she would look as though she was resting in a tranquil state. A serene state of being is what she longed for. She headed to the bedroom to make preparations when her telephone rang. She answered.

"Hello, Mrs. Till?"

"Yes, this is she."

"I'm Jamal Peterson, the reporter."

"Oh yes, Mr. Peterson. How are you?"

"I'm fine, but please call me Jamal. I'm calling to request to do a follow-up story on you. I hope you will grant it. People want to know the things you're doing and what you have planned for the future. So, what are you plans?"

Mamie was caught off guard. She was thinking that she wasn't about to say that she was about to commit suicide. She thought to herself that that would really be an exclusive story. Suddenly a strong wind entered the room from a window she hadn't remembered opening. The wind flipped pages of a newspaper that was on top the coffee table. She looked and saw an advertisement for Chicago Teachers College. She said, "One thing I plan to do is to return to school and study to become a teacher."

"That sounds great," Jamal said. "I know you would make a wonderful teacher and make a valuable difference in the lives of children. That's great…."

After Mamie got off the phone her mind was made up. She no longer considered ending it all. She was going to become a teacher and impact the lives of children as she knew she had done with Emmett.

Chapter Twenty-Nine

December 20, 1956
Montgomery, Alabama

Just a little more than a year after the bus boycott began, Negroes in Montgomery were jubilant when United States marshals served a court order on Montgomery city officials that directed them to integrate the seating on its buses. The United States Supreme Court had affirmed a lower court ruling that held Montgomery's bus segregation laws unconstitutional. Negroes considered the ruling an early Christmas present, although there was no organized celebration or public display. Though they were euphoric, the boycotters were equally tired and emotionally exhausted.

Negroes displayed no bitterness toward the white bus drivers, toward the police, or toward the white authority who all had been immutable in regard to changing any aspect of the hard-line segregation statues of the Montgomery City Lines' buses.

A meeting of the Montgomery Improvement Association was called and held at the Dexter Avenue Baptist Church. Hundreds of Negroes attended and the media were barred. After opening prayers, Dr. Martin Luther King Jr. approached the microphone and said, "We, as a people, have much to be thankful for and excited about this evening, for U.S. marshals have served a court order on the city's fathers to immediately integrate the city buses. It's a victory for humanity. It has been a long, grueling thirteen months arriving at this victory, and many of you have suffered beyond reason. But you hung in there and helped make this day possible. Why don't everyone give themselves a hand?"

Thunderous applauding erupted and shouts of "Hallelujah!", "Praise God!", and "Thank you, Lord!" engulfed the sacred edifice.

Voices grew silent as Dr. King raised his hand. He said, "Although we've won a glorious victory, it is not the time for public display and gloating in the faces of white people. Many of them are hurting because they believe that separation of the races is right. So instead of us being bitter and hateful, I ask you to pray for our white brethren who are misguided, not in our eyes, but in the eyes of God Almighty. Pray that their hearts will be healed by love. Love is redemptive, not for just white folks but for Negroes as well. Hate is more injurious to the hater that the hated. The state of mind and the body of the hater responds to hate in harmful ways just like an illness. Hate deteriorates the mind and body like cancer, which can cause illness and result in death. I ask you to treat our grand victory with dignity and don't flaunt our hard-earned victory to white people, though for some it might be difficult. And remember that not all white people in Montgomery agreed with the segregated buses and that it was a white lawyer, Attorney Clifford Durr, who aided us in our court battle and he has suffered on account of it…"

After the meeting, Negroes went home and felt uplifted by Dr. King's words. Many of the boycotters harbored pity for the white people who had bitterly opposed the integration of the busses. A new day had dawned in the lives of Negroes in the cradle of the Confederacy, and they took on a prayerful demeanor and rendered silent prayers of thanksgiving.

* * *

The following day the court order was enacted and for the first time in over a year, Negroes in Montgomery returned to ride the city buses and were allowed to sit wherever they pleased.

News photographers snapped pictures of the historical event and the most notable photo was that on Rosa Park, Dr. Martin L. King Jr. and Reverend Ralph Abernathy who all boarded an early morning bus and occupied seats in a section that had once been reserved for white passengers. No longer were Negroes assigned to sitting in the back of the bus, standing over empty seats reserved for whites, or surrendering seats to white passengers.

A broad smile encompassed Rosa Park's face as she sat in the front of the bus and took the victorious ride in the early morning. She reminisced about all the humiliation of the past in regard to the segregated buses. She thought if it hadn't been for the anger and bitterness she'd felt as a result of Emmett Till's murder that she likely wouldn't have been defiant when she refused to vacate her seat to the white man as the bus driver demanded. She was thinking that the bus boycott was over, but Emmett Till's memory would always be a part of her.

Reverend Abernathy asked Dr. King what he was looking at. Dr. King showed the reverend the piece of paper he was holding.

"It's a picture of Emmett Till," Reverend Abernathy remarked.

"Yes it is. I've been carrying it since it appeared in *Jet magazine*. Emmett could've been one of our kids and it's how I always think of his death. There's still much work to be done, reverend, in regard to achieving equal rights, fair treatment, and dignity for Negroes in this country. We have just begun. I pray that we'll leave a better world for our children and that in doing so, young Emmett Till's death wouldn't have been in vain."

"Amen, Dr. King."

* * *

Mamie Till had followed the Montgomery bus boycott from its beginning and rooted for its success. She was proud that the boycotters had used *Remember Emmett!* for their slogan throughout the boycott. She knew that if Negroes in Montgomery were successful then perhaps other barriers that deny Negroes equal rights of citizenship might be demolished.

Mamie rejoiced when the news broke across the country that federal marshals had served Montgomery authorities with a court order to desegregate the buses. She applied a gentle kiss to the photo of her son Emmett that she held in her hand. She said, "Baby, you can rest in peace because your death has given so much courage and inspiration to Negroes in this country."

Mamie went to her bedroom and secured the Mason jar with the *Freedom Soil* from a dresser drawer. She took the jar out to the backyard, dug a hole in the ground, sat a seedling in the hole, sprinkled some of the *Freedom Soil* into the hole and then covered it with dirt. It was the beginning of her pledge to plant a tree whenever Negroes won major victories in regard to civil rights and use the *Freedom Soil* to nourish it.

* * *

Jamal Peterson drove from Detroit to Montgomery, only purchasing gas and grabbing a bite to eat on the way.

He desired to witness the victory in Montgomery and report on it. He understood that the outcome in Montgomery was a monumental achievement in regard to Negroes' thirst and desire to achieve equal rights.

After Jamal arrived in Montgomery he checked into a room at the Ben Moore Hotel. Bright and early the next morning, he ate breakfast in the hotel's restaurant, returned to his room to freshen up, and later drove to E.D. Nixon's home in the Centennial Hill area of the city. He was treated like a long lost friend when he arrived.

"Keep your coat on, Jamal. We're leaving. We can chat on our way to the bus stop," E.D. said, catching Jamal by surprise.

"The bus stop?" Jamal asked. "Why are we going to the bus stop?"

"To catch a bus; what else?"

"I thought we were going to visit with each other, so I can prospect your mind about the victory achieved in regard to the bus boycott."

"You can prospect on the way to the bus stop and on the bus. I think you'll be more enlightened about what you see rather than what I tell you," said E.D. as he grabbed an overcoat and hat from a closet near the front door. He opened the door, nodded at Jamal to exit, then closed the door behind them.

The two men strolled to the bus stop under a bright sky and into a gentle, cool breeze. They bordered a city bus with other Negroes passengers at the bus stop and took seats together in a section that used to be reserved for whites.

As they rode on the bus, E.D. asked Jamal, "What's your observation? What do you see on this bus?"

"I don't see any white passengers."

"Not yet because the bus stops in the Negro sections of town first in order to get 'em to their jobs downtown and as domestics in white areas. But there haven't been many white passengers riding yet because lots of 'em ain't happy about havin to share seats with Negro passengers." E.D. hesitated as he considered his own statement then said, "Suppose it's gonna take white people's gettin used to. What else do you observe?"

Jamal took time to contemplate. He said, "There's a quiet reserved, not a lot of talking or any celebrating. One wouldn't know by these Negroes' demeanor that they were successful with the boycott."

"Exactly," E.D. said. "And it's by design. Dr. King said it well at a meeting of the MIA the other night. Our victory has been won, but it was a hard fought battle and lots of Negroes suffered as a result of it, and many lost jobs. For us to celebrate would seem sacrilegious and, besides, there needs to be some racial heelin, so like Dr. King advised: We don't need to gloat about our victory. Negroes passengers plan to ride the buses with dignity and pride."

"It shows," said Jamal. "It really does. I think it's amazing in consideration of all the hardships and indignities suffered."

"It's not over, Jamal; not hardly. We can't forget that Montgomery is the cradle of the Confederate and though the buses have been integrated, there's still vestiges of segregation in this city and lots of racial animosity."

"So, the struggle goes on."

"That it does, Jamal. That it does. And for the rest of our lifetimes I'm afraid the struggle will continue."

"That's a sad contemplation," said Jamal.

"Certainly it is. Do you have kids?"

"Yes, a five-year-old son."

"Well, let's just hope, Jamal, that we will leave this world a better place for your son and all Negro children. That's the best we can strive for. Some of us will fight the battles, and some Negroes will sit back and watch. Some will even criticize; just like we had a handful of Negroes here in Montgomery criticizing the MIA for seekin complete integration of the buses as opposed to our initial request to merely assign more seats for Negroes. Now they can freely ride the buses and sit anywhere they want. But like Dr. King said: Some Negroes were just too afraid to take a stand and thank God that a great majority of the Negroes understood the struggle."

Jamal looked away from E.D., leaned back in his seat, shut his eyes, and reflected on what he'd just been told. He opened his eyes and asked, "What became of that little Negro lady who told Dr. King that her feet were tired but her soul was rested?"

"Strange you asked. I was just thinkin of Mrs. Ellingsworth. She's in the hospital. I was just thinkin that I need to get by and visit with her."

"Why is she in the hospital?"

"Mrs. Ellingsworth is up there in age; more than eighty. Her health was bad all during the time of the boycott. She had cancer and had it all the time, but said she just wanted to live long enough to see her grandchildren ride on the buses and take any seat they pleased."

* * *

After Jamal returned to Detroit, he received a telephone call from E.D. Nixon who informed him that Mrs. Ellingsworth had gone home to be with the Lord. Jamal was pleased that he'd had the opportunity to visit the elderly lady at the hospital, along with E.D. And he would never forget her saying to him and E.D. that every step she walked during the boycott, she thought about Emmett Till and her grandchildren, which kept her going.

Jamal remembered looking into the old woman's face and in her eyes and sensing that indeed her soul was at rest.

Chapter Thirty

Christmas Day, 1956

Christmas was again a paid holiday for many Negroes in the Mississippi Delta, which they'd attributed to Emmett Till's ghost virtually serving as a union steward. White bosses, overseers, and hunchos hadn't started serving field-hands, laborers, and domestics lemonade like some Negroes bantered, but gifts of chickens and the better parts of hogs – loins, roasts, and chops – were surely appreciated in regard to Christmas dinner and the holidays. And now Negroes in the Delta knew what it meant to eat *high on the hog,* which induced them to intone "Merry Christmas" like never before and really mean it.

* * *

Roy Bryant and J.W. Milam and their families were living like paupers and in exile in nondescript locations outside the state of Mississippi; all but forgotten by white citizens who were once their allies and supporters. Both men were in failing health; barely able to work and to pay the notes on the shacks they occupied, or put food on their tables.

In the Bryant household, Christmas dinner consisted of potato soup and hot water cornbread. Milam's family wasn't fairing any better by having to settle for turnip greens and fatback. Each household was devoid of Christmas decorations and gifts, or any merriment. The men's wives were planning to leave them.

* * *

Jamal felt that Francine was more and more trusting in him, and he continued to try to convince her that the second time around he would be a most loyal, devoted and loving husband; but Francine still wasn't ready for the commitment of marriage. Jamal hadn't giving up. He realized that his ex father and mother-in-law were another challenge because they hadn't forgiven him. He wasn't keen of accompanying Francine and Thurgood to his ex in-laws' home for Christmas dinner – no matter that Francine assured him that everything would be all right.

As Jamal sat in the Florida room of Francine's parents' large, two-story, Tudor-style home in the Palmer Park area of Detroit, which was an upscale community where a number of professional Negroes lived, he felt uptight and very much wanted to make a favorable impression on Francine's mother and father. He didn't know whether to refer to Francine's parents as Mr. Daniel and Mrs. Daniel, Attorney Daniel and Dr. Daniel (being that the father was an attorney and the mother was a pediatrician), or as Mom and Pop. He quickly dismissed Mom and Pop, understanding that he'd used those monikers when he was still married to Francine and on good terms.

Jamal's rumination ended when Francine's older brother, Ray, offered him a cocktail before dinner. He refused the drink, which prompted Francine to smile and say with pride, "Jamal gave up drinking."

"Who gave up drinking?" Francine's father asked as he wandered into the room.

"Jamal did, Daddy. He hasn't had a drink in well over a year."

"What's wrong, Jamal? Are you sick and on some type of medication?" Mr. Daniel asked.

"Daddy!" Francine said.

Jamal said, "No, I'm not taking medication. I'm very healthy. Just knew I needed to stop drinking because it caused problems in my life."

"You've got that right!"

"Daddy!"

"What, Francine? I was just agreeing with Jamal. Dinner is ready. Let's go to the dining room and eat."

Jamal sat at the large, freshly polished, oak wood dining room table between Francine and Thurgood. He marveled at the large spread: A roasted turkey with dressing, a spiral, glazed ham, mustard and collared greens, sweet potatoes, macaroni and cheese, red beans and rice, homemade rolls, thick slices of yellow cornbread, and an ambrosia made from an assortment of fruit.

Mr. Daniel blessed the food.

Although famished, Jamal found it difficult to enjoy his meal. He felt Mr. and Mrs. Daniel's eyes trained on him. He pretended not to notice as his undershirt got moist from perspiration. He was convinced that coming to dinner was a bad idea. He felt like prey.

"Carolyn, did you know Jamal stopped drinking?" said Mr. Daniel to his wife.

"Well good for him."

Francine's younger sister, Judy, a teenager in high school, noticed the tension. She said, "In our social studies class, I told my teacher that Jamal had gotten shot in

Mississippi, while down there trying to help Negroes to vote." She looked directly at Jamal and said, "Jamal, you are so brave! Mr. Briggs, my teacher, said he knew about you because he'd read some of your articles. He asked me to invite you to come to our classroom and speak about your experiences as a writer. Will you do that, Jamal?"

Jamal smiled. He said, "I would be happy, Judy. Let me know when."

Judy smiled and said, "Thanks, Jamal. That'll be cool."

Mr. Daniel said, "Jamal, I've read your articles, too. I liked that *Remember Emmett!* piece you wrote, and I really liked your editorial about *My Soul is Rested.* I was sorry to hear about you getting shot. You're a very good writer, no question about it. You're most talented in that area. Just too bad some of that talent couldn't have rubbed off in regard to you being a good, loyal husband."

"Daddy!" Francine uttered.

"Well, I spoke the truth. I'm not one to bite my tongue. I call it like I see it and give credit where it's due. Constructive criticism doesn't hurt anyone. Judy said that it would be cool for Jamal to speak to her class, but I'll tell you what else would be cool," said Mr. Daniel. He allowed his statement to purposely hang.

"What, Daddy?" Francine asked.

"It would be cool if Negro men would keep their families intact by honoring their wedding vows. What about it, Jamal? Don't you think that would be cool?"

"Daddy!"

"What, Francine? You shouldn't have a problem with what I'm saying. You were the one around here bawling and going out of your mind when you discovered Jamal had cheated on you. How do you think that made your mother and me feel?"

"Daddy, I know, but this isn't the time nor place for this conversation. I didn't bring Jamal over here on Christmas day to be interrogated and insulted."

"Insulted? Since when did it become insulting for a man to be loyal to his wife and family? Didn't you feel insulted when you discovered Jamal had cheated? So, when is the time and place right for this discussion? Hell, this is the first time I've seen Jamal since, since… Well, you know when it was."

"It's okay, Francine," Jamal said. "Your father is right. I can take it and deserve it. I agree, Mr. Daniel, that it'd be cool for Negro men to keep their families intact by honoring their wedding vows, and that's exactly what I wanna do and will do if I'm given another chance by Francine. I made a terrible mistake when I cheated on Francine. I admit that I was selfish and immature. I'm not going to try to defend what I did because I was as wrong as two left feet. I deserve your scorn, Mr. and Mrs. Daniel. I understand your anger and disappointment. I'd probably feel the same if someone cheated on my daughter and hurt her. I know I hurt Francine, and I'm so very ashame about it; I truly am. I've even hurt myself by hurting her. But I've changed. I'm not the same Jamal who hurt your daughter before. I want Francine back in my life as my wife, and I want our family back. I promise you that I would never hurt your daughter again or do anything to jeopardize our family should Francine ever agree to marry me again."

Francine held Jamal's hand and said, "I believe Jamal. He has changed."

Jamal and Francine shared loving glances, which didn't go unnoticed by either Mr. or Mrs. Daniel.

Mr. Daniel said, "Well, you can't change spots on a leopard, and it's said that once a cheater always a cheater. What do you say to that, Jamal?"

"I respectfully beg to differ," Jamal retorted. " I don't concur with that any more than I think all lawyers are shysters; present company included. I've honestly changed. I'm no longer that cheating worm you knew. I consider my life, attitude, and outlook on life to be a metamorphosis and much like a butterfly that has transitioned from a caterpillar – or a worm if it pleases you."

Judy placed her hands to her mouth and chuckled.

Francine smiled.

Thurgood didn't understand any of it.

Francine's brother, Ray, and his wife looked amused as if they were being well entertained.

Carolyn Daniel got up from the table and said, "Time for dessert. I'm going to the kitchen."

Mr. Daniel's said, "That wasn't bad, Jamal; not bad at all if what you say is true. And for Francine's sake I hope it is. Bring on the dessert. Something sweet tasting is needed about now. I'll tell you one thing; Jamal has spunk. I like that in a person. Sometimes a man's mind gets clearer when he lays off the sauce."

Francine squeezed Jamal's hand and murmured, "Daddy always has to have the last word." She kissed Jamal and said, " Merry Christmas, baby."

"Merry Christmas, Francine. I love you."

"I love you, too, baby."

Chapter Thirty-One

The day after Christmas, Jamal, Francine, and Thurgood traveled back to the Harlem section of New York City for the National Negro Press Association Awards. Unlike last year, they shared a room at the Negro owned and operated Drake Hotel. On their first day in the city, they did exactly as last year: went to dinner, saw a few sights, and returned to the hotel room to relax.

Francine nestled the side of her head against Jamal's chest. He wrapped an arm around her as they lay on top the bedcovers. They admired their son as he slept on a rollaway bed. Jamal said, "Francine, when did you start trusting me again and believing that I'd changed?"

"Well, first I became aware that you'd really stopped drinking, which very much impressed me because you've drank ever since I've known you. At first your drinking wasn't a problem but later in our marriage it became one, especially when you'd come home late at night reeking of the smell of alcohol and intoxicated. So, I realize that not drinking was a major change in you, and it convinced me that you were really trying. I knew how much you loved your parents, so when you told me that you'd swear on your parents' grave that you had changed, that touched a chord in my heart. But still, trusting you with my heart again was another matter because I never wanted to be hurt by you again, or, to that regard, by any one, especially like I'd been hurt by you. So, my trust was hard to come by, even though I began to think you had honest intentions. What happened is that you passed the head and neck test after we started dating again."

"The head and neck test?" Jamal asked.

Francine nudged Jamal gently in his rib cage with her elbow and said, "Don't pretend not to know what the head and neck test is. We've discussed it enough times when we were married because you were notorious with it and not a bit discreet."

"You mean looking at other women?"

"No, Jamal; not just looking. I'm not an insecure woman who's threatened by my man checking out an attractive woman. I mean, after all, women are no different. We notice attractive men. But in your case you'd stare and I could see lust in your eyes. It was almost like you'd forgotten that you were with me."

Jamal said, "Guilty as charged. I admit it. But I hadn't done that since I can remember because I have no interest in other women. I really don't, Francine."

"Well, like I said, you passed the head and neck test because since we started dating again I've found your focus and concentration on me and not on any other woman, which makes me feel very good, really special, and comfortable. So, with your quitting drinking and doing all the sweet things I love, I began trusting you again. And I realized it was very difficult and most uncomfortable situation for you to go to my parents' home for Christmas dinner. The fact that you went told me that you were willing to take the heat and place yourself on the firing line for us."

Jamal kissed Francine on the lips, chuckled and muttered, "It certainly was a firing line." He got serious and said, "Francine you are the only woman for me. I know that, sweetheart; I really do. I've got an idea, let's slip down to the hotel's lounge like we did last year."

Francine smiled and said, "Why? Last year you invited me to come to your room, which I refused, but now I am in your room. So, why do we need to go downstairs?"

"Correction! This year we are in our room."

"I stand corrected."

Jamal said, "Last year things didn't work out so great when we went downstairs. I thought it'd be nice to do it again and make the situation more of a pleasant memory."

"Sounds good, baby. I would like that. Give me five minutes."

Downstairs in the hotel's lounge, Jamal and Francine looked for the same table they'd sat at the year before but found it occupied by a young couple, so they sat at another table not far from it. A very attractive waitress came to the table to take their orders. Jamal ordered two ginger ales.

The waitress left. Francine uttered, "You passed the test again." She smiled then said, " I remember a time when you would've practically fallen off you chair looking at a woman that attractive."

"What woman?"

"The waitress, Jamal. I know you had to notice that she was very attractive because I did. Baby, there's nothing wrong with noticing; it's the way you do it and what goes on in your mind when you do."

Jamal kissed Francine and said, "She is attractive, which is only her cover. Francine, I've learned that it's not what you see on the outside of a person that's important, but rather what you discover on the inside. I surely know what it means when they say you can't judge a book by its cover. You have a lovely cover but more importantly, you have so many good qualities about you that I love and adore. You are a woman of both beauty and substance. And if you were a book, I would always want to turn your pages, read you over and over from cover to cover, and never, ever put you down because I would never grow tired of you."

Francine held Jamal's hand, kissed him, then said, "Baby that was so sweet; real sweet. I love you"

"And I love you too, sweetheart; and always have." Jamal excused himself and went to the jukebox.

Francine saw him turn toward her and smiled.

Jamal returned to the table and as he arrived, the Platters' hit song, *Only You,* began to play.

Jamal held out his hand and said, "May I have the honor of this dance, lovely lady?"

"Yes, you may. It would be my pleasure."

Francine took Jamal's hand. They strolled a few steps to the dance floor. As they danced and held each other close, Jamal borrowed words from the song and whispered them into Francine's ear: "You do make my world seem right... You've certainly made a change in me... You are my destiny... You are my dream come true and you will always be my one and only." He placed a hand gently underneath Francine's chin, raised her head from his chest, and gazed into her glistening brown eyes. He lowered his head toward hers and savored her lips, which he thought to be as sweet and soft as cotton candy.

The two of them were impervious to their surrounding and the other people in the lounge. And for that moment they felt as though they were the only two people who existed. Unlike last year, they danced the whole song through and returned to their room together holding hands and exchanging utterances of love. They retired for bed and held and kissed each other until they blissfully fell asleep, smiling, happy, and at peace with each other.

* * *

The hotel ballroom was packed with people attending the National Negro Press Association Awards ceremonies. Again this year, Jamal was a nominee for the *Ida B. Wells Editorial Award* in regard to his two editorials: *My Soul Is Rested,* and *Dying to Vote.*

Jamal, Francine, and Thurgood were sitting at a table with five other people who they chitchatted with during dinner. There was respectful quiet in the room as the award presentations began.

A tall, thin, thirty-something Negro man with a full beard came to the microphone and announced, "It's my pleasure to present the recipient of the *1956 Ida B. Wells Editorial Award.*" He provided background information on Ida B. Wells, stated the criteria for the award and then said, "This year's recipient is Jamal Peterson and I might add the second consecutive year he's won this award."

Jamal kissed Francine, rose from his chair, and left the table to go to the rostrum to receive his award. People stood and clapped as he approached. He was handed his award, a striking large plaque in the shape of a scroll with a fountain pen engraved upon it.

Jamal spoke into the microphone and said, " On the way up here, someone in the audience asked me if I was going for number three next year."

There was laughter and applauds from the audience.

Jamal continued and said, "The fact is that I never write anything with the notion of winning awards. I write from my heart. I write honestly and with conviction. I write hoping that what I write will make a difference to those who read it. There are other very talented Negro journalists out there who are writing some real good stuff, so I feel most honored and privileged to be this year's honoree and I humbly thank the association for selecting me. But just one more thing before I leave the podium. I wanna recognize two very important people in my life who are sitting down front: my son, Thurgood, and a lovely and charming woman who has accepted my proposal of marriage, my soon-to-be bride for the second time and Thurgood's mother, Francine Peterson."

A thunderous applause broke out, accompanied by hardy cheers. Jamal smiled all the way back to his seat and kissed Francine at the table in the midst of all the adulation.

Chapter Thirty-Two

Jamal felt a sense of peace, wellbeing, and stability in his life since being married to Francine for the second time. He was committed to staying faithful, never desiring to stray from their marriage again. He vowed never to forget that he'd broken Francine's heart once before and constantly told himself that he'd rather rot in hell than to hurt her ever again; and he meant it. And he continued to pass the head and neck test during the three years he and Francine were now remarried.

Jamal found himself very busy on the speaking circuit and away from his family more than he desired, but Negroes' struggle for civil and equal rights was both the substance and catalyst for his appearances and speeches throughout the country.

Francine supported him. She understood the significance of what he was doing, and she let him know how proud she was of him. Each appearance he made and every talk he gave, he never failed to make reference to Emmett Till because in Jamal's mind Emmett Till's murder -- nearly five years earlier -- jumpstarted the modern-day civil rights movements, starting with the bus boycott in Montgomery.

It was mid-February of 1960. Jamal was in Nashville, Tennessee at the invitation of the Nashville Student Movement that was replicating sit-in demonstrations started by students at North Carolina Agricultural and Technical College in Greensboro, North Carolina. Just like the students in Greensboro had done in regard to segregated lunch counters at Woolworth's stores, college students in Nashville and in ten other southern states were staging sit-ins at national chain stores in the South that segregated services to Negroes and whites.

Jamal positioned himself on the ground floor of the student protest movement by having earlier interviewed the four Negro students who'd started the demonstrations in Greensboro. He saw the student protest growing expeditiously. He mulled that if Emmett Till were still alive he would've been the same age of many of the college students in the audience this evening at the Nashville African American and Episcopal Church.

"...I see Negroes in America engaged in a struggle in this country that's much like the Revolutionary War when Americans believed that they were participating in a just and noble cause in regard to the creation of a society free from oppression and evil. The *Brown vs. Board of Education of Topeka* decision that outlawed segregated schools was just and noble. Outlawing segregated buses in Montgomery, Alabama was just and noble. Struggling for the right to vote is just and noble. Students' demonstrations and sit-ins to desegregate public facilities and businesses that accept Negroes' dollars is a just and noble cause."

Students and adults present inside the church to hear Jamal Peterson's talk stood and applauded.

Jamal waited for the audience to settle back down and then said, "The Declaration of Independence clearly states that *all men are created equal.* It doesn't say that only white men are created equal. It says all men, which includes

Negroes. But since the end of legalized slavery... And I stated 'legalized slavery' for a reason because yet today – on plantations throughout the south – one can witness Negroes laboring and toiling under conditions that are not much better than when slavery was legalized with Negroes living in abject poverty, near starvation, and residing in unpainted, tar-paper shacks. I've seen it with my own eyes in the Mississippi Delta, and I'm certain such conditions also exist here in the state of Tennessee."

Loud applauding, statements of "Amen!" and an assortment of vocal affirmations resounded in the church.

Jamal continued. He stated, "Negroes continue to struggle against tremendous barriers in order to achieve equal treatment under the law and the Declaration of Independence. The student demonstrations and the push for equal treatment here in Nashville are both just and noble causes. What isn't just and noble in this country is the lynching and killing of Negroes who dare to pursue the right to vote. What isn't just and noble is to treat Negroes like second-class citizens. What isn't just and noble is for white men to get away with brutalizing and killing Negroes with impunity and be able to boast about it and get paid for murder as Roy Bryant and J.W. Milam did when they murdered young Emmett Till down in Mississippi! For money they told their heinous story to the nation and to the world and made a mockery of justice in Mississippi and in America! I say to you this evening that we can't let America forget about Emmett Till because he was a symbol of every Negro in this country when he was brutally murdered!"

The audience rapidly stood as though bolts of electricity penetrated their seats. People shouted support. Some flung their arms and acted as though they were embodied with the Holy Ghost. And some sniffled and cried softly.

Jamal said, "We can't ever forget what they did to Emmett Till in Mississippi. Negroes in Montgomery didn't forget. They used the slogan 'Remember Emmett!' as a battle cry during their long, hard, and difficult struggle to desegregate the buses. And as the sit-in demonstrations continue, I urge the students in the movement to also use 'Remember Emmett!' as their mantra in the struggle for justice and equality."

Students and adults in the audience rose to their feet and began citing, "Remember Emmett!, Remember Emmett!, Remember Emmett!..."

* * *

A week after Jamal's appearance, the Nashville Student Movement mobilized more than two hundred students for sit-ins at the city's major stores. The movement grew and galvanized students from the North and South – Negroes and whites. The movement became known as the Student Nonviolent Coordinating Committee (SNCC).

Chapter Thirty-Three

Jamal and Francine were asleep upstairs in the master bedroom of the two-story, three-bedroom home they'd purchased on Detroit's westside near West Grand Boulevard and three blocks from Motown Records. Jamal thought he was dreaming upon hearing the words "Oh God! No! Oh, God!"

As Jamal grew fully conscious he became keenly aware that it was Francine uttering the words while she lay next to him in bed.

He gently nudged her. "Francine! Francine, wake up! Wake up, Francine!"

Francine awoke. She gasped as though she'd run a marathon.

"What's wrong? What were you dreaming about?"

Francine sat up in bed, held her hands to her breast, and allowed her strident breathing to subside. She said, "I had a dream that you were seriously hurt; maybe dead." She slid close to Jamal and embraced him as she buried her head into his chest. She said, "Jamal, I don't want you to go with the freedom riders to Birmingham. I've got the feeling that something awful is going to happen."

Jamal squeezed Francine in his arms, kissed her forehead, and said, "Francine, I'm not going to lie and say that I know everything will be all right because you never know. But this is something that I feel strongly about and something I feel I need to do."

"Why, baby?"

Jamal planted his lips on Francine's forehead again and said, "I've been following stories about Negroes fighting for justice and equal rights, but I've always been on the outside like a spectator. Francine, too many Negroes in this country are spectators who look to other Negroes to fight the battles, take the risks, and endure all the hardships, but in the end all Negroes benefit when civil rights are won. I don't wanna be a spectator. This time I wanna be part of the action. I wanna be a participant. I wanna see, smell, hear, taste, and feel what the freedom riders endure as they attempt to get the government to enforce laws that have already established that the segregation of interstate travel is illegal. I need to be on the inside of this thing this time, which means on the bus with the freedom riders."

"But, Jamal it's dangerous. We both saw the picture of how they firebombed that bus in Alabama with the freedom riders on it."

"I know, Babycakes. And I'm not going to say that I'm not nervous about it, because I am. I'm real nervous, but, Francine, this is something that in my heart I feel I have to do. I've written editorials about the fight for civil rights and beseeched readers to remember Emmett Till, but what have I done besides write about these things? I haven't tried to register to vote in a hostile environment. I didn't help integrate one single school after school segregation was declared unconstitutional. I didn't march one block during the bus boycott in Montgomery. And I wasn't a part of the sit-in demonstrations. I just wrote about these things and appealed to other Negroes in the trenches to remember

Emmett Till as they placed their bodies, health, personal welfare, and sometimes their lives on the line. Well, it's my turn to remember Emmett Till by not just writing about it, but, rather, by putting myself on the line for justice and equality. So, Babycakes, that's why I need to board that bus and join the freedom riders. I want our son to be able to go any place in this country and enjoy the full rights of citizenship. I wanna be able to stand and say that I did something to make it happen other than write and talk about it."

"I don't understand," Francine said. "If it's the law why are white people fighting it and being so violent?"

"It's just like when the Supreme Court ruled against segregated schools, a lot of white people in the South became awfully bitter and violent about it. Segregation is all that a lot of white people know in the South. They grew up believing it is right"

"Damn, white people don't want us to vote or sit next to them anywhere. They must think our blackness is a disease or something that will horribly rub off on them." Francine raised her head off of Jamal heaving chest, looked into his face and said, "I'm proud of you, Jamal. You're a good man. You have a good heart, and I do understand what you've said to me about needing to go. But can't a woman be afraid for her man sometimes?"

"Yeah, Babycakes, you can, and I appreciate it." Jamal gathered Francine closer as he reflected on her words and loved her for them.

Francine said, "I remember you clinging to death in that Mississippi hospital and I just don't want anything else even close to that happening to you again, Jamal." She glanced forlornly across the room, not looking at anything in particular, but her mind revisiting being by Jamal's bedside when it appeared he was dying.

Jamal said, "I know it might be dangerous, but I keep thinking about what they did to Emmett Till and then I think about his mother and our son. Francine, I don't think I'll be able to live with myself if I don't join the freedom riders. What they're doing is just and right. And I believe God is on the side of Negroes when it comes to fighting for civil rights."

"I think God is too. Just be careful, baby. That's all I'm asking."

* * *

Jamal was up early the following morning packing a single bag, making sure he traveled light as instructed. Francine was downstairs preparing breakfast. Jamal tossed the last item in his bag, and then left the master bedroom to look into Thurgood's room where he saw his son sleeping peacefully as though his world was tranquil and abiding; the way Jamal wanted life to always be for his son. He kissed him gently on the cheek, not wanting to awaken him, though he would be gone for a few days on a journey in the South that in most everyone's opinion could be most treacherous. Jamal knew his son didn't understand all the contention over civil rights, but was aware that he had seen racism in Detroit, although he wasn't yet old enough nor sophisticated enough to recognize it as such. Jamal contemplated that his son had witnessed the uncongenial manner in which people of his pigmentation were treated in various sections of the *Motor* City and especially by racist, white policemen who paroled the city and brazenly victimized Negro citizens.

Jamal recalled the time when he and Thurgood were on a father and son outing and got pulled over by a white policeman for a tail-light being out on his car and was questioned and treated by the policeman as though he'd robbed a bank or done something else criminal. He remembered Thurgood asking the reason the policeman was so mean. He didn't have the heart or the desire to tell his son that being a Negro was why; so he said to Thurgood, "He's having a bad day" and left it at that.

Jamal returned to his bedroom where the early morning sun shone brightly through the window. He ambled to the large picture window and watched robins perched regally on the banister of the upper deck as the feathery ambassadors of spring chirped melodiously. He saw green lawns and hedges and colorful flowers that were the product of the warm weather. His mind fixated on the love he had for his family. He fantasized remaining in that moment of mental tranquility he was experiencing.

Chapter Thirty-Four

Jamal flew out of the Detroit Metropolitan Airport to Birmingham, Alabama, where he was to meet with representatives of the Congress of Racial Equality (C.O.R.E.) and other freedom riders who were to make the bus ride from Birmingham to Montgomery.

Upon arriving in Birmingham in the early afternoon, Jamal caught a cab to check into a motel in the Negro section of the city. He went to his room to rest and read some literature before his orientation meeting later this evening. It was his first time in Birmingham, which was a city he'd heard much about and foremost its police commissioner Eugene "Bull" Connor, who was known to be a staunch segregationist and an antagonist to civil rights workers and particularly the freedom riders. He'd been informed that Commissioner Conner had purposely held back policemen during an earlier freedom ride into Birmingham in order to allow an angry white mob to assault the freedom riders, which left one rider paralyzed for life. Jamal lay on top of his bed, closed his eyes, and pondered the freedom riders' trek into Montgomery.

Later that evening, Jamal was picked up and taken to a church, where he was greeted by a casually attired, short, dark complexioned man in his mid to late thirties by the name of Charles Marshall, who introduced himself as a C.O.R.E. official.

There were nearly thirty people in the room -- all men and six of them white.

Charles Marshall stood before the gathering along with a tall, heavyset Negro man wearing spectacles and said, "I'd like to introduce Reverend William Troublefield, pastor of this church, who will lead us in prayer."

After the prayer and self-introductions, Charles was back before the group. "We thank all of you who have volunteered to make the freedom ride into Montgomery, known as the 'Cradle of the Confederacy'. What you can expect when we arrive in Montgomery is hostility and perhaps violence perpetrated against each one of you. Nothing can be ruled out. Is it worth it? Well, hopefully that question has already been answered by each of you or otherwise you wouldn't have volunteered. You all understand your personal risk, so I won't dwell on it. But a note of encouragement is that freedom riders are making a difference. The freedom rides have caught the attention of President John Kennedy and his administration. The violence against freedom riders has drawn international attention and national press coverage. C.O.R.E. can report that the Kennedy administration is very concerned about the negative impression that the violence is creating abroad. President Kennedy is aware that nothing could be worse for America's prestige abroad than to have this country's racial problems exposed to the rest of the world. The freedom rides have compelled the president to pay attention to our noble struggle and to take some decisive action by getting the United States Department of Justice involved."

Applause broke out.

"Another thing," Charles said, "keep in mind that you aren't breaking the law. The purpose of the freedom rides is to test compliance with the United States Supreme Court ruling which established that the integration of bus stations and terminals that serve interstate travel is legal. So, it's the law of the land. The ones in violation of this federal law handed down last year are those who oppose it, although it's the freedom riders who are getting arrested in Southern states. But we'll keep pressing on until the victory is won. The law is on our side."

"And so is God!" someone shouted, which received verbal support from others.

Charles said, "All of you are motivated to make this journey into Montgomery for various reasons and I'm sure some for the same reason. But whatever is your motivation, hold on to it and let it sustain you because your journey won't be easy. You will be called vile names, maybe spat on, and perhaps subjected to physical violence. Be strong, stay strong, may God be with you all, and to the righteous be the glory."

* * *

At mid-morning on May 20, 1961, twenty-one freedom riders, black and white, and Jamal Peterson among them, left Birmingham to travel by bus to Montgomery. Jamal wore a white T-shirt with the words *Remember Emmett*! embossed on it in red letters on the front. On the back, the inscription *The Struggle Continues* was printed.

The scene presented itself as surreal to Jamal. He'd never seen anything like it and never was involved with anything of such magnitude. Their bus was being escorted by a phalanx of Alabama patrol cars with planes flying overhead as part of the entourage. It seemed to Jamal to be a script from a movie. It was an ominous scene that made Jamal both proud and nervous. He felt like he was headed off to war.

The riders sat in quiet contemplation as the bus pulled out of Birmingham for the hour-and-half journey south to Montgomery. Jamal attempted to psyche himself up by conjecturing that the United States Department of Justice had intervened and brought Alabama's governor to his senses in regard to protecting the freedom riders.

Jamal soon discerned that he'd engaged in wishful thinking when the bus approached the outskirts of Montgomery and all the patrol cars suddenly left and the planes disappeared.

The bus arrived at the terminal and was greeted by hundreds of enraged white people who were waiting and shouting, "Kill the niggers!"

Not a single city policeman or state trooper could be seen. Jamal sensed that he and the other freedom riders had arrived in a purgatory of hatred.

A white man who Jamal only knew as Jim from Wisconsin was the first off the bus. Jamal saw the mob subdue him and beat him unmercifully. Some of the legion boarded the bus and began beating the other freedom riders. Jamal looked into the faces of wild-looking men who seemed to have the visages of pre-historic animals, snarling and growling as they pounced on the freedom riders, flinging their fists and pounding the riders with sticks and various instruments of torture.

Jamal curled into a fetus position and attempted to protect his head and face with his hands and arms as he was punched, beaten, and repeatedly called a nigger. Jamal's body ached miserably from the blows and the agonizing pain that permeated his head and body. He felt blood flowing in his eyes.

The beatings and violence seemed to go on interminably before federal marshals arrived on the scene and restored order. The most seriously injured freedom riders were triaged and taken to a hospital. The others were patched up and taken to Negroes' home in Montgomery for sanctuary. Jamal was taken to one of the homes. His *Remember Emmett!* T-shirt was covered with blood. He was bruised, battered, and swollen. He thanked God to be alive. He had firsthand seen, smelled, tasted, heard, and felt the vicious opposition to civil rights, got baptized by the hatred, and shed blood, sweat, and tears for the cause.

Chapter Thirty-Five

August 6, 1975

Jamal was clad in pajamas in the study of his home and slumped in a padded leather chair behind a cluttered desk and in a room lined with shelves of books, four large filing cabinets, and with awards and citations adorning the walls. He was happy on one hand but sad on the other. He felt joyful about his family. Francine was a loving wife who'd earned a doctorate degree in education at Wayne State University and now was dean of instruction at the University of Detroit. His son, Thurgood, was a sophomore student at the University of Michigan majoring in Political Science with aspirations to become a lawyer and to enter politics. Jamal's newspaper, *The Michigan Trumpet,* was doing really well during the five years it'd existed. So, Jamal, now forty-six years of age, was most pleased as to how things in his life were going. But what he was sad and upset about, as he pondered alone in his study, was the fact that ten years to this date when President Lyndon Baines Johnson signed the Voters Right Act, too many Blacks were not going to the polls to exercise their right to vote. Jamal recalled the hard fought battles and the lives lost to win the right for Blacks to vote without harassment and threats, and thus the reason he was in his study composing on an IBM electric typewriter an editorial entitled *Self-Disenfranchisement: When Blacks Fail to Vote.*

Jamal lifted his body off the chair to fetch a book off the shelf. He had a slight limp in his gait as a result of the beating he'd sustained in 1961 as a freedom rider, along with blurry vision in his left eye that necessitated him wearing corrective lens.

After retrieving the book of *Black Statistics in the United States*, Jamal resumed sitting at his desk. The book's title with the word "Black" printed in its title reminded Jamal of how it'd taken an adjustment for him to abandon the use of "Negro" for "Black". He contemplated that his conversion was a result of the black pride and cultural identity upheaval during the late sixties and early seventies when young black people were ubiquitously using the mantra "Black is beautiful!" and soul brother-extraordinary, James Brown, sang the hit song *I'm Black and I'm Proud.*

Jamal reflected on how he'd naturally gotten caught up in the vertex of black pride that swept through the country and how, as some others of his race, he debated whether modern day Negroes in the United States should be referred to as Black or African-Americans. He finally decided that Black was more acceptable to him, but not that he disparaged any reference to African-Americans and he proudly wore his hair in the style of what was known as an Afro.

Jamal contemplated that black pride was a good thing: psychologically healthy and in many ways invigorating. But he found himself infuriated by the statistics that established that Blacks – particularly outside of southern states – were not registering to vote in large numbers; therefore, not casting votes in high percentages and, in fact, at a lower percentage than any other racial group.

Jamal worked on writing his editorial into the late night and early morning and more than once he shed tears during the process. With agony he remembered the church bombing in Mississippi when lives were lost, and when he almost lost his, because they were championing the right for their people to vote. He recalled that during that time they were referred to as "Coloreds" or "Negroes" and when the mantra was "We shall overcome" and when Black pride was more in deeds than in words. Such thoughts resonated in Jamal's mind, which he transferred on paper as he wrote his editorial.

* * *

A bit more than three weeks later, Jamal was back in the Mississippi Delta at the invitation of Reverend Joseph Masolt who'd sent him a formal invitation on letterhead of *The Mississippi Delta Orchid Company* and on which the reverend was referenced as the *President & CEO.*

Reverend Masolt's letter informed Jamal that *The Mississippi Delta Orchid Company* was located on the grounds of the Masolt Homestead and grew orchids that were sold throughout the country and abroad. The reverend further apprised Jamal that the company had contributed money to erect a statue of Emmett Till on the bank of the Tallahatchie River near where Emmett's body was found and that he was invited for the dedication.

Jamal had gladly accepted the invitation and hence the reason he, Francine, and Thurgood were in Mississippi on the twentieth anniversary of Emmett Till's death as guests of Reverend Masolt at his well-kept and impressive mansion.

Jamal was up early before seven, restless, and most eager about the dedication. Francine and Thurgood were still asleep. He quietly went to the bathroom to take care of business, got dressed, gently closed the heavy bedroom door behind him, and ambled down the wide, winding staircase as his right hand slid across a white handrail gilded with gold etchings. Halfway on his descent he was met with a delightful aroma that signaled something delectable cooking in the kitchen. The aroma of freshly brewed coffee sensually guided him to the bottom of the stairs, where he saw offices that gave the glorious edifice the appearance of a corporate headquarters on the inside. He marveled at the assorted colors of potted orchids that decorated the hall and the vestibule he passed as he followed his nose in the direction that the fragrance was tempting him.

He heard voices and arrived at a room where he saw Reverend Masolt sitting with a short, stubby white man and a bearded black man. The men were seated at an impressive-looking, relic wood table with porcelain dishes on top and under the glare of a large, white chandelier that cast shadows along the edges of the chamber. The men had decorative cups in front of them that emitted wee vapors of steam.

Reverend Masolt looked up and said, "Ah, Mr. Peterson, come on in and join us. I was just discussing you with my colleagues. Would you care for a cup of coffee?"

"Sure," Jamal replied as he made his way into the room and took a place at the table.

"We were just discussing how you'd so valiantly helped us out during our struggles back in the fifties as a journalist when you came here to cover the Emmett Till murder trial and then returned to report on problems associated with Negroes registering to vote. And the latter nearly cost you your life. We'll be eternally grateful to you, Mr. Peterson, for all you did."

"Please call me Jamal. I was happy to be of assistance and pleased that I had the opportunity to assist as a journalist. But I'll be lying if I told you that I wasn't scared and didn't fear for my life."

"That establishes you as a brave person. We all had some sense of fear, Mr. Peterson. Ah, Jamal. If the powers-that-be at that time and members of the white citizen council had discovered the work of the John Brown Christian Society, none of us would be sitting here today. These gentlemen were all members of the Society. George Mason here was known as Brother Justice Nine and Robert Samuel next to you was Brother Justice Fifteen, so they're very familiar with you. And we all greatly appreciate you and thus the reason I invited you to stay here at the Masolt Homestead and home of *The Mississippi Delta Orchid Company* for this auspicious occasion."

A tall black elderly woman wearing a white apron deposited a cup of steaming decaffeinated coffee in front of Jamal and said, "Cream and sugar is on the table, Mr. Peterson."

Jamal thanked the pleasant woman, stirred sugar in his coffee, sipped from the cup, placed it on the table, and asked, "Is the Society still in existence?"

"No," Reverend Masolt said. "After the passage of the Voters Right Act and Civil Rights Act, we thought our purpose had come to an end, though not to say there isn't racial bias, prejudice, and discrimination in the Delta that need to be addressed. The orchids we grow became a very popular and most sought-after product in major cities and locations abroad. So, we began growing and selling more of them and our orchids became a most productive and profitable enterprise. We now employ nearly one hundred people producing and shipping orchids to such places as New York on the east coast, California on the west coast, and overseas to places like Rome, Paris, and London."

"Wow! That's amazing," Jamal uttered.

"I like to believe it's all in the providence of our Lord and Savior," said Reverend Masolt. "We believe the good Lord was looking out over us and still is. The employees, both black and white and working side by side, make good wages and above the standard. We have established a foundation and make contributions to worthwhile causes. And when we thought the climate was right in Mississippi, we proposed to pay for the construction of a life-like statue of Emmett Till to be erected near where he was killed."

"That's great. How did you get local politicians to agree to that?" Jamal queried.

"The Voters Right Act helped," Reverend Masolt responded. "Black citizens in the Delta always accounted for a large percentage of the population, so when the Voters Right Act was passed, black citizens went to the polls in large numbers and elected members of their race as well as white office seekers who were sympathetic to their causes. Black voters comprise a large and significant constituency in the Delta, which hasn't gone unnoticed by white politicians, so when the statue of Emmett Till was proposed, it met some white opposition, but in the end it was approved. Members of the Ku Klux Klan and other white diehards of segregation and racial bigotry aren't happy, but the faithful hearted and those who look to God for guidance will forever prevail over the forces of hate and evil."

"Amen!" uttered the other men sitting at the table.

* * *

Jamal and his family arrived at the site of the dedication on the east bank of the Tallahatchie River along with Reverend Masolt and an entourage of black and white representatives from *The Mississippi Delta Orchid Company* as throngs of people began to arrive. Portable bleachers were set up to accommodate the crowd. It was a bright, sunny day with not a cloud to be seen. Jamal thought the sun was beaming a warm smile. He contemplated that God had crafted the weather just for this occasion.

Jamal, Francine, and Thurgood took seats in folding chairs down front that were reserved for speakers, dignitaries, and special guests.

Francine asked, "Isn't that Thurgood Marshall?"

Jamal looked in the direction of his wife's gaze and saw a tall, distinguished-looking, fair complexion black man with gray streaks in his fine hair make his way to a seat up front.

"Yes, it is," Jamal confirmed. He said to his son, "That's the man your mother and I named you after."

"I know," Thurgood said. "Do you think I can meet him? I want to be a lawyer like him and fight for the rights of black people."

Both Jamal and Francine gave their son an adoring smile. Jamal affectionately patted his son's leg; Francine kissed him on the cheek. Jamal said, "We'll see if you can meet him after the ceremony."

Thurgood smiled.

Jamal looked up and pronounced, "There's Emmett Till's mother, Mamie."

Francine said, "She looks good and so dignified. That's a black woman with lots of character and inner strength. I really admire her."

Jamal observed the notable personalities he was aware of. He then contemplated who wasn't at the dedication. He immediately thought about Dr. Martin Luther King Jr. who'd been assassinated in 1968 in Memphis, Tennessee at the Lorraine Motel and considered a "Drum Major for Justice" and referenced as "The Prince of Peace". Jamal recalled how proud he and other black people were when in 1964 Dr. King was awarded the Nobel Peace Prize. His thoughts drifted to Medgar Evers, a field secretary for the NAACP in Mississippi, who was assassinated eight years after Emmett Till died because of his voter rights efforts on behalf of blacks in Mississippi and was buried with honors in Arlington Cemetery in Washington, D.C. Jamal pondered that King and Evers had put down their lives for civil rights, equality, and justice, but not in vain.

Jamal felt happy to have witnessed that young Emmett Till's death wasn't fruitless, and like others, he thought the nature of Emmett's demise was actually the catalyst for the modern day civil rights movement.

"Remember Emmett!" Jamal mumbled.

"What did you say, Daddy?" Thurgood asked.

"I said remember Emmett!"

Thurgood said, "I will, Daddy. I'll always remember Emmett Till. How old would he have been if he was still alive?"

"He would've been thirty-four years old, the same age as Dr. Martin Luther King Jr. when he died."

Jamal looked behind him and saw all the seats filled and the bleachers packed with both black and white people, sitting side by side with no protest and without signs that cited *Coloreds* and *Whites* sections when the institution of *Jim Crow* was alive.

Jamal contemplated that it was a new day in Mississippi and throughout the country and that it was much brighter times than in the past, starting with Emmett Till's murder trial. He considered that Emmett wasn't the only young black boy to die in Mississippi and in other southern states due to racial hatred, intolerance, and violence. He mused that it was Emmett's death that received national attention and if it hadn't been for that, then perhaps civil rights wouldn't have come this far at this time.

Jamal sat there along the bank of the Tallahatchie River in deep contemplation, observing the swarm of people and the excitement of the occasion. He looked out at the river and couldn't help but wonder how many black bodies probably have found watery graves in Mississippi and other southern states. He looked at his son who was well and safe and who had a bright future in front on him. He observed Francine, his beloved *Babycakes*, and felt fortunate to have a woman like her in his life who was beautiful from the inside-out, intelligent, loving, kind, and forgiving.

The Ghost of Emmett Till

Jamal reflected on times when he thought he wouldn't see his family again. The first time being right in Mississippi when he was shot and clung to death, and the next time was when he was a freedom rider in Alabama. He felt that he was one of the lucky ones, because so many lives had been lost in the struggle for civil rights.

"Soldiers," Jamal whispered.

"What, Daddy?" Thurgood queried.

"I said *soldiers,* son. I was thinking of all the people in the civil rights movement – both black and white people – who sacrificed their lives. Don't ever forget that, son. Always remember that the rights you have as a young person today didn't come easy and without human sacrifices."

"I won't, Daddy. I promise."

"Good, son. I love you."

"I love you, too, Daddy."

Francine smiled and said, "I love you both."

* * *

After the ceremony, hordes of black citizens who weren't anybody's dignitaries, but just common people, who worked on plantations and as manual laborers throughout the Delta, left to return to their homes. Many of them did not have seats during the ceremony, but stood for its duration without a complaint because Emmett Till had meant so much to them. They credited his ghost for making life so much bearable in their jobs, and they were grateful that they were no longer working sunup to sundown, and that a forty-hour workweek with fifteen minutes breaks in the morning and afternoon and a decent lunch period was now the standard. And they gave the credit to the ghost of Emmett Till.

That night, early in the morning, when they thought the time would be strategic and the darkness accommodating, four white men parked their truck into the woods off the Tallahatchie River about a half-mile from where the bronze statue of Emmett Till stood. They stole through the night carrying a slug hammer, crowbars, and an ax. They came upon the statue angrier than a disturbed nest of yellow jackets and seething with hate. They were about to apply their tools of destruction to Emmett Till's statue when suddenly the wind grew strong and knocked the men to the ground. They heard a loud splash and then a painful moaning that emanated from the river that made their flesh crawl. The wind grew considerably stronger and howled as it rolled the men down the riverbank into the swirling water.

* * *

The next morning, two county workers, one black and the other white, were off into LeFlore County performing maintenance work and came upon the statue of Emmett Till, where they saw suspicious tools lying on the ground. They checked the statue for damage but found none.

The white worker took off his cap and scratched his head. "Why would someone bring these tools here and leave 'em?" the man asked.

The black worker pondered the questioned and then said, "I think someone was intent on harming Emmett Till's statue."

"That's what I thought at first, so what stopped 'em?"

They looked at each other.

The black worker had an epiphany. He said, "Emmett Till's ghost probably stopped 'em."

The summation of what the men saw and what was conjectured about Emmett Till's ghost got spread throughout the Mississippi Delta, and no one else ever considered harming Emmett Till's statue after what was tattled like gospel.

THE END

About The Author

He is a retired educator who served as a classroom teacher, coach, and school administrator. He started his own business by the name of Write Stuff and works as an independent contractor. He has won honors in the field of education and community service. He resides in Michigan and is a member of the Detroit Writer's Guild. His first published novel is "Misbegotten." Readers have praised his writing and are eagerly awaiting his novel "The Ghost of Emmett Till."

He is a graduate of Central Michigan University--holding three degrees.

Printed in the United States
129235LV00001B/58-81/A

9 781418 464776